ELLA'S DESIRE

MADELINE MARTIN

Copyright 2019 © Madeline Martin

ELLA'S DESIRE © 2019 Madeline Martin. ALL RIGHTS RESERVED. No part or the whole of this book may be reproduced, distributed, transmitted or utilized (other than for reading by the intended reader) in ANY form (now known or hereafter invented) without prior written permission by the author. The unauthorized reproduction or distribution of this copyrighted work is illegal, and punishable by law.

ELLA'S DESIRE is a work of fiction. The characters and events portrayed in this book are fictional and or are used fictitiously and solely the product of the author's imagination. Any similarity to real persons, living or dead, places, businesses, events or locales is purely coincidental.

Cover Design by Teresa Sprecklemeyer @ The Midnight Muse Designs.

To my sweet minions

You fill my life with joy and you fill my heart with love. Thank you for always being so proud of me. I love you both to the moon and back again, and back again, and back again...

1

April 1338
Brampton, England

Lady Ella Barrington, the third daughter of the Earl of Werrick, knew there was trouble the moment she found her older sisters waiting with her father in her solar. A parchment was pinched between Marin's fingers. It had been months since she'd seen either of her elder sisters, and from the sternness of Marin and Anice's faces, this wouldn't be a pleasant reunion.

"What is it?" Ella asked, her words slow and wary.

Her father's forehead crinkled above his worried gray-blue eyes. "I've received a missive from the king. He is questioning my loyalty despite the many decades I've faithfully served the crown."

Ella's mouth gaped. Never had there been a man more loyal to the crown than her father. It was why they lived on the dangerous border between England and Scotland. It was why Ella and her sisters had been trained to fight as warriors. It was why her mother was dead.

Heat flared in Ella's cheeks. "How dare the king question your allegiance?"

"It's our fault." Anice put a hand to her stomach, which was now flat after the recent birth of her new son. Not that one would be able to tell from her face, still lovely and glowing with good health. But then, Anice had always been the most beautiful of all of them.

If they were having this conversation prior to Ella being introduced to the babe, the news must be grave indeed.

Anice continued, a pained expression on her delicate features. "With Marin and I both having married Scotsmen, our dowry lands are now in their possession. Lands that were meant for Englishmen."

"The war against Scotland is not going well." Marin set the parchment onto the surface of the desk. A lock of her pale blonde hair fell forward, but she brushed it back absently. "Most of England's strongholds in Scotland have been taken back by the Scottish. He is..." she paused, considering her words carefully. "...not pleased."

"But the circumstances of your unions were extraordinary," Ella countered. "What will happen to Papa, then?" She looked to her father's weary face. "Will you be arrested?"

He lowered his head.

"It's possible," Marin replied.

Ella's heart dropped into her stomach. If Marin had to be the one to share this news—if it was more than Papa could bring himself to say—the situation must be truly dreadful.

Marin put a supportive hand on their father's shoulder. "There's an alternative that will keep him from such a fate."

If Ella had been wary before, she was absolutely on edge now. "What is it?" She looked about for her younger sisters. "Why aren't Cat and Leila here?"

Anice hesitated and nodded toward Marin, who finished with

the news both were struggling to unveil. "Father's eldest unwed daughter must marry the Earl of Calville."

Ella stiffened. No wonder they had not wanted to speak, when they brought such unwanted news. As Marin and Anice were both married, the eldest unwed daughter was Ella.

"Nay." She shook her head. "There must be other options to prove your loyalty, Papa. A witness to tout your glory on the battlefield in England's favor. Mayhap Geordie when he returns from his campaign with the king. Or even Drake could…" The words died on her tongue, slain by the flat expressions reflecting the futility of her suggestions.

None of Werrick Castle's soldiers would be able to sufficiently vouch for their lord. Even she knew that.

But *marriage*? Her heart threatened to race from her chest. This was not how her marriage was supposed to be.

"I could join a convent," she offered weakly. Desperation might save her yet.

"Oh, pish." Marin spoke tenderly, moving around the desk to approach Ella. The blue silk of her kirtle rippled around her ankles from the sunlight coming in through the precious glass window. "You'd be miserable in a convent. The rules are far too strict."

"I don't love the Earl of Calville. I don't even know him." Cracks splintered through a lifetime of her carefully spun dreams of marriage and love, threatening to shatter. But Ella held tight to the vision, as she always had.

She'd read enough tales, and had heard enough stories from troubadours, to know how a marriage built on love began. An honorable and wonderfully handsome man would notice her at a banquet, or something of the like. He would think her the most beautiful woman he'd ever seen and then spend months wooing her, writing sonnets and bringing flowers in the hopes of securing her affections. Mayhap, he'd even give her a kiss.

Once he had proven his worth as a warrior to her father, and as a chivalric suitor to her, he would seek her hand in marriage. They would wed in an elaborate marriage with cloth of silver and gold sparkling throughout the church. Then they would have half a dozen children and live with their hearts glowing bright with their eternal love.

It was a dream she'd clung to. One that had helped her survive the childhood attack on their castle, the dark days following her mother's death, the sieges and every other terrible event in her life.

An arranged marriage was not love.

A hot tear slid down her cheek. When she was a girl, her father had promised her that she could marry who she liked. But even she knew the situation now to be out of his control. His drooping shoulders said as much, as did the deep creases lining his face.

The bag at her side wriggled where she held her pet squirrel. The poor thing had been in the woods several summers prior, near death when Ella had found him. Moppet, empathetic creature that he was, clearly sensed Ella's unrest.

Ella pulled the squirrel from her bag and cuddled his furry warmth against her chest.

Marin recoiled. "Is that a rat?"

"'Tis a squirrel," Anice replied in a droll tone. "Be glad there are no acorns about."

Ella's comforting embrace with her pet became protective. "His name is Moppet and he's very sweet."

Marin looked to Anice for confirmation, but she simply glanced in the opposite direction rather than verify Ella's claim.

"Ella, sweeting." Marin met Ella's gaze.

Ella wanted to shrink away and keep right on shrinking until she fell through the floorboards, never to be seen again. She knew this tone of Marin's. Ella didn't remember much about their mother, but she recalled that same tone well, and the kind of request that followed such cajoling endearments.

Ella choked back a sob. It was terrible and selfish, but she could not help her sorrow any more than she could stop the ache in her chest.

"I have it on good authority that he is young," Papa said. "Lord Bastionbury says the earl's father only recently passed and left the earldom to him. He's quite handsome, per what is said around court."

Ella's head snapped up. Lord Bastionbury was nearly a day's ride away. As was Marin for that matter. Apparently, it had all been discussed prior to that morning: her marriage, her life, the smashing of her dreams.

"Ella, you have been left to do as you wish for far too long." Marin smoothed Ella's long blonde locks. "That is my fault. I didn't have the heart to be strict with you, not after Mother died. But you are a woman of two and twenty now."

It is time to grow up.

Marin need not speak the implied words when they hung so obviously between them. There was no hope for any of Ella's dreams. Her heart had been dashed upon the floor.

But Papa's life was worth all the love in the world, and Ella would be proving it with this action. She lowered her head and kissed Moppet's twitching ear.

"I will do it," she whispered. "I will marry the Earl of Calville."

❦

BRONSON BERKLEY, THE NEW EARL OF CALVILLE, HAD NEED OF many things. Funds, the king's favor in supporting his newly inherited earldom, and forgiveness for the taxes the late earl had overlooked paying. What Bronson did not need, or want for that matter, was a wife.

Unfortunately for him, the king refused to give him anything without agreement to the latter. It was the reason for Bronson's surprise visit to his boyhood home, prior to any consideration in accepting a new bride.

If Berkley Manor was in good order, Bronson could put aside the idea of marriage and bide his time while he came up with an alternate solution. There had to be something else he could do to gain favor with the king.

All hope was not yet lost.

Bronson's horse slowed to a stop in front of the country manor house and his heart dropped into his stomach. Bits of plaster had crumbled from the exterior, revealing the cracking gray stone beneath, and the roof sagged inward like a sheet hung slack over a rope.

This was not the opulent home he'd grown up in, with the manicured lawn stretching before it, practically gleaming with wealth.

A pinch-faced woman showed him inside. If memory served correct, her name was Jane, or something of the like.

The interior of the manor was as dilapidated as the outside. The tapestries were faded and moth-eaten in areas, the carpets threadbare. Not a speck of dust coated any interior in the neat home, but it was evident that his father had not sent his wife's stipend in some time.

His stepmother, Brigid, approached him with a look of kindness, executing a respectful curtsey. She no longer appeared as young as she did in Bronson's memory. Her brown hair had lost its rich luster and the smile she'd always readily given him had dimmed to nearly nothing.

"My Lady Brigid, if I may," he said softly. "What's happened?"

Her face flushed, and he immediately regretted the question.

"Forgive the appearance of your home, my lord." She ducked her head, revealing the top of her wimple where several small holes showed against her dark hair beneath. "We've tried our best." Her gaze wandered the room, no doubt seeing everything through his eyes.

"Please call me Bronson as you did before." He took her hand in his. Her nails were bitten to the quick and rough calluses rasped against his palm. No doubt she was doing as much work as the servants. He gave her fingers an affectionate squeeze. "I'm still the same lad from fifteen years ago when you married my father."

Her eyes crinkled with the happy memory. "Aye, though you are a few feet taller."

"Did Father not send funds?" Bronson asked.

The joy fled her expression and her gaze dropped to the tops of her shoes. They were badly scuffed, worn to tearing in some spots. Most certainly they wouldn't last to winter, let alone through it. Were they her only pair?

As if hearing his silent assessment, she swept her skirt forward to cover her insufficient footwear. "He stopped sending anything several years back. He said we were spending too much. But we weren't, truly. It was only what was needed."

Bronson frowned at his father's egregious oversight. He and his father had lived a luxurious life at court, while the countess lacked the bare necessities.

A shy face peered around the corner at him and then quickly disappeared behind the wall again.

"Is this Lark?" He peeked around the wall as he asked.

A girl with brown hair and eyes as green as his own, as green as their father's had been, stepped forward. Her skirt came only to her shins and her sleeves to her elbows. The child was nearly splitting from her clothing and her feet were bare. Nay, not a child, for though she appeared to be nearly ten, she was fourteen.

She nodded and gave him a tentative smile.

"Aye, this is my Lark." Brigid ran an affectionate hand over her daughter's hair. "Do you remember Bronson, your brother?"

"Nay, my lord, but I've heard much of you." Her voice was small, and her shoulders curled forward as if she wished to hide herself.

An uncomfortable silence congealed between the three of them, one borne of an unexpected visit and the revelation of hard times. He felt the fool, standing in his silk brocade doublet when his sister could scarcely fit into her dress.

"I've heard you were ill for some time." To fill the heavy quiet, Bronson pulled the tidbit from his memory.

Lark lifted her brows. "When I was a girl. I'm much recovered now."

Ah, that was correct. It had been some time since then.

"We were preparing for supper," Brigid said. "Would you join us and regale us with tales of court? It has been some time since I have been."

Bronson hesitated. He had planned to stay at Berkley Manor. Now he dreaded taking supper with them and diminishing what stores of food they possessed. Knowing it would be insulting to decline, he agreed and found himself set before a table decorated with wildflowers and nicked cups.

He was right to be concerned about their supply of food. Supper was a simple soup with several lumpy bits of something that might be barley, unidentified chunks of greasy meat he couldn't chew and a couple of peas. His bowl had been filled to the brim while theirs had barely covered the bottom. He wanted to refuse it, to let them eat the lot of it, but did not wish to cause offense. At least he'd left his servant, Rafe, in the stables, lest they felt the need to fill his bowl with what little remained in theirs.

Bronson forced himself to eat their generous offering as he shared courtly gossip rather than extravagant descriptions. They didn't need to know how Bronson and his father had lived then. How he and the former earl had slept on feather beds and ate sumptuous meals, leaving more on their plates than they could possibly fit into their bellies.

In the small space of time that he spoke, Brigid's eyes lit up with joy and she gave the same radiant laugh he'd remembered from the few times he'd met her as a boy.

At last, Jane cleared away supper and Bronson gave his excuses to repair to an inn nearby where he intended to sleep that night. It was a lie, of course, but he would not eat any more of their food than he already had.

Brigid allowed Lark to offer Bronson a shy farewell before sending the young woman to her room. Once Lark was gone, she regarded Bronson. "May we talk a moment?"

He nodded. "Of course."

She balled her hand into a fist and drew a deep breath. "I must seek your favor." Her words were whispered, as though she didn't want anyone else to hear. She closed her eyes, her expression pained. "Could you perhaps provide me with a small stipend? I would not ask for myself," she rushed on. "It's for Jane who has stayed on for over four years now with no pay, and to buy Lark's winter shoes. She has none to fit her feet."

Bronson regarded his stepmother, a woman only several years older than himself. The hope in her eyes made the hole in his chest widen. How could he tell her the truth? That there was no money, that even the immaculate and rundown manor could soon be taken back by the king?

"I will provide you with as much as I have on me presently and will send additional funds when I can. You will have more than a stipend," he promised. "You need wait only awhile longer and I promise I will give you your life back as it ought to be."

He did a quick inventory of the coin on his person. It was not much, but he had more in the apartments he'd shared with his father, as well as items of worth to sell. He handed her the small coin purse. She accepted the weight of it in her cupped palm, the contents within clinking.

She stared down at the small purse and remained silent. Shame squeezed through him. His offer was not enough. And how could it be, after so many years of shameful neglect?

"Forgive me," he said. "It is all I can give as yet. There will be more soon…"

Brigid sniffled and finally lifted her head. Tears shimmered in her pale blue eyes. "Thank you." The words came out on a sob. She pressed her lips together and swiped at her eyes. "I think God has finally heard our prayers, because he brought you to us."

It was unworthy praise and her stated poignancy plunged into his chest.

He gave her what coin he had, ignoring her protests when she declared it to be far too much, and rode on back to London that night with Rafe at his side.

There were no more options available to him now, not when his father had so neglected Brigid and Lark. They were Bronson's responsibility now, and he would not be remiss. He and Rafe would depart again as soon as they arrived in London, to head to Werrick Castle on the border between England and Scotland where the Earl of Werrick also served as West March Warden on the English side. Where Lady Ella would be waiting to wed Bronson.

For whether he wanted one or not, he was getting a wife.

2

Ella spent the next fortnight coming to terms with her dismal fate. She was by no means happy with it, but she had at least begun to accept it. Or rather, how she might work around it.

She strode across the courtyard, her steps purposeful. However, as she neared the stable, her knees went soft and her steely resolve began to melt. She could turn back to the castle. No one would be any wiser, as the first part of her plan was known only to her.

She had left Moppet back in the castle, and now regretted having done so. His furry warmth was always such a comfort. And yet, how ridiculous would it look for her to have a squirrel nestled in her hands? The image that conjured was so amusing that she might have laughed were she not so terribly nervous.

She sucked in a deep breath and entered the stables. The Master of the Horse was the only one within, as she had hoped. Peter's broad-shouldered back faced her, a pitchfork clutched in his fists as he hefted a load of straw into a nearby stall. He turned at the sound of her approach and the frantic race of her heart went completely still.

His sleeves had been rolled up to keep him cool in his labor, and sunlight played over the corded muscle at his forearms. His strong chest was visible through the notch at his tunic, lightly sprinkled with dark hair. His eyes looked hazel from where she stood, but she knew they possessed flecks of green as vibrant as summer grass. He fixed her with his beautiful gaze now and shook a dark lock from where it had plastered to his brow.

She tried to breathe and found she could not. How could she, when he was so perfect? When she was actually going to do this thing she had imagined for so long?

Peter frowned slightly. "Lady Ella. Are you well?"

"Aye." She stopped, uncertain how to go about speaking. "Nay. I..."

He rushed to her. His arms were wonderfully strong, left bronzed from years of work under the sun's rays. How she wanted to fall into them, to feel those powerful hands gently cradling her face, running down her neck, her shoulders...

He hovered where he stood, not touching her, but poised to in case his assistance was needed. "My lady, what is it?"

"I need your help." Lightheadedness nearly overwhelmed her. She had practiced what she would say, and this was not it. "Please."

His gaze searched hers in earnest concern. "Of course. What do ye need?"

Her pulse flickered with fear. Could she truly do this?

"Lay with me," she breathed.

Peter's eyes went wide. "I beg your pardon, my lady?" His gaze flicked frantically around the empty stable, as though seeking confirmation no one had heard her brazen request.

"I'm to be married off." She stepped toward him and lowered her head in supplication. "The maids talk. You are an extraordinary lover, and I've always found you to be terribly handsome." She was speaking too quickly, her words pitched with desperation.

Heat burned in her cheeks. She hadn't meant to sound so pathetic.

Peter backed up. "My lady, please. This isna a conversation we ought to be having."

"No one need know." She stepped closer. "It will only be between us. Show me passion before I enter this forced union."

"Nay, Lady Ella." He clenched his jaw.

His words slammed into her like a fist. Rejection.

She stopped short in surprise. Unexpected tears prickled at her eyes. "Do you think me unattractive?" she asked in horror.

Peter had lain with most of the women at Werrick Castle, if rumors were to be believed. Surely, she was as pretty as those who had warmed his bed before.

His gaze danced around the room, landing everywhere but on her. "Nay, my lady. But ye're the earl's daughter. No' just any earl, but a border warden, and one I hold in high regard. I've too much respect for him, and for ye, to do what it is ye request of me."

"I see." But she did not see. If no one was to know, why would any of it matter?

"And if I was a laundress instead of my father's daughter?" she pressed.

He shook his head and those unique, exquisite eyes met hers finally. "But ye're not a laundress, Lady Ella." His tone softened as though he meant to take the sting from them. "And ye never will be."

Emotion welled like a fist in her throat, nearly choking her. She nodded as if she understood, as if everything was right and well between them. She stepped back, but a small stone caught the heel of her shoe and she stumbled.

Peter reached out to her, but she pulled away, preferring to trip than accept his aid. "Lady Ella." There was a gentleness to his voice. Pity.

It was impossible at that moment for her to be any more humiliated. The one thing she had planned to do solely for herself had gone so miserably wrong. Now she was left with rejection in addition to an unwanted impending marriage.

※

Bronson rode from the civilization of London into the wilderness of the border. He'd been traveling at a steady pace for a fortnight, and still he and Rafe had not arrived at Werrick Castle.

A low rumble came from overhead. The second one in several minutes.

The rain had been a constant companion throughout their travel. Initially, they had stopped several times to find shelter. After a short time, they'd given up. Fortunately, the majority of Bronson's belongings, and several of his prized hunting dogs, were in the large covered cart being driven by Rafe.

Regardless, it was hard to shake the idea that all the rain was a bad omen. As though the heavens themselves were frowning upon the union.

"Do you think she will be beautiful, my lord?" Rafe asked. The young man looked up at him through a fringe of wet, blond hair.

"The king says she is," Bronson answered.

And indeed, he had said all the daughters of Werrick were stunning beauties. All but one had golden locks and beautiful blue eyes. Appearances were pleasant, but they did not make this decision for him.

Bronson would marry her if she looked like the back end of a goat. Anything to give Brigid and Lark the life they ought to have lived these past fifteen years.

Bitter anger tightened along Bronson's back at his father's carelessness. It was the late earl who always told Bronson to look after women, to see to their needs and wants. Apparently, he had only meant women who might offer him favors for an evening rather than his own wife.

"If she is lovely," Rafe said with careful consideration, "then the journey is worth the effort."

Bronson's leather cloak had soaked through and there was a chill deep in his bones. Despite his ire, he could not help but smile at the younger man's enthusiasm.

"I hope you're right." Bronson nodded to the castle looming in the distance. "Because it looks like we're about to discover the truth soon enough."

A curtain wall encircled the lush grassy hill surrounding the structure. Werrick Castle was rustic in appearance, no doubt built more for defense than for comfort. He'd heard such things about life in dangerous areas and was glad he'd purchased a sword prior to leaving London.

The rain ceased all at once. Little good it did now, though. Bronson was drenched and eager to change from his wet traveling clothes.

The portcullis was down when they arrived and there was an unsettling quiet about the surrounding area that left Bronson straining his eyes and ears for another soul. An arrow whizzed down from the battlements and stuck at an angle in the soft ground. The white fletching caught the wind and made the arrow bob slightly.

"Far enough," a female voice shouted.

Rafe shot Bronson an incredulous look as he shouted up to the castle wall. "My Lord, the Earl of Calville is here upon the request of the Earl of Werrick to discuss contracting a marriage with his daughter."

Silence followed the declaration and continued for several beats before the portcullis groaned and slowly creaked upward. As it lifted, Bronson swept at his hair and straightened his clothing. After days spent in the storming weather, trudging through mud and wearing sodden, wrinkled clothes, there was little he could do.

By some miracle, the downpour had not resumed. Rather, the

clouds had cleared away, revealing a blue sky filled with the brilliance of a full-faced sun. Except it only made his appearance all the more disheveled.

Lady Ella would no doubt take one look at him and refuse to accept him into her home. And he wouldn't blame her. He coaxed his horse into the courtyard, expecting the earl to come forward and present his daughters.

There was no earl, but a woman instead. She wore a fine blue kirtle of costly silk and her hair was bound into braids coiled beneath a gilt caul. Her attire was dry and absent any wrinkles or mud.

If he had expected a pretty woman as his bride to be, he would have been taken aback. This woman was not merely pretty: she was beautiful. Beyond beautiful. Her fair skin was flawless, her cheekbones high, her lips full and sensual.

He sank to one knee before her. "Lady Ella." His three hunting dogs crowded around him, silent as though they too were in a state of awe.

"That isn't necessary, my lord," she said. "Please, do get to your feet."

Bronson rose obediently. It was then he noticed a man standing beside Lady Ella. A man who put his hand possessively about her waist.

Bronson narrowed his eyes at the intimate gesture.

The woman inclined her head in greeting. "Forgive me, my lord, I am not Ella, but her eldest sister, Marin. This is my husband, Bran Davidson." She cast a glance at Bronson's wet, wrinkled clothing. Though it was quick, it was enough to leave him practically wincing at her assessment.

"It rained for the majority of our trip," he offered by way of apology.

She smiled in such an understanding way, it eased some of the tension from his shoulders. The kindness she exhibited only enhanced her appearance. After a lifetime at court, Bronson had come to be something of an expert on women and knew well what sort of reaction a woman like her would elicit from the courtiers. She would have every man in the palm of her hand.

If one sister was so finely featured, what must her younger sister look like?

"At your leisure, my lord, you may recover from your journey before you are introduced to the rest of my family," Marin said in a congenial tone. "My father, the Earl of Werrick, is Warden of the West March on the English side as I'm sure you are aware. He is presently at Truce Day and will join us on the morrow."

Bronson nodded as though he understood what Truce Day was. Mayhap a border thing. At any rate, he would not meet his bride in such a disheveled state and allowed Marin to lead him into the keep where the interior redeemed the old castle. While the outside was gray and bland stonework built for defense, the interior was luxurious and meant for comfort.

Tapestries hung from the walls, exquisitely worked with resplendent thread, and all the furniture was ornate and polished to a high shine.

No wonder Werrick was held in such high esteem. It was evident he had considerable wealth. It made sense now that a man with such a fortune could afford to supply a considerable dowry for his third daughter.

The chamber Bronson was shown to was far grander than his own in London and nearly four times the size. Rafe set about hastily preparing the room and before the hour was up, Bronson was ready to meet his intended.

He opened the door to his room and nearly tripped over a black cat.

He muttered a swift apology to the animal. His mother had chattered on with the hunting dogs and other household animals when he was a lad. It was a part of her that had never left him, a small piece of himself that reminded him of her.

He strode down the hall, in search of Marin or someone who

might introduce him to the betrothed he was suddenly very eager to meet.

The black cat trailed behind him and attempted to wind about his feet as he walked. "Are you following me?" he asked. The cat stared up at him with bright green eyes.

"Do ye know what they say about Bixby?" Marin's husband, Bran, grinned at him from across the hall.

The man's accent was heavy with a Scottish brogue. Bronson straightened in surprise. Was the king aware Werrick's eldest daughter had married one of his enemies?

"I do not," Bronson replied warily. He'd heard enough about Scotsmen and what they did to the English to be on guard. When Rafe had dressed him, he'd attached the sword to Bronson's belt. It was an awkward accessory as it was heavier than the decorative blade he'd worn at court. He was glad for it now.

Bran simply laughed at Bronson's reply and bent to scratch the cat's head.

Bronson ignored the rude response. "Where might I find Lady Ella?"

"Lady Leila and Lady Catriona are down in the garden." Bran scratched under the cat's chin, making its eyes squint in pleasure. "Ye might start by asking them." With that, he stood and made his way down the hall in the opposite direction.

The Scotsman had offered the information like something wondrously helpful when it was anything but. Bronson hadn't any idea where the garden might be.

He found it eventually, with the assistance of an errant servant he happened upon in the hall who had been far more helpful than the damned Scotsman. The garden smelled of wet soil and was filled with many flowering plants. It was rather a fine garden, more than he had expected from the primitive exterior of the fortified castle.

Two young women were picking carefully through a small garden of plants that had been marked off with a waist-high wooden fence. One was light-haired as Marin was, while the other possessed dark hair.

A foul mood had settled over Bronson during his search through the many halls of Werrick Castle, but he covered it with a courtier's smile as he approached.

"Good day to you, my lord." The blonde young woman smiled at him, her loveliness equal to Marin's. "You are Lord Calville, I presume?"

No servants appeared to be about, not for protection of their person, nor to dig about in the earth for them. He regarded their dirt-stained hands. "Where are your servants?"

"In the keep," the blonde woman replied casually.

The dark-haired girl did not speak, merely glancing at him from the corner of her eyes.

He glanced about. "Should you be out here alone? Without a guard present?"

The blonde laughed. "We can handle ourselves well enough. I'm Catriona, but everyone calls me Cat, and this is our youngest sister, Leila." She nodded to the dark-haired girl, who faced him with a curious expression. After a long moment, she inclined her head in greeting.

"I'm pleased to meet you both." Bronson offered his best courtier's bow. When he straightened, however, both women had resumed their task in the dirt.

He cleared his throat. "I've yet to meet my betrothed. Have you seen her about?"

"Nay," Lady Catriona replied with a pleasant smile.

He'd been a courtier long enough that he could bury his growing irritation with the barbarity of this place. The lack of manners and decorum was truly deplorable. "Do you know where I might find her?" He kept his tone pleasant with considerable effort. "Or perhaps you might introduce me?"

Lady Leila bent to pick several leaves from the plants while Lady Catriona looked around with a little hum of contemplation.

"You can try the orchard." She shrugged and gave him a brilliant smile.

God's teeth, this was exasperating. He had anticipated the borderlands would be different than what he was familiar with in London, but this was getting ridiculous.

"And that would be in what direction?" He pointed toward a cluster of trees. "There?"

"Aye." She gave an enthusiastic nod.

He hesitated before leaving and glanced at the two young ladies. "Are you sure you do not need someone to stand watch over you? I've heard it's dangerous here."

"Oh, it is," Lady Catriona replied brightly. "We're fine."

Lady Leila nodded and tucked a fistful of leaves into her basket.

Bronson slowly walked away, but kept his ears trained on the girls to listen for any sign of a call for help. He entered the quiet orchard and was disappointed to discover no sign of Lady Ella, or any other person for that matter.

Heat crept over his chest at his own foolishness. What would a lady be doing in an orchard anyway?

Fully vexed, he strode through the orchard. Something dropped down in front of his face from a tree above and he stopped short.

A woman's leg kicked back and forth only inches from his nose, languid and naked. Absent a skirt, stockings or even a slipper.

Surely *this* was not his betrothed.

3

Bronson stared in surprise at the shapely, naked leg. It was a fine example of what a woman's limb ought to be. A trim ankle, petite feet with well-formed toes and a firm calf. His gaze trailed indulgently upward to where the delicate knee disappeared in a cloud of red silk brocade. For the most part.

A bit of the gown had shifted apart, giving him a glimpse of her smooth thigh. He ought to look away, and yet found himself stepping back for a better view.

"Who is down there?" The woman tucked her leg back beneath her skirts with haste.

He straightened in surprise. "I am Bronson Berkley, my lady. The Earl of Calville." Guilt at having been caught made his tone brusque.

She peered down at him through the leaves. Wavy blonde hair hung over her shoulders, obscuring her face. "That isn't true," she said. "He isn't due to arrive for another few days."

"I have a fast horse."

The woman didn't reply.

"Might I inquire as to who you are?" He queried.

Still she did not answer.

"Are you Lady Ella?"

The face of the woman with shapely legs disappeared.

He leaned to the side in an effort to peer through the branches to see her once more. "You ought to get down from there. It isn't safe."

An acorn came hurtling down from the tree and smacked his forehead. He slapped a hand over his smarting brow. Had she just thrown an acorn at him?

He stared up into the leaves as a bedraggled looking squirrel scampered to the end of the branch and launched another acorn at him.

"Moppet, cease that at once." The woman's hand reached out toward the squirrel.

"My lady, please." Bronson lifted his arms in an effort to assist her descent. "Come down before you injure yourself."

"I'm perfectly fine." The squirrel evaded her grasp and chattered irritably to itself. She rose with slow care, balancing on the branch in her bare feet. The full skirt of her scarlet kirtle billowed gently in the breeze and offered a teasing glimpse of those slender, shapely legs.

This time he did glance away, surveying the orchard. "My lady, someone will see you in this state of indecency." And he certainly didn't wish to be caught taking advantage.

"Are you *looking*?" She spun about and clutched at her skirt.

The branch, however, was only so thick and there was not enough room for both her feet at once. Her feet slipped from the bark and down she went in a stream of red silk and ribbons of golden hair.

He leapt to her aid, rushing toward her and she landed perfectly in the cradle of his arms. He hadn't anticipated the impact would be like having a sack of grain dropped on his chest and only just managed to mute his grunt at the impact.

She blinked in surprise and slowly turned her face toward his. If having her land on him hadn't knocked the wind from him, gazing upon her threatened to steal every breath he'd ever taken. She had the same pale hair as her sisters, with long-lashed blue eyes. The crimson of her gown made the flush of her cheeks and the pink pout of her mouth stand out.

He held her weight easily against him, reveling in the warmth of her body, the sweet scent of the fruit trees clinging to her skin. Her hair was unbound and blew lightly in the gentle breeze.

He wanted to crane his head forward, to brush her lips with his own to see if they were as soft as he imagined they were. "Are you Lady Ella?"

"I am." She pulled her bottom lip into her mouth very much the same as he'd wanted to do. "And you were not supposed to arrive for several more days." She squirmed in his embrace. "Release me."

"Are you injured?" he asked.

"I assure you, I am quite well." She wriggled again. "Do release me, please."

Obliging her request, he settled her to the ground. She bent and picked up something. A leather-bound book. Strange that she would have an item so valuable out of the castle.

"What were you doing up in the tree?" he asked.

She shrugged. "Reading."

He glanced at the book once more. "Psalms?"

She shook her head. "Nay, stories."

He looked at the blank cover. The books he'd seen had scrolling titles and colorful images painted on them by monks. "What story is it?"

"You wouldn't know it." She pursed her lips, considering him, as though unsure if she ought to go on or not. Finally, she lifted her shoulder. "They're stories my sisters and I created."

"You mean you wrote them?" he asked.

She nodded and pulled the book to her chest, arms crossed over it like a shield.

Was she intentionally making him dredge every bit of information from her? Because he would. If need be. "What are they about?" He took a step closer and she backed up.

Her brow furrowed, and she stared hard at the ground. "Love," she whispered. The full effect of her glare hit him like a blow. "They're about love." She threw the statement at him with heavy accusation. Before he could reply, she shook her head. "You were not supposed to arrive yet. Do excuse me." With that, she dashed out of the orchard with bare feet and the acorn-wielding squirrel racing after her.

Bronson watched her go and absently rubbed the ache on his brow where he'd been struck by the acorn. Where did that squirrel get the acorns from in the middle of an orchard?

It was a silly musing, and one he'd rather place his focus on than the blatant truth of his encounter with his beautiful betrothed. For it was quite obvious that Lady Ella did not wish to marry him.

ELLA WAS CURLED INTO A BALL OF MISERY ON THE BED SHE shared with Cat and Leila when they entered some time later.

By all rights as eldest daughter at Werrick, she ought to have their mother's former rooms, but she hadn't wanted to take them. Memories of her mother's screams, of the cloying odor of blood, were too much for Ella to bear. And besides, after over twenty years of sleeping with her sisters, she did not wish to sleep alone. They were warmth and comfort, laughter and love. She would remain in this room, in this bed, with them until she was forced to marry. Which might very well be soon.

"Did Calville find you?" Cat flopped on the bed beside Ella.

"Aye, I saw him." Ella flipped onto her back. "Or rather, I fell into his arms."

"That sounds romantic," Cat said.

Leila nodded her head in agreement. "You *are* partial to that sort of thing."

Ella scoffed. "Perhaps if he hadn't made me fall, it would have been romantic. Catching me was the least he could do." Shame heated her cheeks. "I wasn't very kind to him afterward. I imagine he'll have his own hesitations in marrying me as well."

"He didn't seem like the type to intentionally cause a woman to fall from a tree." Cat rolled onto her back too and stared up at the wooden underside of their canopy. "He was quite concerned when he found Leila and I alone in the garden." Cat nudged Ella's foot with her own. "*I* thought he was handsome."

Ella almost scoffed again, but then stopped herself. He was handsome. She would grudgingly admit it to herself but refused to say as much aloud.

He had light brown hair and deep green eyes. His lower lip was fuller than the top and it softened the hard lines of his angular face. His body had been firm when he caught her, and then he'd continued to hold her as if her weight was insignificant.

But handsome was not love.

"Cat can marry him." Leila sat on the bed and stroked Ella's hair where it lay splayed against the coverlet. "But I don't want either of you to go away. Soon I'll be the only one left."

"I don't wish to wed either." Cat wrinkled her nose. "It seems terribly bothersome. Leila, you and I can grow old together in this castle." She sat up abruptly as though something had just occurred to her. "What if you made him not wish to wed you, Ella?"

"I'm sure he already feels that way." Ella sighed. Surely, it hadn't been enough to dissuade his intent to wed her, and she hated how thoughts back on her behavior made her stomach twist with guilt. She had just been...surprised...and overwhelmed.

"What if *he* refuses to marry *you*?" Cat grinned. "You cannot be faulted for agreeing to the marriage and having him not going through with the union."

Ella and Leila looked at each other and both turned to Cat at once. "That's brilliant," Ella said. "Though I cannot do it by being rude. I already feel awful about how I treated him in the orchard."

"You'd better think quickly then." Leila nudged Ella with her elbow. "Because now it's nearly time for supper."

"Quick, help me put my hair up." Ella scooped up her locks. "Once he sees how large my ears are, he will not think me very attractive."

Her thick, wavy curls rebelled against her attempts to gather it all. She'd always hated her ears and took desperate attempts to hide them. While she would never be as beautiful as Anice, she did ordinarily try to look her best.

Not tonight.

Leila rushed to her aid, twisting the mass. Cat got a ribbon and secured the locks with a giggle. "I don't think we've ever seen your ears."

The two younger sisters stepped back to regard Ella with wide smiles. Leila's wilted somewhat. "Your ears aren't all that big."

Ella frowned slightly and touched her ears. They felt huge and exposed. "Are you certain?"

"We could dress you in one of my old gowns." Cat rushed over to her clothing trunk. "They are too small, and the ill fit will be unflattering."

"I suppose," Ella agreed. "Though we'll need more than just my appearance." And she refused to do anything that might shame their father. Like dipping her fingers into the salt bowl instead of using the tip of her knife. After all, she was a clever girl, she could surely find a way to dissuade Calville's attentions without being crude.

Cat set to work on Ella's gown, removing her kirtle and replacing it with one of Cat's. The fit was tight across the shoulders and chest. It was horrendously uncomfortable, if Ella was being honest, and restricted her movements. However, when Cat held up the small mirror and Ella saw how the front strained at her waist and breasts, she was forced to agree the gown was indeed terribly unflattering.

The three sisters held hands on their way down to the great hall. Ella had nearly brought Moppet with her, but feared doing so might be disastrous, to the point of humiliating her family. Papa was still at Truce Day and Anice had returned to her own manor. Marin and Bran had remained at Werrick Castle and were already at the table, along with the steward, William. Calville was the last to arrive with three dogs in tow.

Ella lifted a brow. "You brought your hunting dogs to Werrick?"

He grinned. "Aye, it's rumored there is great hunting to be had in these lands."

The castle priest, Bernard, blessed the meal and bowls of water were brought out to each of them at the family table. Ella and Calville dipped their hands in the water and servants wiped them clean.

Trenchers of meat and stewed vegetables were brought out along with baskets of bread. While they were indeed a noble family, they did not go through the pomp of several courses. Not on the border where airs were not required to the same effect as one might expect in the rest of England. No doubt Marin was dying inside at the lack of time to prepare a more respectable dinner for their guest.

"Do you not think it's cruel?" Ella asked.

The earl gave her his full attention despite the trencher of food placed between them. "I beg your pardon, my lady?"

"Hunting," she clarified. "Do you not find it cruel?"

If he was offended at having received the first meal in its entirety without a fruit, broth and a lighter meat served first, he offered no comment. He sliced into the venison at the joint, carving out the choicest, tenderest piece. "I only find it cruel if one does not intend to eat what they have caught, and if they aren't good hunters and the poor beast suffers."

"And what of the animal that's been hunted down?" she demanded.

He slid the best cut of meat onto her trencher and her words suddenly went dry in her mouth at the show of kindness.

"If the hunt is over quickly, the beast does not suffer. Not with anticipation, nor with fear or pain."

A snuffling sound came from beneath the table and the head of a gray hunting dog lifted to reveal a pair of hopeful brown eyes.

"Hardy, be gone with you." Calville gently nudged the dog. It didn't move. "Hardy. Now." The dog continued to stare up at Ella.

"Hardy, go lay down," she said. The beast obediently turned and flopped to the ground with a grumble of disappointment.

Calville nodded with approval. "I'm impressed. Hardy doesn't listen to anyone."

"I hold great affection for animals," she said pointedly. Then she cut a piece of the venison he'd given her, pulled it from her blade and slid it into her mouth.

"Like deer?" he asked with a smirk.

She nearly choked on the mouthful she was swallowing. "Do you have any siblings?"

"A sister." His reply was amicable enough, and he did not seem to mind the shift in conversation. "She's several years younger than me."

"What does she enjoy?" Ella picked around the meat and plucked a bit of cabbage.

"I confess, I do not know." He cut off a piece of meat for himself. "I haven't been able to spend much time with her."

Ah, a perfect topic to prod. Ella tilted her chin in the haughty way she'd seen the ladies at court do, the one time that she'd been there when she was a girl. "Men often do not take the time to learn of a lady's interests or pursuits as they are often too busy engaged in their own amusements."

He placed a bite of food in his mouth and chewed, his expression one of consideration. Something nudged Ella's foot. Most likely Hardy. She ignored it. The second nudge was more of a jab. Surprised, she looked up and found Marin's hard gaze fixed on her, sharp with warning.

"I don't disagree," the earl said at last. "I've seen deplorable examples of exactly such things."

"Have you not taken an interest in your sister's life, then?" A full-on kick this time from Marin, directly to the shin. Pain bloomed just below Ella's knee and she discreetly put her hand over the injury under the table. No sooner had she done so than a warm tongue lapped greedily over her fingers. Now *that* was definitely Hardy.

"Alas, my inability to visit her was due to circumstances outside of my control." Calville appeared genuinely regretful. "I'd like to hear more about the books you and your sisters wrote."

Ella took a big gulp of wine, but it did little to help her swallow her disappointment. He hadn't appeared to be at all perturbed by her goading, and he hadn't once even bothered to let his gaze settle on her ears or the straining waistline of Cat's dress. Now she was simply being a deplorable person, eating food she now felt guilty for consuming and wearing a kirtle she could scarcely move in.

Her plan was not working.

4

Bronson hid a smile at Ella's antics. It was quite obvious she was attempting to lure him into a heated discussion of some sort. In truth, he was enjoying it, this sparring of words, like verbal chess.

She'd worn her hair up that evening, the glossy mass of wavy hair bound up with a bit of ribbon. While he'd enjoyed seeing her hair unbound and falling softly around her face, he equally enjoyed being able to see the sensual curve where her long, graceful neck met her shoulders. He wanted to brush his lips over that spot and feel her shiver with pleasure.

Her dress, however—that was a curious thing indeed. It was obvious the green kirtle was ill-fitted and left her movements hindered. Her firm bosom strained at the front where the neckline cut into the soft flesh and pressed tempting mounds of creamy skin. It looked terribly uncomfortable. His hands itched to unlace her dress, to free her poor breasts and ease their discomfort with caresses.

"We have been writing them for some time," Lady Catriona piped up.

He dragged his gaze from his intended wife and focused on the younger, blonde sister.

"The books," she said. "It was Ella's idea to write our own stories. First from what we'd heard from troubadours that came through, but then we started our own. We all like those better, as much as we enjoy the French books Papa brings us sometimes. Ella is the best at coming up with ideas."

"Aye," Ella replied. "Stories of love."

"Not arranged marriages?" He'd meant it as a light jest.

Ella, however, did not laugh, nor did she offer a goading remark. She stared down at her food, her expression shuttered.

"When we are wed, I shall buy you hundreds of books," Bronson promised.

Still, she did not look up.

"My marriage was arranged," William said. They all regarded the steward. He ducked his head and a tender, affectionate expression softened his face. "We were happy. I c‑couldn't imagine my life without her." He paused and ran a hand over his auburn hair to smooth what had not been out of place. "She d‑died in the childbed, along with our newly b‑born daughter." He smiled regardless, in the way kind people often did, even when divulging sad news. "Arranged marriages can bring great happiness. Those years with my Annie were the best of my life."

"Many marriages that start with strangers turn to love." Lady Marin regarded her Scots husband with a quiet smile. "You simply need to get to know one another."

At least it appeared the others were championing Bronson's efforts. He glanced to Ella for her reaction and found her cheeks red. She pressed her lips together as though restraining words she'd rather say and reached for her wine.

The sound of rending fabric filled the solemn silence. She sat up straight and her eyes went wide.

At her back, a seam had split behind her right shoulder, revealing smooth fair skin beneath fraying green cloth. Ella's mouth fell open while Lady Catriona and Lady Leila covered giggles behind their hands. Lady Marin touched her fingertips to her brow and slowly closed her eyes.

"Excuse me." Ella shoved back in her chair.

Before Bronson could get to his feet, she was already out of her seat and partway across the hall. He leapt up and went after her. He'd half-expected someone to stop him, especially once he was in the corridor, where they might be alone, but no one did. He continued on in his pursuit.

"Lady Ella," he called after her. She did not stop. Of course. What had he possibly expected? That she would stop, turn to him and race into his arms?

He shook his head at his own stupidity and quickened his pace until he was directly behind her. "Lady Ella." He spoke with more authority this time.

It did the trick. She spun about, her eyes flashing with indignation. "Why are you following me?"

He offered a smooth smile that slid easily over his mouth. "I simply wish to walk you to your chamber," he replied. "To learn more about you."

She stared at him for a long moment. "That isn't necessary but thank you."

"I would enjoy it." He offered her his arm. "Being at your side, knowing you are well-protected." His courtier's manners had always pleased women.

Ella, however, did not appear impressed.

Not that it mattered. He would win her over the same as he won everyone over.

Ella looked at his arm but did not take it. "I will hardly be abducted on my way to my room."

He dropped his hand and contented himself to walk beside her. "How long ago did William's wife and child pass on?" If she wouldn't share anything about her own life with him, sharing things about others would still enable him to get to know her.

"About fifteen years ago."

"And he's not remarried?"

Ella slowed her brisk pace. "Nay."

"He must have loved her very much." Bronson could not stop his thoughts from trailing back to his own mother's death, and how his father had married Brigid before the year was out. It had been impossible to resent his stepmother, though. She had been such a source of comfort to him as he made his slow, painful way through grieving.

"Mayhap marriage causes considerable stress." Ella's tone was nonchalant with the pragmatic assessment. "Papa never remarried either after my mother died."

"You write stories of love, and you assume their lack of remarriage is due to stress?"

Ella didn't answer but began walking more quickly. "Here is the door to my chamber, and no fiend has attempted to abscond with my person. Are you pleased?"

He stopped in front of her and took in her face. Sconces lit the corridor with small flames and cast a gilded hue to her lovely face. Her blue gaze flicked away and back up to his face, bits at a time, as though grudgingly studying him as well.

It was her mouth which most drew his attention, pink and lush, gently parted as though she wanted him to kiss her. He knew better.

"You aren't going to attempt a kiss now, are you?" Her tone confirmed his suspicions so perfectly, he nearly laughed.

"You should be so lucky." He smirked. "But, nay, I've no intention of kissing you."

"Lucky indeed." Ella crossed her arms over her chest.

"Oh, aye, because kisses aren't just sloppy things meant for mouths. I'd touch my lips to you. Gently at first, and not on your mouth, but here." He lightly ran a fingertip down the graceful dip between her shoulder and neck. "Then here." Slowly, he drew his finger to the hollow of her collarbone. Her pulse ticked with wild frenzy beneath his fingertip. "Then I'd cup your face in my hands and slowly, tenderly kiss your mouth until you felt your whole world melt away from beneath you."

Her lids lowered, her eyes hazy with unmistakable desire. "I would hate that," she whispered.

He nodded with a serious expression. "Which is exactly why I didn't bother trying." He looked about. "Shall I fetch a maid to assist you in changing into a new gown? Mayhap one with a proper fit?"

Her arms had relaxed to her sides as he'd spoken about the kiss, and now pulled up to cross over her chest once more. "Nay, I will not be coming down. I should like to stay in my room."

"I shall miss your conversation. There is a fire in you that greatly appeals to me." With that, he took her soft hand in his, kissed the air above it and departed, leaving her to slowly simmer in his wake.

ELLA SCRAMBLED INTO HER ROOM AND TRIED DESPERATELY TO reach the ties of her kirtle. The unforgiving fabric was so tight about her, she could scarcely breathe. She'd nearly fainted dead away when Calville had gone into detail on what he would do to her if he were to kiss her.

Ugh. The man was beyond arrogant.

She hated how sure he'd been of himself and hated even more how her body had stirred with heat in response. Her fingers grasped and missed the ties of the kirtle several frustrating times before finally catching one and yanking. It unraveled quickly, as if it were as desperate to be rid of the strain as she was to be free of the squeezing pressure.

She drew herself from the garment and resisted the urge to kick it aside. After all, the tear could be mended. She laid it over one of the chairs near the hearth, drew on a night rail and curled into the large shared bed.

The night had been a failure. Ella's heart sank. Mayhap she ought to have done something more drastic. And yet part of her was glad she had not. Her goading had done nothing more than reflect poorly on her character.

She squeezed her eyes shut and tried to will sleep to come, to still the churning thoughts in her mind. While sleep did not come, images did. Ones of Calville leaning over her, his mouth brushing across the skin of her neck. She traced the path he had with his fingertips. Her skin prickled with pleasure.

She opened her eyes. Nay. She would not think of such things. But no matter what she told herself, when she tried to sleep again, she imagined him kissing her collarbone. She cast a longing glance at the chamber's door and silently begged her sisters to walk through it soon, to save her from her own mental torment.

A sudden thought came to her: not only had she failed that evening, but Calville had won.

Eventually, sleep finally did come and on the morrow, she received a summons from her father to see him in his study. She quickly broke her fast and went to the solar to meet with her father. He sat at the large desk with his forehead propped in his hand.

"Welcome home, Papa," Ella said pleasantly.

The earl lifted his head and glowered at her. "I heard of your behavior at supper last eve." He sighed heavily and pinched at the bridge of his nose. "Coming home from Truce Day with tidings such as those was most unwelcome."

Her stomach twisted with guilt. Being Warden was difficult, she knew. He often spoke of the perfidy of others in power he had to deal with, of innocent men punished for crimes they did not commit, while wicked men were freed. All this paired with the king questioning his loyalty.

Her father was losing weight as he aged, and now the large

chair he'd once filled seemed to swallow him up. It made him appear vulnerable in a way she'd never noticed before. And it made her feel all the more wretched for what she'd done.

She was exceedingly grateful she had not brought Moppet to supper or acted rudely at the table. "It was simply a discussion. I am sorry if it offended him."

If Calville had been offended, however, hopefully it had been enough that he would return to London and leave her be.

Lord Werrick narrowed his eyes. "Are you truly, Ella? Or have you and your sisters come up with some scheme to run him off so that he won't want to marry you?"

Ella dropped her gaze to the ground lest he see the truth written on her face.

Her father saw through the paltry guise. "Ah, exactly as I figured." He sighed. "Marin told me you wore Cat's kirtle and tore it."

"I'm sorry, Papa."

"And I am sorry as well, Ella." He pushed up from his large chair and came around the desk to embrace her. "I know this is not the marriage you had wanted. I know what you are forced to do is unfair."

She nodded, unable to speak. It all was unfair. Terribly so.

"It breaks my heart that you have to make this choice." There was a heaviness to her father's tone, and it tore deep into Ella.

He pulled her into an embrace against his skinny chest. Never once had he asked her to take on this burden of a marriage to Calville. Anice and Marin had, but never Papa. It was a reminder of why she had accepted this marriage in the first place: to save her father. A man worthy of saving, no matter the sacrifice.

Her father released her, and she looked up at him. "Why did you never marry again after Mother died?"

Her father drew in a hard breath. Her question had taken him aback.

"I..." He blinked and looked about the room, clearly gathering his thoughts.

"Was it because marriage is so difficult?" she pressed. If nothing else, at least she could win an argument.

"Nay. It isn't that, it's simply..." Papa's eyes went watery with unshed tears. "How can I fall in love again when my heart died with her?"

She murmured her thanks, then offered her father one final hug by means of silent apology for having hurt him, first with her childish behavior, then with her question, and fled the room.

She could not think on it anymore, not when it made her head ache and her heart pound. She grabbed the green leather-bound copy of *Floire et Blancheflor*. Never had she related more to Blancheflor, feeling as though she herself had been sold by King Felix to the merchants traveling to Babylon.

But rather than being sold to keep her from love, she was being married off.

5

Bronson walked the length of the orchard with his hunting dogs trotting behind him. Rafe could have easily taken the dogs to run them a bit, but Bronson had hoped to find a lady tucked in a tree. He wouldn't have complained should a naked leg dangle in front of him once more.

He'd thought about it often enough to border on being rather ridiculous. How could a single limb be so wonderfully tantalizing? And while he didn't know the answer to that, he knew only that it was.

He could almost feel the heat of her silky skin as he imagined palming her shapely calf and sliding her skirt up those creamy thighs, gazing openly at what he'd only been able to peek at before.

After a second pass through the orchard, Bronson accepted Ella was not about. Upon entering the castle, Bronson passed his beasts onto Rafe and went in search of Ella. He wouldn't want the excitable beasts jumping and racing about as he told her about the conversation he'd had with her father that morning.

The Earl of Werrick had been quick to apologize for Ella's behavior, claiming it was his own fault for spoiling his middle daughter. Bronson had told the earl that no apologies were necessary, and that he was still interested in the marriage. Negotiations for the union had proceeded smoothly. Now the marriage was fully settled, the documents signed.

He had implored the earl not to tell Ella. At least, not yet, not before Bronson could speak with her.

At least not until he found her, which had proven to be a difficult task. At last, he caught sight of Cat as she passed through a doorway. He followed her into the castle's kitchen, rich with smells of various cooking foods. Food stores hung on strings overhead and were bottled in clay pots.

Cat beamed brightly at him. "Good morrow, Lord Calville. Did you sleep too late, and sneak down for a bit of bread as well?"

He chuckled. "Nay, I'm searching for Lady Ella. Have you seen her?"

Cat lifted the cloth off a wooden bowl and peered at a pile of freshly baked rolls. "Have you checked the orchard?"

"Aye, I didn't see her there."

Cat pulled out a roll and held it to him. He shook his head. She shrugged, biting into the bread as she let the cloth fall back into place over the bowl.

"Ach, what are you doing here, my Cat?" A rotund woman with bright blue eyes and gray hair came out of what Bronson presumed to be the larder.

Her apron streaked with flour suggested she was the cook. A female cook was an interesting thing to be certain, but if she had made the food the prior night, she'd done it as well as any man.

The woman lifted a brow at Cat's full cheeks. "Overslept again, did you?"

Cat nodded vigorously.

She peered into the bowl and tsked. "You could've taken the ones I'd made from this morning rather than the ones just out of the oven. Did you burn your tongue?" the cook asked.

Cat nodded vigorously again.

The woman poured a cup of ale from a pitcher near her and handed it to Cat. "Serves you right, you know."

Cat drank deep from the cup and set it down with a happy sigh. "Aye, I know, Nan. Thank you."

Nan nodded to Bronson. "Who is this you've brought into my kitchen?"

"The man Ella has to marry." Cat winced. "Er, I mean, Ella's betrothed." She shot him an apologetic smile.

Something nudged at Bronson's shins. He glanced down and found the small black cat from the day before. Apparently, the dogs had scared it off until now.

"I see Bixby likes him." Nan chortled with laughter.

"Why does everyone find that so funny?" Bronson asked warily.

Cat giggled. "Because Bixby loves rats."

Bronson failed to share their humor. "It's unfortunate Lady Ella isn't a rat then, or I might have more ease in locating her."

"Ach, we're only jesting, my lord." Nan smiled good-naturedly at him. "The lady is most likely in the orchard."

"I checked there already."

"Perhaps the solar then?" Cat broke off a piece of the roll, blew on the chunk, then popped it into her mouth.

Bronson inclined his head with gratitude. "Come along, Bixby." But as he made his way to the doorway, the cat remained where he'd stretched out on the floor. Bronson grinned at having been abandoned by the little beast.

Apparently, he was not a rat after all.

"Have you heard from Geordie recently?" Nan asked Cat as if he had already left the room. No doubt not noticing Bixby hadn't followed him at all.

Cat's wide smile wilted. "Nay. I suspect he's terribly busy on campaign to not have written."

Bronson slipped from the kitchen, giving the ladies their

privacy. He found the solar easily. The room appeared empty, but then he spied Ella.

There she was, on a padded bench seat beneath a large glass window. Sunlight streamed in and poured over her. Her back rested against the wall; her legs were propped in front of her with a book settled in her lap. She had a whimsical expression, something far away and dreamy as she read, completely oblivious to his presence.

She bit her lip and her fingers lightly curled over the next page in anticipation to turn it before she'd even finished reading.

"It must be a very good book." He said it as softly as he could, lest he startle her.

She jumped slightly regardless, and her brow furrowed. "It is."

"Is it one you and your sisters wrote?" he asked.

"Nay, 'tis *Floire et Blancheflor*." Her eyes went to the book once more.

He approached her. "My mother had a fondness for reading."

"Mmmm..." Ella settled deeper into the cushions. Her bare feet poked out from beneath the fine linen of her pale blue gown.

"My father said books were far too expensive and so he didn't buy her many." He glanced around the room at the shelves of books. It was not nearly so many as in a monastery, but there were easily four dozen or so. A veritable fortune. Their leather spines faced out in a colorful array of dyed leather. No doubt some were books the women of Werrick had written.

"I imagine hunting dogs and destriers far surpass the cost of a book." She turned another page and her attention trailed to the upper left-hand corner of her book. She looked up and shook her head slightly, as though chastising herself. "It sounds like you know what she liked." Her gentle smile was evidently offered by way of apology.

"Aye, I know everything my mother liked." Bronson settled against the wall opposite the one Ella leaned against to better see her, to watch her captivating expressions and the way the light played in her glossy hair.

"She liked animals," he continued. "Cats, especially. We had several in the house and it was riotous when my father would return from court with his hunting dogs." He laughed at the memory of chairs being overturned and tapestries falling. "Cats running about in every direction, dogs darting about after them."

Ella chuckled and her eyes slid back to her book.

"I don't think she ever read *Floire et Blancheflor*," Bronson continued. "But her favorite book was *Roman de la Rose*."

Ella's head lifted with interest. "*Roman de la Rose?*"

"Aye. Penned by Jean Renart. Do you know it?"

Ella sat straighter, her gaze focusing on him fully for the first time since he'd entered the room. "I do. I read it once when I was at court. It was a beautiful story."

"I have it still at Berkley Manor. It was the only book I kept after my mother died. You can have it if you like."

"You would give me her book?" Ella looked at him wonder.

The victory, though small, had made him glad to have mentioned it. It would make the news he would share more welcome. Or so he hoped.

ELLA HAD ALWAYS WANTED A COPY OF *ROMAN DE LA ROSE*. SHE never asked her father for books; he simply bought ones he thought she might enjoy. To ask for more had seemed greedy when he was already so generous. Now Calville was offering her exactly what she'd coveted for years. Giddy excitement quickened through her.

And yet, it had been his mother's book. He obviously had cared greatly for her, enough to have kept it after she had died.

Ella set her book aside and hugged her knees to her chest. "How old were you when your mother died?"

He shifted his gaze from her to the floor on the other side of the room. "I was ten." He shrugged. "Too old to need my mother."

He did not look away from the invisible spot on the floor. Despite his flippancy, it was obvious her loss still pained him.

"I was seven," Ella said. "I think it's difficult no matter what age you are. Did you ever read it?"

He frowned slightly. "Read what?"

"*Roman de la Rose*."

"Nay. I tried it, but..." He shrugged again. "I don't enjoy reading stories."

She eased back into her seat. Was that a pull of disappointment at her heart? Ridiculous. "Do you find them silly?"

"Boring."

"Boring?" She gaped at him. "How could you possibly consider them to be boring? They are full of deceit and adventure and love and travel. They have everything." She got off the bench and came to his side.

He looked up at her, surprised. Her stomach gave a little twist of shyness at how close she stood. There was a pleasant scent about him, like soap and sandalwood.

"I presume you have not read *Floire et Blancheflor*." She held out the book to him. "I'd like for you to read it."

He did not pull it from her hand, but instead simply continued to watch her. "Here? Now?"

She laughed. It wasn't what she'd meant, but it would at least ensure he read it. "Aye."

He took it from her and opened it to the first page. It did not possess the beautifully painted pictures as some of their books did. As much as she would like to see the story painted out in bold blues and vibrant reds, the ones with more detail were far more costly.

"It's in French, as *Roman de la Rose* is," he mused.

"Aye, all books with stories are French." She leaned over his shoulder, desperate for him to start. "English texts are only ever on religion. Read."

He smiled lightly, held the book aloft and began to read. She tried to keep from cringing at his monotone voice. He'd only gone through two lines when she knew it would not get any better. His reading was awful.

While his French was immaculate, his words were without inflection, without color or taste or vision. They were simply said, read aloud like London's caller blandly announcing another hour passed.

"No wonder you hate to read." She hadn't realized she'd spoken the words out loud until his droning ceased.

"Have I done something wrong?" he asked.

"Aye, egregiously so. You read without passion."

His mouth lifted at the corner. "'Tis a book."

"Nay, 'tis a world." She held out her hand. "Let me show you."

He closed the cover and passed it to her. She cradled the cool, smooth leather spine in her palm and reveled in the soft creak as she opened it. Her pulse thrummed faster with nervousness. She'd read aloud many times before for Papa and her sisters. Why was she now suddenly anxious to do so?

She began to read, her voice shaking slightly, breathless. At least, until the story took her away. By the time she got to the queen accepting the knight's widow as her lady-in-waiting, and both delivering their babies on Palm Sunday, Ella was lost in the story.

Page after page, she read, continuing on through the adventure as the two grew up together and the king became wary of Blancheflor possessing his son's affections, and so sold her to the merchants. By the time Ella got to the part where Floire was mistakenly taken to Claris's room in the tower rather than Blancheflor's, she'd idly sat down on the bench and Calville had joined her.

Far too soon, the book ended and the hum of her own voice in the room went quiet. She blinked, lost for a moment in the tale she'd read, and reorienting herself in the solar, sitting next to the young earl. He sat so closely that his thigh rested against hers. His body heat pressed against her in an act more intimate than any she'd ever experienced with a man.

Her shyness returned. Her cheeks flared hot with a self-consciousness she could not help, especially with the awed way he gazed at her.

"That was...incredible." He shook his head, almost disbelieving. "You brought it to life in a way I've never heard before. I could see the characters, feel their struggles." His searching gaze swept over her face. "*You* are incredible, Lady Ella."

Her heart thundered in her chest and the heat of her cheeks spread to her ears, her chest, even her stomach. Aye, he was too close, but she did not mind. Indeed, she would not mind being closer still.

He leaned toward her, so their faces were nearly touching. His eyes locked with hers, a deep, perfect green. "Will you read for me again someday?"

"Aye." She tilted her chin upward, so their mouths were only a whisper away. "Is it not the most passionate thing imaginable?"

"Not the most passionate." He lifted his hand and gently brushed his fingertips down her neck and in the shallow dip of her collarbone. She sucked in a soft inhale. Would he kiss her there?

His other hand came up and he cupped either side of her jaw, careful, gentle, as though he worried that she might break. Her heartbeat came faster until it was hard to catch her breath. All she could think of was his detailing of how he would kiss her; how the simple touch of his fingertip on her skin had elicited such delight.

His lips brushed hers, surprisingly soft and wonderfully warm. He pressed his mouth to hers once, twice, then he parted his mouth to kiss first her top lip then the bottom, then both at once. Ella's head swam, her thoughts whirling in a tangle of desire and excitement.

He nudged apart her lips and dipped his tongue between them. Prickles of pleasure danced over her skin. His hands slid down her arms and over her back, holding her to him.

Her breasts crushed against the strength of his chest. She wanted to touch him as well, to let her fingers trail over his chest, which had been so firm when he'd caught her as she fell from the tree. But she stayed her hand for fear of being thought of as wanton.

His mouth descended down her chin to her neck. Her heart raced faster still. Was he going to make good on his promises the night before? He pressed kisses to the dip between her neck and shoulder. Exactly where he'd said he would.

It was far more wonderful than Ella had imagined. So much pleasure, so much anticipation for more.

A throb had begun between her legs, thundering to the same beat as her heart. His kisses trailed down, to the hollow of her collarbone. Ella moaned and dropped her head back. Her breasts pushed forward of their own volition. The action pressed her aching nipples to the fabric of her dress. Bliss rushed through her body.

Would he touch her breasts? She knew it was something men enjoyed doing with women. It had always seemed silly, until now.

Calville leaned back and gazed at her with half-lidded eyes. Though she'd never seen a man regard her thus, she knew the expression to be one of sensuality. Of lust. That *she* had caused. A gasp slipped from between her lips.

"Kiss me again." She sat forward and tentatively reached out for him. "Please, Calville."

He released her body to caress her face. "Call me Bronson."

"Bronson," she repeated.

He nodded and brushed his thumb over her lower lip. Her eyes swept closed in expectation.

"Soon, Ella. We can kiss like this and so, so much more." His wonderful, hot mouth found hers again. "After we are married on the morrow."

Her eyes flew open. "I beg your pardon?"

He leaned back with a grin. "We'll be wed on the morrow, Ella. Does that not please you?"

She stared at him in horror. It did not please her. Not when they were only just beginning to know one another, not when there was still so much to learn.

All the pleasure he had elicited, all the anticipation he had awoken, went cold. Ella was not ready, not when there was still so much to learn of one another.

Not when she did not love him.

6

Ella's father had obviously been anticipating her arrival. He didn't look at all surprised at her appearance in the steward's room, where the earl often went over ledgers. William, however, regarded her warily.

"I assume he's told you." The earl rubbed his brow.

"I can go, my lord." William half-rose from his seat in preparation to flee.

"Why would you not have told me?" Ella tried to keep her tone even, a difficult feat in the light of such betrayal.

"Because I asked him not to." Calville entered the room. "You're to be my wife, Lady Ella. I thought it best that I should tell you, to begin to establish trust between us."

A fire roared in the large hearth and sunlight streamed in from the window. The room had become too hot. Suffocatingly so. Ella fought the heat choking the air from her lungs and making her head spin. "It's so soon."

"It is," Calville agreed. "There are matters at hand that require us to join in our union sooner rather than later."

Surely that did not mean... was the king so ready to accuse her father of disloyalty? "Papa," she gasped.

Her father shook his head. "We are not the only ones who stand to gain favor from your marriage."

"I'm not ready." Ella drew herself upright. "Please, could we delay, just for a sennight?"

She glanced at Calville who frowned slightly. Would he not agree to it?

Her father glanced through a stack of parchment and paused to gaze down at one with the king's crest on it. "I suppose waiting a sennight might not cause issue..."

He handed the parchment to William who scanned over it with considerably more care. "It can be done if both parties are amenable."

The suggestion hovered in the air, not meant for Ella so much as it was for Calville. After all, the negotiations were from England where women had no voice.

Calville cast a questioning glance in her direction and she silently begged him with her eyes. Looking at him thus, a connection tightened between them, making her recall the kiss they'd shared only moments ago. Her body hummed at the memory.

His lips had been wonderfully soft, his touch tender. And her response...that had been the most surprising thing of all. She'd reveled in his touch, his kisses. She tucked her lower lip into her mouth as she savored the remnant feel of his lips on hers.

His gaze shifted to the subtle action. "I am not opposed to granting such a request," he answered slowly. "This marriage has come upon us all rather abruptly. I do, however, have a request of my own."

Ella bit back a scoff. Of course, an agreement could not be made without negotiation.

"Would it be agreeable to you if we extend the date by a fortnight instead?" He asked the question as though he expected an argument.

Certainly, he would get none from her. She knew it best to

hold her tongue in such a situation and instead looked to her father to offer his final answer.

"You see," Calville continued, "it would please me greatly to have my stepmother and half-sister in attendance. They are all the family I have left, and I know it would mean a great deal to them to join us." He slid a smile in Ella's direction. "I've been inspired to get to know my half-sister better and feel this would be an ideal opportunity to do so."

Shame lowered her gaze to the ground. She had been rude to him and he responded only with more kindness.

"That's perfectly reasonable," her father replied.

"And you, Lady Ella?" Calville came to her side.

She looked up at him, startled.

He inclined his head. "It is your life too, Lady Ella. Would you be comfortable extending the day of our union out by a fortnight?"

"I would be amenable to it," Ella said graciously. "Especially with such a good intention as you spending time with your sister."

He smiled at her and something inside her stomach gave a pleasant little flip.

Papa clapped his palms together and rubbed his hands, the matter clearly settled with him. "William, please see to it that Lord Calville's family has all they need to make their journey here as comfortable as is possible."

"Aye, my lord." William closed the ledger he'd had open and practically leapt from his seat to slip out the door before he could be called back.

Ella was just as eager to flee as William had, but did not move from where she stood. And while she maintained her demure expression, she was crying out with joy within. An extra fortnight! It was practically a lifetime. Mayhap in that time, Calville would decide he did not wish to have her as a wife. After all, women who climbed trees and read books were not especially prized at court.

Her father did not appear as pleased as she was. He indicated the door. "If you will, Calville, I'd like a moment with my daughter."

Ella's stomach slithered lower. This did not bode well.

"Of course." Calville bowed and removed himself from the room.

She had expected her father to yell, or at the very least chastise her. Instead, he merely frowned. "When you make a commitment to something, you must make good on it." He put his hand on the surface of the desk, his fingers spread. "You could have said nay when I asked you. I will give you the final option one more time, daughter." He went to the window where he unlatched the shutters. Fresh, cool air rushed in. "Will you agree to marry the earl of Calville?"

She opened her mouth to immediately reply, but he put up his hand to stop her. "If you do, you will cease this nonsense of trying to dissuade him from marrying you. With that in mind, I ask you again: will you marry the Earl of Calville?"

She hesitated in her response. This time, it was a different thing altogether. This was full capitulation.

And yet with her father's freedom, mayhap even his life, at stake, she could not refuse. "I will marry him, Papa."

Her father waved her over. She went to his side and looked out to the garden below. Calville was there with his dogs, running them about. Two of them frolicked together while the gray one carried something over to him and set it at his feet. Hardy: that was the dog's name.

Ella smiled weakly, recalling Hardy's antics at supper the night before.

"I granted that extra fortnight for you with a purpose in mind," the earl said. "And it was not for you to have more time to discourage the earl's interest."

Papa settled his hand on her shoulder and gently squeezed with the same affection as when she'd been a girl. "I promised I would let you marry for love. I know the circumstances have changed, but I do not see my promise as being out of reach yet. Ella, my romantic, whimsical daughter, you have a fortnight to let yourself soften toward the idea of marrying the Earl of Calville. It is enough time, I pray, that the two of you may find love."

Papa pressed a kiss to the top of her head. He still smelled as he had when she'd been a child, of leather and parchment and sealing wax.

He regarded her once more. "Let go of your stubbornness and accept this gift most are not afforded."

His words broke through her walls and finally she did see the opportunity she'd been given—the chance to not marry a stranger after all, but, despite the circumstances, to marry for love.

※

Bronson's neck prickled with the sensation of being watched. His gaze lifted to find the window to the study open with Ella and her father both staring out. At him.

They could speak of him all they wanted, so long as Brigid and Lark were able to join him at Werrick. At least their visit would ensure they had enough food to eat and a comfortable place to sleep. Somewhere outside of Berkley Manor where repairs were sorely needed.

Ella had obviously been grateful for the stretch of time as well, relief practically shining in her eyes that she could put off marrying him for just that much longer. He should be grateful for the reprieve too.

Except the kiss they'd shared had awoken something within him. Ella was so unwilling to trust, so very wary. And for that brief moment in time, he'd lowered her shield and saw the beauty that lay beneath.

It was intoxicating, that trust, and he wanted more.

Hardy rushed by and nearly knocked his feet from beneath him.

"I spoil you," he said quietly to the dog, so no one else would hear.

Hardy's ears perked and he cocked his head with a questioning look in his deep brown eyes. Imploringly.

"Very well, but only once more." Bronson bent to retrieve the stick Hardy had brought back from the forest, careful to pick it up by the end not darkened with saliva. He hauled his arm back and launched it as far as he could.

For their part, Wolf and Bear panted in the shade, their ears perking with every passing of the stick. They were adequately trained hunting dogs. Not as spoiled as Hardy had become. It was Bronson's own fault though.

The stick spiraled through the air as Hardy flew with impossible speed to clamp it in his teeth. If training Hardy were possible, the beast would be a damn fine hunting dog. He had proper breeding, hawk-like focus, and he could run faster than the very devil if the old demon ever decided to give chase.

It was then that Bronson saw Leila in the garden once more with a large basket beside her, far too large for a young woman her size to manage. She was without a guard. Again.

Bronson headed toward Ella's youngest sister.

"You've trained Hardy well." Leila clipped several lengths of flowers from their stalks. A milky white substance oozed from the snipped stems.

"Not so well for a hunting dog, I'm afraid." Hardy appeared at that moment and dropped the stick on the ground in front of Bronson.

Leila gently laid her clippings in the basket with the other leaves and blooms and got to her feet. Hardy leaned his head back to watch her approach, his long, pink tongue lolling from his mouth. His tail thumped wildly on the ground.

She regarded the stick. "May I?"

Bronson lifted it from the ground and handed it to her, dry end first. "If you do, you may just become his favorite person.

Mind the bits where pieces have been snapped off, they're sharp."

Leila smiled quietly and took the stick with a nod of thanks. Before he could offer a word of advice, she hurtled it through the air with surprising force. Hardy leapt with excitement and dashed after his prize in a blur of gray.

"Do you want some help with your basket?" Bronson asked.

She hesitated as though intending to decline his offer, and then thought better of it. She nodded as Hardy approached with the stick jutting out of his mouth like a tusk. He dropped it in front of her and sat expectantly, filling the silence with the rapid thumping of his tail.

Bronson hefted the basket into his arms. "I told you you'd have a friend forever."

When she didn't throw the stick, Hardy wriggled closer to her and nudged his head under her hand.

"You need to remain patient, Hardy." Bronson scolded the dog like a child before he caught himself.

Leila smothered a giggle. "Do you talk to animals too?"

"Not all the time," Bronson started defensively. "Only when I need to tell them something." He winked at her and this time she didn't bother to hide her amusement.

He indicated the basket with his chin. "Where am I carrying this?"

"Just outside the kitchen. I'll show you."

He issued a sharp whistle and the other two dogs ran toward him. Hardy trotted after Leila with the retrieved stick in his mouth, his eyes bright with adoration.

"Ella can be hard to manage sometimes." Leila twisted her lips and flicked a shy glance in his direction. "She's been allowed to do what she likes."

"And now she's being forced to marry me," Bronson stated.

"And you're being forced to marry her." Leila shielded the sun from her eyes with one hand and found Hardy's head with the fingertips of her other. "You didn't choose her either."

Bronson gathered from the comfortable quiet settling between them that he didn't need to reply. Not with this young woman who was barely out of girlhood and yet saw more than most adults.

"Over there." Leila pointed to a small stone building with a thatched roof.

He ducked into the hut attached at the back of the castle and found various herbs and flowers hanging from the rafters, shelves, and anywhere else bits of string could be strung. The sweet perfume of drying herbs scented the air as they spun about by an unseen breeze. He set the basket on a stone table.

"Is that all you need?" he asked.

Leila nodded, her fingers still working over Hardy's ears. Hardy, for his part, was laying against Leila's legs in his attempt to be closer to her. The two were quite a pair to be sure.

"Mayhap he should stay here with you." Bronson indicated Hardy. "Until you come back to the keep."

Leila ducked her head, but not before he caught her small smile. "Are you certain?"

"Aye, Hardy hasn't had this much affection in years."

The dog didn't even bother to lift his ears at the sound of his own name. Besides, he would be good protection for little Leila, though Bronson sensed it was best not to mention that last part aloud.

"I'll bring him with me to supper this evening," Leila said.

Bronson nodded and made to duck out of the small stone hut.

"She's always dreamed of being wooed," Leila called after him.

He popped his head back in the sweet-smelling room. "I beg your pardon?"

"Ella." Leila scratched Hardy under the chin. "She's always loved the idea of heroes in stories." She shrugged. "Be her hero and you'll have an easier time winning her heart."

Her hero?

Bronson offered his thanks and slipped from the hut. He'd always been one to win over people, and Leila had just given him the key to unlocking Ella. If being a hero would be what was necessary to win her over, then he would become a damn hero.

7

Since Ella's determination to soften herself to Calville, she hadn't seen him. She'd wanted to thank him for his generosity in allowing them both more time.

Though she doubted she'd find him in the solar, she entered and discovered Cat sitting perched on the end of the window seat with a square of unfolded parchment in her hands.

"Have you seen Lord Calville?" Ella pulled Moppet from the little bag at her side. He tended to display a temper when she carried him about too long. He scampered out, drawing several acorns with him from the bag's depths.

Cat beamed at her. "It's from Geordie." Her shining gaze skimmed over the missive and she elicited a laugh. "The knights told him they've never seen a bowman more skilled than he. And he said when he told them about me, they didn't believe a woman could handle a bow like that. He wishes I could join him to show them all." She sighed wistfully "I wish I *could* be there."

It was still a strange thing to see Cat without Geordie, like the sun without a summer day to shine upon. It had been a long two years since Sir Richard had retired and Geordie had gone on campaign with the king's knights for the rest of his training.

Cat hadn't been the same without him.

"Not much longer now," Ella offered hopefully and put Moppet into Cat's hands.

Cat offered a sad smile and rubbed at Moppet's belly. "It'll be another winter at least until he's home. Why did Papa have to send him away?"

"To give him the experience he needs to become a knight." Ella softened her tone and ruffled a hand over Cat's silky hair. "You know that. You supported it too."

"I did." Cat traced a finger affectionately over Geordie's looping script. "I still do." She sighed. "Lord Calville was in the courtyard when I saw him last. It was not too long ago, and I imagine he could not have wandered far."

Ella watched her younger sister for a moment. It was a rare thing to see Cat fall prey to melancholy. Rare and sad.

Wordlessly, Ella pressed a kiss to her sister's smooth forehead.

Cat smiled up brightly at her. "May I read you the whole missive tonight as we ready for bed?"

"I'd love nothing more," Ella replied affectionately. She missed Geordie; they all did. Though he'd entered their home as prisoner years before, a sacrifice for his father's lies, he had become one of the family. He was a good young man with a good heart, always eager to please, quick with praise. He'd been Cat's closest companion.

"You can leave Moppet here, if you like," Cat offered. "His company is pleasant."

As if understanding what Cat had said, Moppet snuggled into a tight ball in her lap and his beady eyes slid closed.

Ella embraced Cat, careful not to disturb the sleeping squirrel, then navigated her way out of the castle and into the courtyard. Several of Werrick Castle's soldiers passed this way and that, but the bailey was otherwise empty. She turned to go back into the castle when she heard a familiar voice.

Calville.

"I suspected that was the case," he said. "When can we expect them?"

She followed his rumbling baritone all the way to the stables and stopped. The familiar sweet scent of hay mingled with the mustiness of horse sweat. An ache settled in her chest. She hadn't been to the stables in several days. Not since...

Shame heated through her. Not since she'd thrown herself at Peter and been rejected. Her hesitation to enter made her grit her teeth with frustration. This was her home. She ought to feel comfortable going anywhere. Even the stables.

"They'll be along in a month or so, I suspect," Peter said.

Ella's heart slapped her ribs at the familiar sound of his deep, smooth voice and her feet refused to pull her forward.

She glanced inside at the two men. First to Peter, who made her stomach flutter with the same giddy excitement he always had, but there was something else sitting heavily within her—a rock of regret. Next, she studied Calville, who stood slightly taller than the Master of the Horse, his back straighter, prouder.

Calville's body was bulkier, his arms thicker, his shoulders wider, and his features were not so fine as Peter's. Nay, they were hard angles and those soft, soft lips. Her pulse quickened and the memory of their gentle kiss flitted into her thoughts.

She backed up, eager to get far from the stable where the man who had rejected her spoke with the man who refused to reject her.

"Lady Ella." Calville leaned to see her easier and offered a wide smile. "I was just seeking advice on Wolf here and have discovered she'll be having pups soon." He indicated the hunting dog, laying in a pile of hay.

Ella's gaze wandered to Peter who nodded at her in greeting. As though nothing had ever happened. As though she hadn't sauntered into the stable in a dress as red as sin and asked him to deflower her. Her cheeks went hot.

Calville was talking still about the dog. She returned her attention to him.

"Would that please you?" Calville asked her. "To take one of her pups? As a wedding present."

The harrier lay in a slant of sunshine with motes dancing about her like fairies. Her velvety brown ears hung over her white and brown spotted face. Ella bent to stroke the weary dog and found her fur to be silky. Wolf lifted her head at once, her eyes bright and eager for attention. Her pups would undoubtedly have loose brown and white fur, floppy ears and sharp little needle teeth. How could Ella possibly turn down such a wonderful gift?

She grinned up at Calville. "I'd be honored to have one of her pups. Thank you."

"Then you may have first pick." He held out an arm to her. "Will you walk about the orchard with me?"

"Aye, of course." Ella slid her hand to the warm crook of his elbow.

He gave a short whistle. "Come, Wolf."

The dog leapt up despite the roundness to her belly and trotted over to them. Together they left the stables and Ella forced herself not to look back at Peter.

"Thank you." Ella kept her gaze forward as they left the courtyard and headed in the direction of the orchard.

"Wolf's pups will be fine beasts," Calville said with apparent pride in his tone. "If you enjoy dogs, I will give you a small army of them."

Ella laughed. "I prefer the animals I find in the forest to heal, generally. I was actually thanking you for the extra time." She bit her lip. "Before our wedding."

He was silent a moment. "It means a great deal to me that my stepmother and sister be here. I think it will do them much good to get away from Berkley Manor."

It was the first time he'd offered any indication at his own hesitation for their wedding. Mayhap he had doubts too, that he did not wish to marry either. If so, he was handling it far better than she. A man set on doing his duty while she balked against responsibility.

"Do you wish to marry me?" she asked.

His smooth gait faltered. "I beg your pardon."

Ella stopped walking and turned to face him. "Do you truly want to marry me?" She repeated the question and hated the way her insides clenched in anticipation for his answer.

❦

BRONSON DETECTED NO MALICE IN ELLA'S QUESTION, NOR HURT or excitement or any other emotion. Regardless of her apathetic delivery, he considered for a moment to offer a delicate reply.

"I did not wish to marry when I was first given the news," he replied carefully. "Yet now that I have met you, I think I should like to know you more."

She tilted her head and studied him as though trying to read through the diplomatic response. "What do you want to know about me?"

He lifted his shoulder and tried to act as though he didn't care. "Whatever I can find out in a fortnight, I suppose."

"What do you want from a wife?" Ella asked. "From me?"

Honestly, when offer for the marriage had been pushed upon him, he'd been eager to get his new wife with child so he might leave her at Berkley Manor with Brigid and Lark while he continued on with his life at court. As most men did.

Except that was not a heroic answer, not like the men from one of Ella's books. The proof of its lack of heroism was evident in the lives Brigid and Lark had led. The very idea made his muscles tense, with anger, and with betrayal. For all his life, his father had told him to care for women, to see their needs met, to be a man.

And in all those years, his father had lied. They had jaunted about on hunts, at court, at parties. Together, they had lived in the silk-lined lap of luxury while Brigid and Lark endured the torture of poverty.

"My lord?" Ella squeezed her hand on his arm gently. "Is it such a horrid answer that you hesitate to put it to voice?"

He chuckled. "Nay, 'tis nothing so grave. I am unsure what I want from you, Lady Ella. I know only that I wish to be a better man than my father."

Her brows pinched together, but before she could open her mouth with a question, he spoke. "And what do you want from me as a husband, Lady Ella?"

Ella stopped and trailed her fingers through the raised pond, sending ripples through the still, reflective waters. "I want love." But it was said in a tone flat with defeat. As though he was not worthy of it.

Resolve steeled him. He would get Ella to fall in love with him. By being a hero. Whatever that meant.

He would figure it out though, and then he would be that man. It was a far cry better than the man he had been: a courtier with expensive taste in clothes and women, who gave in to his desires, who shifted masks to be whoever was necessary to earn him more favor.

Life at Werrick Castle did not seem based on such foundational principals. It seemed honest, which terrified him. At court, honesty might cost one their head.

Ella drew her fingertips back and forth through the water again. The action was slow and graceful. Silence filled the space between them, and Bronson found himself lulled by it, by the gentle sweeping of her hand. The garden around them was only just beginning to come to life again after winter, with pale green leaves unfurling from withered shells of plants that had gone dormant. Life was beginning anew.

"I think one of the important things about a forced marriage is finding commendable things about one another." He approached her and propped himself against the edge of the pond. "I find you beautiful. I have since the first." Ella blushed and ducked her head.

He dipped his hand in the pool. The water was cool against the heat of his palm. "You are kind to animals. I like that too. Though I confess I am still baffled at how you got Hardy, of all creatures, to listen to you. And I find your passion for books to be enjoyable. I look forward to the day you will read to me in bed."

He rubbed at his brow with his free hand. "Although I find Moppet to be aggressive for a corpulent little squirrel." Lowering his arm, he dramatically glanced at her side for the pouch she transported the demon-beast in.

"He's being cared for by Cat." Ella smiled and swept her fingers over his brow. "Moppet can be the devil sometimes, but he's sweet and means well."

Bronson doubted as much but didn't wish to speak for fear of breaking the fragile moment. She was touching him, smiling at him—this wild and rare creature slowly easing toward his trust.

"You are good with your hunting dogs." Her touch fell away and her cheeks went pink. "I find you handsome and..." She tucked her lower lip into her mouth and slowly released it. "I liked your kisses."

He couldn't stop the grin spreading over his lips if he wanted to. And he bloody well didn't. "Then I shall have to give you more."

She drew in a soft breath. He stroked her jaw with his thumb and her eyes fell closed in anticipation. Aye, she was lovely. Achingly so.

He leaned in, intent on her lush mouth. A lapping sound filled the air, wet and sloppy. Ella's eyes opened and a baffled expression took over her face.

Bronson met her confusion when a weight barreled past their legs, sending them both sprawling back. Bear leapt up with his front paws, bracing himself on the end of the pond, and joined Wolf in greedily drinking the pond water. Their pants suggested that while Ella and Bronson were talking, they'd been running about.

Ella sat on the ground, no doubt thrown there by the impact, laughing good-naturedly at the two dogs. The clear, joyous sound of her mirth rang out in a way Bronson found immensely pleasant. He offered her his hand and gently pulled her to standing.

Something slipped from her pocket. Bronson immediately bent to pick it up and his head connected with hardness and pain. He shot up with his hand to his brow and found Ella doing likewise. They laughed together.

"I'll get it for you," Bronson offered. After all, wasn't that what heroes did? Watching her to ensure she stayed upright, he bent to retrieve what was a small book. Apparently, she had one on her person at all times. He handed it to her and dramatically cowered away as though afraid of her.

She took her book with a smile and shook her head at his antics. And they were foolish. That had been his intention. After all, the idea that this woman could hurt anyone was preposterous.

But picking up the book did give him an idea. Ella and her sisters had spent countless days dreaming up stories of adventure, and of romance. If Ella needed the perfect hero to fall in love, he knew exactly where to find examples of what appealed most to her—in the solar, from her own hand.

"Ride with me tomorrow," Bronson said. "I would love to see the land and the village, and I imagine you would know all the best places to go."

"I do," Ella agreed.

"Then it is done. I'll inform the Master of the Horse of our plans, and I shall see you at supper." He bowed to her and indicated the orchard. "I leave you to your trees, my lady."

While he knew he could press his hand for another opportunity to kiss her, he was a man who knew best how to anticipate the odds. And his would be considerably better with her idea of a hero locked in his mind.

✣ 8 ✢

Bronson spent the better part of the evening after supper and a portion of the next morning in the solar with the wealth of Ella's books. Her carefully scripted handwriting made it seem as though her words were dancing across the page, bright with resplendent descriptions and emotion. Though she was not there with him to read aloud, he imagined what had been penned by her hand being read in her voice, infused with passion.

He became buried in her stories, turning each page with haste to see what might happen. One was of a knight who happened upon a nymph pretending to be a lady lost in the woods. Another was of a princess locked in a tower and the courtier who fought to set her free. Yet another was about a female knight, of all the fascinating and impossible things, and how she fought alongside a prince with whom she ended up falling in love.

The tales were wild, fantastical and filled with many perfect ideas on how to win her heart. In reading her stories, she had unwittingly opened her heart to him and let him glimpse her secrets.

Something scrabbled in the corner and drew his attention from the troubadour creeping up on a dragon in defense of the fair maiden he sought to protect. Moppet stood in the doorway, his eyes gleaming with menace. The little beast did not possess an acorn in his paw, but that did not mean he couldn't find something else to throw. It also meant that Ella was most likely nearby, being that she was the only one in the castle who enjoyed the creature's company.

Bronson leapt to his feet, closing the book as he did so. Rushing so as not to get caught, he hastened to a shelf and shoved the book into an available gap.

"Ah, Calville," Ella's sweet voice rang out. "There you are. I thought you might have gone on the ride without me."

He spun around to face her. "Good morrow, Lady Ella." He offered a small, respectful bow.

Ah, but he could do better than the simple bidding of a new day. The heroes in her books certainly did.

She was dressed in a yellow kirtle that made her skin shine with youthful beauty. Her blonde hair had been plaited into a long single braid with a bit of ribbon threaded through her silky locks, and a gilt circlet adorned her fair brow. She was stunning, golden and gleaming like the sun.

Aye, that was good. He ought to say as much. Except it did not come out of his mouth as smoothly as it'd been thought in his mind. "You look fresher than the sun," he blurted.

Her forehead crinkled, her expression echoing the wild confusion in his own mind. What had just happened? How had he thought something so eloquently, and yet it had fled his mouth in such an awkward jumble?

He cleared his throat. "You look beautiful. And please, do call me Bronson. I was quite serious about that."

Her puzzlement smoothed away, and she smiled brilliantly at him. "Thank you." Her gaze skimmed the wall of books behind him. "Were you reading?"

"Nay." He said it far too quickly. "I was simply looking at your collection of books to determine which you had in case I had more I could add, aside from *Roman de la Rose*."

"I thought that was the only book of your mother's you'd kept." She came to his side and took his arm. Her hand was warm, and she smelled like sunshine and flowers.

"I meant if there were any more at Berkley Manor," he corrected. "I believe my sister and stepmother may have some."

It was a lie, of course. When one could barely afford food and lacked sufficient clothing for the upcoming winter, one hardly bothered with costly books. But it was better than admitting he'd come into the library to read through her stories and sift through her dreams to find the key to making her fall in love with him.

It was pathetic even to his own internal assessment and would certainly not be something he could voice aloud. She peered over his shoulder to the shelves and tilted her head. He followed her gaze and found he'd left the green book with its spine not pushed in completely, so it jutted out from the others.

"What is that one doing there?" She reached out to retrieve it.

Bronson's heart stopped for a breath. She walked to the other side of the wall and put it onto another shelf. "That's where you belong." She said it in a soft, maternal tone before turning to Bronson. "The horses should be ready for our ride. Shall we go?"

A scraping sound came from overhead. Before Bronson could look up, something hard slammed onto the crown of his head. A book clattered to the floor, followed by the giddy chattering of a small animal. No doubt a gift from the wretched-looking scrap of a squirrel.

"Might we leave Moppet behind?" He smoothed a hand over his head to ensure his hair was in order, ignoring the new lump grazing his fingertips.

"Aye, I'll leave him with Leila." She shook her finger at Moppet. "For being so poorly behaved."

Nonplussed, the little mongrel scampered down the shelf and

perched on her shoulder. They were able to leave him in Leila's care without issue, thanks be to God.

Or at least with minimal issue. Hardy had returned to Leila's side first thing that morning, his slender tail whooshing back and forth like a whip in his frenzied excitement to see her. And while she was all too pleased to add another animal to her retinue, Moppet was not as eager to be paired with a dog.

After much chasing and whimpering and chattering, the two calmed under Leila's gentle voice and the soothing, clean scents of drying herbs, falling into a truce of sorts.

The horses were indeed ready and waiting for them when they arrived at the stable. Bronson followed Ella to her horse, prepared to aid her onto her saddle, when she leapt up on her own with considerable ease.

Bronson straightened his doublet. It mattered not that he was unable to aid her onto her steed. It was simply one missed opportunity. There would be plenty more ways for him to implement his newfound knowledge of being the perfect hero.

❈

ELLA INTENDED TO SPEND THE ENTIRE DAY WITH BRONSON, OF her own volition this time. And not to dissuade him from marrying her, but to actually give the idea of their union an earnest effort.

Marin had left early that morning with Bran, needing to return to Kendal Castle to see to their own matters. Of course, Marin had given Ella advice on love and marriage and making it work. Ella only hoped it was enough information to allow her the opportunity to fall in love. The rest could work itself out at a later date.

She nudged her horse, Kipper, up a hill with Bronson at her side. "Do you enjoy life in London?"

"I enjoyed it for a time." His gaze skimmed the endless sea of velvety grass stretching before them. There was something shuttered in his expression, but he did not elaborate on it. "The border is significantly more different than anything I've ever seen."

"I remember court, though it's been a long time since I attended." Her mother had still been alive then. They'd all donned their finest silks to be paraded about with ceremony. It had felt ridiculous.

"Did you like it?" He led the way down a steep hill and continued to glance back at her to ensure her safety. A kind gesture, but an unnecessary one. After years of owning Kipper, and how often she went riding, she could do it with her eyes closed. Truly. She'd tried once.

"I remember only being laced into a constricting gown and having to be on my very best behavior. Everything was luxurious, but there were a lot of rules." She navigated the uneven terrain with ease in an effort to prove her ability to him.

He chuckled. "Aye, there are a considerable number of rules. Were we in London, for example, we would not be able to be alone together without an escort."

She knew well of this rule. Here at Werrick Castle, escorts were seldom required between an unwed woman and a man, unless Papa was entertaining important guests.

The time Ella had spent alone with Calville thus far had not felt improper. However, the reminder that in a different place this would be inappropriate made the quiet around them feel suddenly heavy with intimacy.

"The sky is enchanting today, is it not?" She tilted her head back to better view the wide stretch of blue overhead. Bits of clouds hung suspended in the great expanse, like tufts of wool spread apart until they were little more than nearly transparent threads and fibers.

"Your eyes rival the beauty of that blue sky, Lady Ella."

The softness of Calville's voice drew her attention back to her companion.

Heat touched Ella's cheeks. "Thank you."

Truth be told, she liked this part of him, the part that made her go warm and squirmy with attraction. It made her recall that kiss in the solar, when his lips tenderly caressed her mouth and skin.

He reached out a hand and skimmed his fingertips down her cheek. "I want to see your favorite place here."

Her heart stuttered. "How did you know I have a favorite place?"

"Mayhap I know you better than you assumed I did." His eyes were as green as the grass they rode over, his smile as warm as the sun.

Had he really learned her so quickly, after such a short a period of time? Was she so easy to read? And if she was, had he been able to tell how she recalled their kiss with such vividness?

He leaned toward her, his eyes closing. Heavens! He was going to kiss her while they were both on horses. How very romantic! Like something from a troubadour's tale.

Ella closed her eyes and stretched in his direction. Their lips had only but grazed one another's when Kipper gave an irritated huff and leapt forward, pulling Ella from Bronson's kiss.

She couldn't help but laugh as Kipper jealously trotted away with her on his back. Calville flashed a charming grin, snapped his own reins and trotted ahead of her. "Point me in the direction and I will lead the way."

Ella couldn't help the smug smile. He did not know her so very well after all. She urged her horse to canter faster. "I can show you where it is."

He navigated his stead in front of hers. "That is not necessary, my lady. I can lead us both. You need only point me in the proper direction."

Ella tightened her grip on the reigns and pushed Kipper to the beginning of a gallop. "Lord Calville—"

"Bronson."

Ella swallowed down her exasperated sigh at this stubborn courtier determined to be the protective man. "Bronson." She tested his name on her tongue. It felt masculine and intimate, and she decided she liked it very much. "I am perfectly capable of leading you. I venture this way all the time and am often alone."

"You are not alone today, my dove." He drew up alongside her, practically shouting to be heard over the thundering of their horse's hooves. "Please indicate where we will go."

Their horses were both moving swiftly now.

A grin curled her lips. If he wanted the direction, she would give it to him. "There is a cottage," she spoke loudly to ensure he heard her. "Go in the direction of the sun over several hills and you will find it."

Bronson's face lit up at the opportunity to lead her. He was so overjoyed, in fact, she nearly felt bad for what she was about to do.

"I'll meet you there." She flashed him a smile and allowed Kipper to fly. The horse had been her father's, a wild foal meant to be broken to become a prize mount. However, the wilderness could never be tamed from the beast. He attempted to throw every rider but her. She'd spent the better part of a month talking to him, soothing him, never once attempting to ride him. Until her father planned to sell him.

She'd begged Peter to let her try. He'd refused, of course. So, when they had all gone to bed, she'd snuck out of her room and took Kipper out to the field. With no saddle, and nothing but the moon to witness what her father liked to call foolish bravery, Ella climbed onto Kipper's back.

She'd expected him to throw her, but he had not. To this day, she was the only rider Kipper would allow on his back. He was the finest horse in the stable, with his black sleek coat, fearless and powerful.

And so, it was no surprise at all to her that she won the impromptu race. Though to his credit, Bronson's horse had put forth a strong effort and he was only several moments behind her.

The cabin was small, a single room that had been abandoned some time ago. Her gaze caught on an axe with part of its head sunk deep in a stump used for splitting wood. She froze.

Mayhap it was no longer abandoned. A heavy thump of horse hooves brought her attention back to Calville, who rode toward her at an impressive speed.

Ella slid from her horse and put her hand on her hip as he approached, acting as though she'd been waiting quite a while for his arrival, rather than having just gotten down from her horse herself.

"You had a head start." He leapt from his steed with an athleticism that appealed to her. "And don't act as though you've been waiting for me when I was right behind you." He chuckled. "You cannot fool me."

A stick cracked in the woods surrounding them. The charge of warning prickling over her skin told her it was not the cabin's new occupant returning home. Or if it was, his intentions were not good.

Bronson stepped closer to Ella, his proximity brazen, and lifted his mouth in a sensual half smile. He was oblivious to the threat nearby. "My sweet Ella, I commend you on your speed that won you the race." He cupped her face in his hands and gazed down at her as though he meant to kiss her.

Before she could protest, he spoke as his mouth brushed against hers. "Get behind me."

"There is someone in the woods," she surmised.

"Nay." He nibbled the area just below her neck, close to her ear. "There are several someones in the woods."

9

Ella peered over Calville's shoulder to the forest behind him where several figures moved in the shadows.

"Several someones...behind you?" She tilted her head slightly, as though in pleasure. In actuality, she was looking for how far the axe was from where they stood. Only several feet. It would require a short leap to grab it.

Calville's mouth grazed along her neck. A small sound came from the back of her throat unbidden. "Stay behind me, my dove. Run for the cottage and bolt the door while I hold them off. I'll keep you safe."

The shadows in the forest began to move, creeping closer.

"You prefer your sword then?" Ella fingers itched to curl around the solid wooden handle jutting up from the chopping stump.

"Aye." He put his fist on the hilt of his sword. "Ready?"

Before she could answer, a battle cry shrilled from the woods. Calville pulled his sword free with a metallic hiss and gently pushed her in the direction of the cottage, which was also in the direction of the axe. She gripped the handle in both hands and swung upward, freeing it. The weapon was no battle axe, the weight being more top heavy than balanced, and the head far too small. But it was better than trying to protect herself with the small dagger tucked in her belt.

The first man fell upon Calville. The earl parried, taking his time as he feinted right, then left. Finally, he drove the sword beneath the armpit where the gambeson was less armored.

Calville stood as the man fell in front of him and watched him. Was he waiting to ensure the man had died?

Footsteps sounded behind Ella. She turned on her heel as she lifted her axe. A reiver gave her a leering smile and made a lunge for her. She swung her weapon and caught the man in the side. He cried out and grabbed for her. Ella jerked at the handle to free the blade. It pulled away from the man's body with a sucking sound and blood gushed from his wound. Behind her came the ringing clash of blades and the grunt of someone being struck.

An arrow shot from the trees and hit the ground where Calville's foot had been braced moments before. Ella trained her eyes on the forest, waiting for movement.

A branch shifted. There. Exactly what she'd been anticipating. In one smooth motion, she drew her dagger from her belt and threw the blade at the archer. A solid thud told her she'd hit her mark.

She glanced back to Calville and found him with three men upon him. He parried and blocked, his movements precise, but slow. If he continued thus, he'd be dead in minutes. She hefted her axe into her hands and ran to his side.

"Lady Ella." He started at her appearance. A reiver took advantage of his distraction and sliced his left forearm. Crimson blood blossomed against his white sleeve. Regardless of the injury, Calville put himself between her and the men. "Please. Get in the cottage."

Three more men rushed from the forest and joined the fight, fresh and ready to kill.

She ignored Calville's request and focused instead on the

reiver trying to get a rope around her. He hadn't seen the axe until it was too late, until it was slamming down on his shoulder. He howled in agony and the rope slipped from his fingers.

Another took his place, but Ella wrenched her axe from one man and planted it into the gut of another.

"Flee," the reiver with the rope cried, clearly the leader. "They're no' worth it"

"Take your dead and injured," Ella called after them. "We don't want them here. You'll stay unharmed as you get them."

Several of the braver reivers grabbed their fallen brethren, three of whom groaned with pain while another four remained silent.

Calville watched them leave before turning to Ella, his green eyes wide in his pale face.

Alarm took hold of Ella. "Are you injured?" Her gaze frantically scoured his body, but aside from the nick on his forearm, she saw nothing else.

"Are...are you..." His mouth worked without words for a moment. "Are you injured?"

Ella regarded him curiously. "I wasn't struck. Are you well?"

"Of course." He looked down at his hands where brilliant red blood smeared across his palms and fingers.

Silence followed, stretched out as Calville continued to stare at his hands in bewilderment and horror. And it all made sense: Bronson had never killed a man before.

※

SO MUCH BLOOD. BRONSON COULDN'T TEAR HIS GAZE FROM THE smear of it across his hands, the way it settled like dark wine in the creases of his palm.

"Lord Calville?"

The men's eyes had gone wide when he plunged his blade into them. Wide and then dull as they ceased to live. What if they had wives at home waiting for them? Children who relied on them?

He had taken the lives of four men.

"Bronson?"

There was a softness to the voice, and it pulled him from his macabre thoughts. Ella watched him with concern pulling at her brows.

"They would have killed us," she said. "Or at the very least taken us as prisoners and held us for ransom. We would be beaten, and I would most likely..." She shook her head, her face crinkling in disgust, but she didn't need to fill in the rest for him to understand.

He'd heard stories of the wild Scotsmen who lived on the border. Still, the reminder helped drag him from his daze. He'd taken lessons with the sword when he'd been a boy and he fought often with his fellow-courtiers, though those bouts were done for sport with blades made for appearance rather than purpose.

He was grateful now for the practice he'd gotten doing those mock battles with his friends. If he hadn't had experience, he would be dead.

He slipped his sword into the sheath and wiped his blood-stained hands on his trews as though he didn't care. He slid the horror and guilt smoothly behind a courtier's smile. "We did what we had to. I'd do it again to ensure you were protected."

Ella studied him. Dots of blood speckled over her face like freckles. "You've never killed anyone before, have you?"

"Not many reasons for running someone through with a blade at court." He winked at her.

Her mouth lifted in a smile. "Life is different here on the border."

"So it appears." He clasped his hands together to keep from staring at them, from remembering that awful moment when the first man had died. "The ladies are as well."

Ella smirked and lowered the bloody head of the axe to the ground. "Aye."

Bronson nodded his head, pretending to understand completely. But he did not. His mind reeled as he tried to take it all in. Not only had they been attacked, not only had he killed men, but Ella had joined in the battle. Lady Ella, who seemed so petite and delicate, had hefted an axe and slain men with the ferocity of a warrior.

He most certainly was not at court anymore, and this wild new land was filled with surprises. No doubt with even more to come.

That was what worried him.

10

Ella relaxed, her concern for Calville eased by the casual expression on his handsome face. No doubt before today, he'd never used the shiny blade on his hip.

Papa wouldn't be pleased about him learning of her skills in battle. He'd asked them all to maintain a pretense of ladylike decorum, which was why he had canceled their practices until Calville departed. With Ella, of course.

However, in a situation such as the one she and Calville had just faced, revealing their secret was a far cry better than perishing or being abducted.

Calville indicated her skirt. "I presume that is not your blood on your kirtle."

"Correct." Ella slid her hand along her belt and realized she no longer had her dagger. The one she'd thrown at the archer. It had been her favorite, a jeweled thing as fine as it was practical. Marin had used it once when she initially meant to kill Bran all those years ago.

It was a pity to have lost it. She glanced toward the thicket where the archer had been. Perhaps...

She made her way through the brambles and over a sodden

layer of undergrowth to where the man had fallen. And where he still laid. She said a quick prayer over his body, the way their priest, Bernard, always did over the dead, and then pulled her dagger free from where it had plunged into his chest.

Calville was waiting for her when she emerged from the thick foliage. "How did you learn to fight? When have you killed men before?"

Ella sauntered over to the tree stump and sank the axe deep into the wood. Blood ran down the blade and stained the pale grain beneath with death. "We fight with the Werrick soldiers."

She knelt in the grass and wiped her dagger against the damp earth to clean the blade as best she could. "Many years ago, we were attacked, and my father learned exactly how vulnerable we all were. We would have all died, were it not for my mother."

She stopped herself from sharing the story. Its pain had always been there in her heart, lodged like a stubborn burr. She could dodge its spines, but never could she be fully free of its insistent presence.

"What happened?" He held out his hand to help her to her feet.

She accepted and rose, but he did not pull his hand away.

"I've never told anyone before," Ella said softly.

Calville met her gaze, his green eyes tender and honest. "You can tell me."

She nodded and swallowed, as though it might help to dislodge the words. "My father was injured trying to save us and so my mother came to our aid. She was beaten, and...ill-used." She clenched her jaw. "She died several months later after delivering a babe, but she was dead before then. In spirit, at least. I remember seeing her walking the halls like a wraith."

"Did the babe die as well?" Calville asked.

Ella's heart gave a fresh twinge of pain. That was when Leila had been born, but it felt almost like a betrayal to her youngest sister to mention it. All the sisters, and Papa too, refrained from ever bringing up that Leila was not like them, that her paternity was so different than their own.

Nay, they loved her like the sister she was, and it was never mentioned. Not even among them.

For this reason, Ella did not answer the question. Instead, she pressed on. "Papa wanted us to leave, saying it was too dangerous. And it was." She shrugged as though it didn't matter, when it so very much did. "We begged to stay with him, and he finally conceded as long as we learned to fight. Our skills in battle have saved our lives countless times."

"Ella..." he rubbed his thumb over the back of her hand.

It was the first time he'd used her Christian name without her title, but she didn't correct him. Surely a man who knew the depth of her secrets was close enough to refer to her so intimately. A man who would soon be her husband.

"We should clean up," Ella suggested.

He hesitated, his gaze filled with concern before he released her hand. "Aye, but mayhap away from here."

Together, they led their horses some distance from the cottage to the nearby stream, which was where Ella had originally intended on taking Calville in the first place. Sunlight streamed through the copse of trees and speckled the forest floor with dots of light. Clear water rushed over smooth stones and the sound of bubbling filled the air around them.

The scene was so drastically different from what they'd left at the cottage, it might as well have been another world. And that was exactly how Ella thought of it. A different world. Her world.

And she'd never brought anyone before to be part of it.

A SENSE OF PEACE WASHED OVER BRONSON AS SOON AS HE entered the small clearing by the stream. The glint of sunlight, the brilliance of the blue sky overhead, the green grass underfoot and the myriad of colors in the surrounding forest, it was almost unreal.

"This is where I meant to take you." Ella closed her eyes and breathed in slowly.

Bronson did the same, inhaling the scents of wet earth and crisp, cool air, as well as the delicate perfume of flowers. Ella's scent.

He opened his eyes and was struck again with the beauty of the area. It was all too easy to see why Ella went there often. All around him was splendor with calming forest sounds, as though one might exist in such a place without ever being bothered. He looked to Ella and found a soft smile touching her lips, her face relaxed and alluring.

A bit of blood showed on one of her cheeks. He wiped at it with his thumb and she started.

"Mayhap we should clean up a bit," he suggested.

"Aye, of course." She led the way to the stream and crouched by the water, heedless of her leather boots or her fine kirtle. Not that it mattered as both were stained from battle, the blood bright red on the yellow silk.

He knelt by the stream and submerged his hands in the icy water and rubbed them together. Gore lifted from them in a cloud of orange-red. Immediately it made him feel better, as though the removal of the stains also helped to cleanse his mind.

He cupped his hands and splashed water on his face, massaging his skin to rid it of blood, before dragging his fingers through his hair. His doublet clung heavy and wet to his body, impeding his movement. Without thought, he slipped free the buttons and pulled it off, leaving only his linen shirt beneath.

What was once white before was now dotted red and pink with the blood of his fallen enemies. Out of the corner of his eye, he saw Ella turn her face toward him. It was then he recalled a scene in one of the books she'd written, with the knight and the nymph, when the knight had stripped off his shirt. Mayhap it was a heroic thing to do. In the past, women had marveled at his physique. He hoped Ella would now as well.

He tugged it free of his trews and lifted the hem upward, over his head. Ella drew in an audible gasp. He would take that as a good thing.

Once more, he bent over the stream and scooped up handfuls of water to let them sluice over his face and body. When he was done, he turned to Ella and found her staring.

"You have...your arm..." she stammered. Her cheeks went pink. "You have an injury on your arm."

He followed her gaze to his forearm where the blade had nicked him. A watery trail of blood dribbled down from it. The thing was little more than a scratch. He was damned lucky that's all he'd gotten, especially when he'd frozen after killing the first man.

"Let me see it." She stepped out of the stream and made her way over to him.

Bronson got to his feet and faced her with his forearm extended.

Her fingers brushed his skin, more of a caress than an inspection of his wound. "It isn't deep. I'm sure I'll live."

Her gaze slid up to his, her eyes wide and blue and innocent.

Lust slammed into him. Hard and undeniable. He'd heard soldiers speak of it before, the overwhelming desire after a battle, when the energy still roared in one's blood and left them restless and unsettled.

Ella ran her tongue over her bottom lip and glanced toward his mouth, as though of the same mindset as he. It was all he needed. He drew her into his arms. Her head tilted back in supplication, her lips parting.

Aye, this was what he wanted. Needed.

He pressed his mouth to hers. He tried to be chaste at first, not wanting to frighten her. Not wanting to move too fast lest he lose control of the powerful, raw longing pumping through him.

She flicked her tongue against his. He groaned at her forwardness and stroked his over hers. The delicate dance of their attraction descended into something desperate then, with mouths slanting, teeth scraping, breaths panting. His body was on fire, his cock raging for release.

His hands were on her, smoothing over the curves he'd imagined. He longed to draw up her skirt and skim his palms over her shapely legs. The image of the long, naked limb dangling in front of him had teased him for far too long.

Ella's hands moved over his bare chest, her fingers roaming in exploration, sending ripples of pleasure prickling over his skin. He wanted her to touch all of him thus.

The very thought sent another surge of yearning through him. He cupped her breast, the move brazen. But she did not nudge his hand away or shy back. Nay, she pushed into his touch, arching into him. Her hips brushed his hard prick and another groan tore from him.

Without thinking, he caught her bottom with his free hand and pushed their pelvises together. Her softness ground against him with the most wonderful friction.

She gasped suddenly and snapped him from his lustful haze.

He released his hold on her and straightened. Ella's hands curled around his neck and she rose on her toes while she tried to pull him down to her once more.

"Where are you going?" Her hand cradled his jaw. "Please don't stop, Calville." She searched his eyes as if she could spend a lifetime doing so. "Bronson."

His name emerged on a breathy sigh, one born of desire and daydreams and exhaled in such a manner, he could not refuse.

He pulled her into his arms and kissed her soundly, with passion infused in the claiming of her lips. Despite the reminder of her innocence, he found himself touching her again, stroking her breasts through the silky fabric of her kirtle, tracing the hard nub of her nipple with his thumb. This time when he caught her fine bottom in the palm of his hands and drew her against him, Ella melted into the embrace with a moan.

She moved against him, grinding against the bulge of his need until he feared the tease of such pressure might unman him. He wanted to lay her out on the bank of the stream and push her skirts up so he could let his gaze caress those beautiful legs.

His fingers clenched a handful of her skirt, the thick fabric bunching in his palm with physical temptation. He need only lift it higher, kneel at her feet, run his hands up her slender ankles and firm calves. "Ella." He'd meant to say her name to tell her they should stop, but the rest of the words did not emerge.

"Ella?" She arched her brow in flirtation. "Not Lady Ella, Bronson?"

"It should be." He didn't bend over her again, despite the temptation to do so.

"Should it?" She ran a single fingertip down his naked chest to his navel.

He drew in a shuddering breath. "Aye." He brushed his thumb over her lower lip. "And we should not be doing this either."

She closed her eyes at his touch, her mouth parting. "And what exactly is 'this?'" Her breath whispered over his finger. "Kissing?"

"More than kissing." His voice came out gruff. "Touching."

She blinked her eyes open. "I like touching." Her fingers eased past his navel to the thin line of hair that disappeared into his trews. With a wicked grin, she dragged her hand up to the back of his neck. "I like kissing too."

He resisted her pull. "Ella, I do not want to take this too far."

"What would 'too far' be?" she breathed.

He hesitated, but only for a moment, just long enough to feel the draw of his own curiosity leading him down a path he knew better than to venture on. "Laying you down on the grass."

Ella sank onto her knees and pulled him down to the ground with her. He froze, poised over her as she lay her head back and stared up at him with those blue, blue eyes.

"Drawing the skirt of your gown up." His attention slid down to her skirt, the hem still wet from the stream.

Her fingers moved over the fine silk, slowly inching it upward. A bit of her slender stocking-clad ankle peeked beneath it.

He stared, transfixed. "Higher."

She did as he asked, revealing the sensual curve of her calf and an elegant knee above the line of her wool stocking.

His breath was coming harder and faster. This foreplay was exquisite, even if it would have no chance of release. At least not here with Ella. He most certainly would be handling himself at the first opportunity and thinking of exactly this moment.

"And then I would touch some more." His fingertips brushed the back of her knee.

She sucked in a breath and bent her leg, propping it up slightly. A triangular gap showed beneath the hem of her kirtle, giving him a tantalizing view of the tops of her legs, and what lay beyond.

"I would trace my fingers up your lovely legs." His fingers eased over the tops of her stockings to where her skin was impossibly soft. He paused, not moving any higher. "Up your thighs to where your most intimate place is."

Ella's cheeks were red and her lids heavy. "Will you show me?"

Bronson curled his hand into a fist so he would not. "In due time, my dove."

Disappointment shone bright in her eyes and made it all the more difficult for him to do the right thing. He got to his feet and held his hand out to help her to her feet.

She accepted his assistance and rose gracefully to her feet. The dress, regretfully, fell back into place over her legs. "When?" she asked.

"When we are not wearing clothing stained with blood, preferably." He nodded toward her dress.

She glanced down and grimaced. "Then next time, when we

are not attacked," she offered hopefully. "Attacks only happen occasionally. We were simply unlucky on this venture."

Unlucky was one way to put it, for unlucky had many sides. One of them was suggesting waiting a fortnight to marry Ella when he'd been ready to take her on the forest floor only moments ago.

The coming wait until their wedding promised to be a long one, indeed.

11

The ride back to Werrick had been exquisitely pleasant. Warmth hummed in Ella's veins and washed over her cheeks. Each time she snuck a glance at Bronson's handsome profile, her heart gave a giddy little flutter.

Sadly, he'd had to put his shirt and doublet back on. Still, she could not stop thinking of his powerful chest, the carved lines of his muscle. His skin was smooth and soft despite the chiseled masculinity of his body. She nearly moaned at the memory of touching him.

But it was more than simply his physical appearance, though that was indeed fine. He was fascinating. They spoke of many things on the way back to Werrick, of Hardy and his affection for Leila, of court life with its many rules and stiff clothing, and of how wild and beautiful the English-Scottish border was. All too soon they arrived at Werrick and Peter was greeting them to take their horses.

For the first time in as long as Ella could remember, Peter's long-lashed hazel eyes did not make her stomach dip with excitement. And when she allowed Bronson to aid her from her horse, she did not once slide a glance in Peter's direction to gauge his reaction.

Suddenly she was glad for his rejection of her, though it had of course been painful. But she was grateful, for that rejection had saved her completely for Bronson, for his kisses, his touches. For him to slide his hands up her skirt and do everything he promised he would.

"My Lady, are you hurt?" Peter's horrified voice startled her from her musing.

She followed his gaze to her dress where blood from the reiver stained the fine silk. "We were attacked but are uninjured. Please see to it whoever is living in the Old Pell cottage is paid handsomely for my use of his axe."

Peter did not balk at the formality of her tone. He merely inclined his head; more servant now than he had ever been with her. "Of course, my lady."

After thanking him, Ella put her hand on Bronson's arm and together they walked into the castle to the new cry of alarm from Rohesia, the castle's Chatelaine. She immediately whisked Ella away and set her maids to work preparing a bath, readying a new gown to be worn and seeing what could be done about those awful stains.

Once her bath was ready, Ella stepped into the hot, perfumed water and sank into it with a sigh.

Bronson.

His name floated into her mind like a daydream. She leaned her head back on the linen-covered back of the tub and let her mind drift back to that moment in the forest. Her blood had still been raging from the fight, every nerve on high alert, incredibly sensitive. The way he'd brushed his fingers over her breasts, her nipples...

She lifted a hand in the bath and did as he had done, gently brushing the buds. Lust immediately blossomed to life between her legs, insistent and ready. She had never been ashamed of her body, or of giving in to her own release.

This time when she slid her fingers between her legs, she imagined they were Bronson's. And she was far, far wetter than ever before.

"Was it the Grahams?" A voice said as the door to her bed chamber opened.

Ella jerked her hand away from her sex and sat up straight, sending water splashing on all sides of the tub.

Cat rushed over with a laugh. "Ella, don't you want the water in the tub with you?"

Ella's face burned at having almost been discovered fondling herself so intimately.

Cat chuckled. "You needn't look so guilty, Sister. It was a mere jest." She was practically glowing with happiness. Most likely due to the letter she'd received from Geordie.

"I assume Geordie is doing well?" Ella settled back into the tub and tried to ignore the large puddles in the floor.

Cat rummaged around in a cabinet and turned back to Ella, her arms laden with a pitcher, soap and a comb. All the essentials for washing Ella's hair. With five girls, the Werrick sisters never bothered with maids for dressing and washing their hair. There was no need when they had each other.

Although soon there would be only Cat and Leila. Would Rohesia be asked to assign a maid to care for them then?

"Aye, Geordie's doing very well." Cat set all the items beside the tub and brought over the small stool they used when helping one another bathe. She settled behind Ella and plunged the pitcher into the tub water. "He said one of the earls there is considering him for his household." A note of sadness pinched her voice. "Tilt your head."

Ella did as she was told. A rush of perfumed water washed through her hair, yet not a drop got in her eyes. But then, Cat always was the best at keeping water out of one's face while washing hair.

"But you will hear all about him and his life now when I read you his letter tonight." Cat scooped a bit of soap from the wooden bowl and worked it between her hands. "Now enough distraction. Tell me of your ride with Lord Calville. Was it romantic? Did you let him save you from the attack? It wasn't the Grahams, was it?" Cat tsked. "That would be so disappointing if it *was* them." Her fingers through Ella's hair, massaging in the soap.

It would truly be disappointing if it had been the Grahams who had attacked them, especially after Anice had offered herself in marriage to make peace between them all. Fortunately, the union was a happy one and Anice had found love in the most unlikely situation.

There was hope yet for Ella.

"Nay, it wasn't the Grahams." Tingles spread over Ella's scalp and she gave in to the luxury of having her hair washed for her. "I'm not sure what clan they were, but Bronson—"

"Bronson?" Cat squealed. "Is that Lord Calville's Christian name? Did he kiss you?" She demanded with a pitch of excitement in her tone. "He must have for you to be refer to him so informally." She stopped scrubbing Ella's hair as she answered her own question. Cat knelt by the side of the tub, her hands still coated with soap. "Did you enjoy it? Do you feel happier about the impending wedding now?"

Ella simply grinned and gave her sister a little lift of her shoulders with her brows raised.

Cat dropped her head forward in exasperation. "You are cruel to be so coy." She spoke with mock indignation for Cat was never actually put out by anything. "You know I will most likely never marry. You, Anice and Ella are all I'll be able to rely on for stories of love and romance."

"That isn't true," Ella chided. "You may be forced to wed your own Englishman."

Cat laughed at that and resumed her place at the back of the tub to continue her task. She chattered on while washing and Ella tried to listen, truly she did. But her mind kept skipping back to Bronson. To that kiss. To his fingers gliding over her stocking clad leg, and all the additional things they would eventually do together.

Mayhap if they were able to share such passion together, they might have a chance at love. She certainly was finding her attentions drawn toward him.

Perhaps it might be time to move from her shared room with her sisters to one with more privacy. Marin and Anice had done it when they were older, and it had not caused issue. And while Ella enjoyed the closeness with her younger siblings, she understood now that it was time for her to become more independent.

She never anticipated it would be so delightful a task.

※

BRONSON COULD SCARCELY REIN IN HIS EAGERNESS TO SEE ELLA at supper. Their time on the ride had been a great success and his attempts at heroism appeared to be winning her over.

She was not the only one who had enjoyed the time alone together. He had found it very pleasant. Enough that he couldn't stop thinking of her, laying on the grass with her skirt delicately pulling up higher, higher, higher to reveal her smooth skin visible over the top of her woolen stockings.

He arrived at the dais and waited, standing, for her to arrive. He was not alone. Bear and Wolf leapt to their feet and took off in her direction as soon she entered the great hall. Her long hair was glossy in the candlelight and she beamed at the sight of the two dogs racing toward her.

Even Hardy slipped away from Leila's side long enough to enjoy Ella's affection without Moppet attempting to intervene. The little beast wasn't allowed at the great hall while food was served. Something about having thrown a wild fit once, and a roasted boar ruined by the wretched little creature. Bronson couldn't say he was disappointed at the squirrel's absence.

Ella knelt to pet the dogs with a genuine smile lighting her face, then rose and glided toward the table, her movements so light and airy, she almost appeared to be floating. Her eyes met his and sparkled with pleasure.

God's bones, she was beautiful. Her crimson kirtle had small gilt flowers stitched on the hem and sleeves. It was a gown to be noticed in. Except he noted what others did not see, the gleam in her eye, the subtle coyness of her reticence. Hers was a dress for seduction.

He guided her to her seat before taking his own next to her as quickly as decorum allowed, lest his eagerness for Ella be humiliatingly aware to all.

"I hear you were attacked." Lord Werrick cast a hard stare in their direction as he cut off a piece of meat from the trencher before him. "Not the Grahams?"

Ella shook her head. "Nay, Papa. I couldn't tell which clan they belonged to but I am certain it was not the Grahams. Besides, we were away from the castle. By the Old Pell cottage."

Lord Werrick frowned. "The Kerrs have been causing trouble about the East March on the English side. I'd not put it past them to coordinate attacks on our land to further cause disruption. He still fancies he can get a grip on England by taking Werrick." He popped a bit of roasted pheasant into his mouth and chewed thoughtfully. "I'm glad I had Drake accompany Marin and Bran home. It might be prudent to bring an armed guard with you next time you venture out." He nodded to Cat and Leila. "You both as well. I will not have you taken from me."

Bronson, for one, was disappointed to hear this news. It meant no more quiet afternoons away from the castle with Ella.

Leila nodded obediently to her father, her eyes wide. Cat kept her gaze fixed on her food, suddenly intent on the roasted vegetables in front of her. Most surprising, however, was Ella's ready agreement to her father's request.

The matter settled, supper went on as normal. Or at least, as normal as it could be with Ella's leg constantly brushing against Bronson's. Though the fare had smelled good to his hungry stomach when he'd first entered the great hall, now it lodged stubbornly in his throat, too thick to swallow in his distraction.

Was there ever a better distraction than Ella?

Finally, at long last, the meal drew to a close.

"It has been a very trying day." Ella drooped in her seat.

Bronson regarded the Earl of Werrick in his great carved seat at the head of the table. "Might I have your permission to see Lady Ella to her chambers?"

Lord Werrick looked between them. His eyes narrowed, suggesting he saw exactly what was there between Bronson and Ella, lying in wait. Emotions played like words over his face, announcing to all what he felt. Surprise. At their new bond, mayhap? Concern. And he had good cause for that given how Ella was like a purring cat at Bronson's side. But then came relief, no doubt that Ella would be more inclined to wed.

"Aye," the earl conceded at last.

Bronson held his hand out to his betrothed. Ella accepted and together they left the clatter and thrum of the noisy great hall behind them. She clasped her hand to his, her palm warm and her pulse thrumming wildly against his wrist.

They turned down one hallway, then a second, their steps growing faster with each corner that led them further from the great hall and closer toward privacy. She spun around abruptly and reached for him. He needed no encouragement, or even words, for that matter.

He pulled her against him, their mouths crashing in a battle of mutual lust. Tongues stroked, lips tasted, teeth nipped. Footsteps echoed around them. As quickly as he and Ella had come together, they now broke apart.

A guard Bronson did not recognize strode past and offered a cordial nod in their direction.

They did not touch again, not even to hold hands. Not until they were down the hall where Ella's chamber was located. Bronson guided her in the direction he knew, but she stopped him with her hand folding around his once more.

"This way." She led him in another direction.

"You don't wish to go to your room?" He asked, his voice deep with lust.

"Aye, I do, and we are." She twirled around briefly to face him. "I've changed chambers." She completed the slow turn and was forward once more, continuing to lead him.

"You've changed chambers?" He found himself grinning.

She stopped in front of a door he hadn't been to before. "I realized I might have need for privacy." She leaned into him and her eyes drifted closed in expectation.

He braced his hands on either side of the doorway, framing her as he pressed her back. His mouth closed over hers and he gently sucked on her lower lip. He released it with a groan. "What do you require privacy for, pray tell?"

She broke away from him with a wicked grin. "Come in and find out."

The clatter of a latch sounded, and the door opened inward, all but spilling them both into a large set of chambers. The ones belonging to the mistress of the castle. Bronson hesitated. "Ella…"

She closed the door with the toe of her shoe and ran her hands up his chest to the back of his neck. Her recent bath left her smelling of wildflowers with a hint of sunshine. He closed his eyes and breathed in her clean, wonderful scent.

Her fingers raked pleasantly into his scalp and sent prickles rippling down his spine. She rose on her toes and pressed her lush mouth to his. Her tongue was sweet with the taste of the blue marzipan flowers the cook had crafted.

If Bronson were at court, he'd gladly accept the offering of a woman's body. But he was not at court where few of the women were maidens, he was at Werrick Castle, and Ella was the woman he would wed.

Bronson steeled himself for the protest he did not wish to make. "This is not why your father gave me permission to walk you to your room."

Ella's mouth trailed down to his throat where she nipped and licked, the perfect pupil in her studies, emulating what he had done to her. His cock strained against his trews.

"He wants me to fall in love with you." She arched against him. "Touch me, Bronson. Like you did in the forest." She settled her hips against his. "The way you said you would next time."

Bronson's thoughts went spinning away without him. Had he said, "next time?"

Even as his mind tried to find objection to what she'd said, his body reacted to her enticement. His hands moved of their own volition, cupping her bottom to fit her more snugly against his prick. His other hand caught her gown. He didn't have enough time to do everything he wanted. Not until they were wed.

Now would need to be quick. Fulfilling.

"Are you certain?" He asked the question, even as he was carefully nudging her back against the wall, even as he was lifting her skirt.

"We are to be married," she whispered, breathless.

"That is not an answer." He had the weight of crimson silk fisted in his left hand. Flickering orange light from the hearth shone on her pale, slender thighs, rising like carved marble from the red hose that came up only to her knees.

"Are you certain you want this?" He asked raggedly.

Ella leaned her head back on the wall. "Aye."

One small, simple word and yet it might as well have been the key to heaven itself. He ran his fingers along her knee, light as a whisper, and let them drift up her inner thigh. She sucked in a shuddering breath and her legs trembled.

He knew all too well that sensation of being overwhelmed by lust, to the point of shaking. His own breath came too fast, the steadiness of his hand compromised by his frenzied heartbeat.

The closer he got to the triangle of golden hair between her legs, the wilder his pulse pounded until it was erratic and uncontrolled. Her skin was hot silk under his touch, and the torment of watching the pleasure play over her face was exquisite.

His fingertip teased along the seam between her legs. Ella cried out and grabbed onto him. His finger came away wet with her wanting. She was so slick already.

Using his middle finger, he traced the slit between her legs, running the digit up and down until she was squirming against the friction in an effort to increase the pressure.

"Do you want more, my dove?" Without waiting for her to reply, he found the bud of her sex and swirled the pad of his fingertip around it.

Ella's legs buckled. She would have collapsed had she not been holding onto him so tightly.

"Bronson." His name came out somewhere between a gasp and a moan. Never had his own name held such appeal as when spoken by Ella Barrington nearing her climax.

He cradled her weight with his other arm and increased the pressure of his ministrations. She panted and nestled her head in the crook of his neck. Mindless and desperate, she kissed the sensitive skin there. Her body tightened under Bronson's hand and he slipped a finger, very gently and not too deep, inside her sheath.

She cried out her release, her warm breath coming in sensual huffs just under his ear. He closed his eyes and reveled in her pleasure, letting it wash over him and stroke against his ego.

His cock was painfully hard with an ache that settled deep on his bollocks, despite having tended to his baser needs with his hand after his bath. But this, the glory of witnessing Ella's release, being surrounded by the erotic perfume of her arousal, this was entirely worth every painful throb.

Ella lifted her head from his shoulder and a lazy smile lifted the corner of her mouth.

"Did you enjoy that?" He kissed her on the mouth, the touch of their lips tender, chaste by comparison to what had just transpired between them.

"Mmmhmmm." She nodded with a dreamy expression. "When can we do it again?"

12

The following afternoon Bronson had the solar all to himself. Or at least, as to himself as was possible with Moppet in the room. The little beast remained perched on the edge of the shelf like one of the nightmarish gargoyles the French enjoyed carving into the corners of their ostentatious cathedrals. A pile of shells lay about the squirrel as he cracked each nut open with his sharp, yellowed teeth.

Bronson had lingered about in the sunny room initially, expecting Ella to join her pet. When she had not arrived after some time, Bronson gave up the pretense of being there solely to find her. The green spine of the book he'd been reading before beckoned him from across the room.

He told himself he needed to continue to read for the additional insight on how to win over Ella. But after the prior evening, after holding her in his arms while her crises overtook her, he presumed he was doing rather well for himself. He had promised to please her so again in the future. The very idea made his cock go stiff.

A fortnight might as well be a lifetime.

He lifted the green book from the shelf. In reality, he was

eager to discover what happened with the dragon and the troubadour.

He'd started reading with his body turned toward the bookshelf, ready to shove the book back into place at a moment's notice. After a while, the shelf digging into his hip became uncomfortable, so he leaned against the wall by the window seat. The light pouring in from the glass window illuminated the pages and made reading remarkably easier.

While he read, Moppet continued to watch him with beady eyes, while cracking nuts open and digging them out with his one arm and his teeth.

Crack.

Bronson gave up all pretense of being prepared to free himself from the book by the time the dragon swooped down on the maiden, fire roaring from its open mouth. Enraptured, Bronson sat on the padded cushion laid out over the stone bench. It was pillowy soft beneath him and warm from the sunlight streaming in. A welcome contrast from the cold stone he'd been leaning against.

Crack.

He settled his back upon the stone wall behind him and tucked his feet up on the bench, as Ella did. The book propped perfectly against his thighs. *Genius.*

"What are you doing?"

Bronson startled at the feminine voice and lurched into an upright sitting position. Ella stood in the doorway with her hand propped on her hip.

Crack.

"Nothing," Bronson stammered. "Spending time with Moppet."

The little beast shot him a look out of the corner of his eye, as if contradicting Bronson's claim.

"Spending time with him?" Ella's brow lifted.

Bronson tried to hide the book in his hands. "Aye, just discussing things as men and squirrels do. Eh, Moppet?"

Both Ella's brows rose this time with skepticism. "He only speaks squirrel."

Bronson was going to offer a simple shrug when Ella craned her neck to see what he held in his hands. It was in that moment of desperation that Bronson began chattering. Like a squirrel.

Moppet staggered back on his fat little legs and blinked at Bronson, who hoped he'd somehow managed to convey something horribly offensive to the beast.

Ella laughed. "What are you really doing in here?" She stepped closer and made a show of examining what he held in his hands. "Are you reading?"

"Aye." He lifted a single shoulder and tried to turn away from her.

"What book?" She touched her hand to his shoulder and, without force, drew him back to her.

He unfurled his fingers from the plain green cover, knowing well enough that he had been caught.

"It's my book." She lifted it from his grip. "Bronson, were you reading one of my stories?"

He nodded his head slowly. "Aye."

"Why?" Her brow furrowed.

He took a breath, hesitated, opened his mouth hesitated.

"Please be honest." Ella watched him with a guarded expression.

Honest.

Bronson had spent almost every day of his life skirting honesty, saying what was needed to make his way at court, to glide out of trouble when favor was scarce. To be honest was to be vulnerable, and that was how one lost their head.

Sunlight streamed in through the window and fell on Ella, lighting her beauty in its full glory. The woman he would marry surely deserved honesty, didn't she?

Bronson sighed. "Falling in love is important to you, I know, and so I thought..." He trailed off, hating how ludicrous this all was to say aloud. She would think him a fool.

He rubbed at a muscle tightening at the base of his neck. "I hoped I could find what sort of things you found romantic, so I read your stories." He shifted on the bench, eager to be done with the whole bloody conversation. "Then they were so interesting that I couldn't stop reading them."

She ran a hand tenderly over the green leather face of the book. "You read my stories to find out what I like?"

It sounded so invasive when worded so. Bronson braced himself for her ire. "Aye."

"Bronson, that is..." She shook her head, clearly so upset she could not even find the words to speak to tell him how deplorable he was.

"I'm well aware," he said miserably. The whole idea had been ridiculous in the first place. He never should have done it.

"That is the most romantic thing I've ever heard in my entire life," she said.

He lifted his head. "I beg your pardon?"

She was beaming at him, joy radiating from her. She set the book on the cushion of the window seat and then took his face in her hands. "You care enough to find out what I hold dear."

"I want you to marry me," he said earnestly. Though he assumed now was not the time to mention his need for her dowry, his pitiful estate and how his continued life at court relied on Ella.

"And I will." She kissed him. "In a fortnight." She kissed him again. "I wish it was sooner." She ran her tongue along his bottom lip and arched her body against him in apparent suggestion.

"I want to learn all the things you like too." Her voice was low and sultry and caressed over every intimate inch of his awareness.

He flicked his gaze toward the open door of the solar. "Not here..."

Ella bit her lip and shook her head. "Nay. Let us go for a ride."

"We'll need to bring a guard with us," Bronson reminded her. The idea of a soldier accompanying their ride did not hold appeal.

Ella scoffed. "I only said that to appease Papa. I don't intend to bring anyone. You and I are perfectly capable of protecting ourselves, as we did yesterday."

"Nay," Bronson said. "Let us stay in Werrick Castle today. We can go in the orchard if you like, with the dogs."

"And Moppet?" She grinned. "Since you are so well acquainted."

The squirrel fixed his beady eyes on Bronson, put a nut to its mouth and...

Crack.

Bronson nodded, looking pointedly at the creature. "Aye, even Moppet."

If nothing else, the animals and being out in the daylight near the castle would keep Bronson's lust in check. For if things continued as they were going, he did not know how long he could continue to rein himself in before Ella broke down his control.

He would want her in a fortnight, of course. He would want her forever. But God help him, he wanted her desperately now.

ELLA COULDN'T STOP STARING AT BRONSON. WAS IT JUST HER imagination, or did he truly become more and more handsome with each passing day?

The color of his eyes shifted between emerald green when he laughed, and a deep forest green when they kissed. When he touched her.

It had been nearly impossible to sleep the night before with her body humming with desire. She wanted to run her fingers through his fine brown hair and kiss him until they were both writhing with need.

And then finding out he'd read her books in an effort to win her heart. It was all so perfectly romantic.

"So, the stories you wrote." He watched where Bear and Wolf roamed about the edge of the woods. "Is everything possible?"

"Dragons and mermaids and female knights?" She smiled to herself. "I wish it were so."

"I mean the heroic things the princes and troubadours and knights do." He lifted his arm for her to hold as they strode through the garden. "Like pulling her to his horse, or kissing on horseback, or taking off his shirt at any given moment to reveal his naked torso beneath."

She couldn't help but laugh. "Is that where you got the ideas from? Kipper sought to thwart your romantic inclinations."

He grinned. "I think taking off my shirt went over rather well by comparison."

The image flashed in her mind and desire immediately pulsed through her veins. The beauty of his muscular frame shifting and flexing as he moved, the way the droplets of water trailed down his naked flesh. She nearly moaned remembering. "I wouldn't complain if it were to happen again." She winked at him in the flirtatious way he often did with her.

She glanced at him and imagined what he might look like if he did remove his shirt again suddenly. It was a sunny day and the clean, open light would leave every bit of him exposed for her slow perusal.

"I'm sure I can accommodate a lady's request." He grinned at her.

Aye, he *was* getting more and more handsome by the day. Truly. His teeth were white and straight, and his fuller bottom lip drew her attention again and again with the yearning to suck it into her mouth and run her tongue over it.

"What do you want in a woman?" she asked. "After all, you know what I enjoy in a man. 'Tis only fair."

He nodded. "Aye, it is." And then he was quiet for a long moment. "I never imagined being married, in truth. My father and I spent the majority of our time at court. We hunted and attended feasts and...did what men do."

"Then I shall fill in the list for you," she offered. "You would want a woman who is intelligent, a lover of the written word, a woman who is in possession of exquisite skill with a battle axe and a mace. One who is slightly stubborn and impertinent, who harbors a penchant for saving animals and has a one-armed squirrel named Moppet. Am I close?"

"I can't say I'm too keen on the squirrel." Bronson peered in the bag hanging from Ella's shoulder and grimaced. "But you forgot beautiful. And passionate."

She couldn't help but smile at such compliments. "I didn't want to fall too hard toward the side of hubris," she offered, earning her a good-natured laugh from him.

It made her smile to hear him laugh. His eyes twinkled and it softened the sharpness of his face, giving her an idea of what he might have looked like as a boy.

Their steps slowed as they strolled through the garden. The day was a fine one, sunny with birds whistling songs in the trees, and the sounds of fat bees humming over flowers that sprang up in an array of vibrant colors. It was the kind of day perfect for laying in the shaded grass beneath a tree where one might be lulled to sleep with the delicate whisper of a breeze playing over them.

Bronson spun her unexpectedly and caught her in his arms.

She chuckled at the sudden gesture and shook her head as he twirled her about again. "What are you doing?"

"We are dancing to unheard music." He grinned and leapt into the air with a hop before taking her hand and walking them both in a circle. "Like in your stories."

She paused to remove the bag from her shoulder. The little squirrel dashed from its depths and darted up the nearest tree.

She returned to Bronson and followed his movements, dancing to music that wasn't there, and she could not help but giggle at the ridiculousness of it all. Despite her hesitation with Bronson, she was enjoying him immensely. His enthusiasm, his enjoyment of life, and the closeness of his powerful body and all the feelings he drew out of her.

Desire flowed through her as they danced, heating her with the memory of everything they had done before. And she wanted to do it again.

"Let us climb into the trees." She stopped spinning to face him. Her kirtle continued to move and wrapped itself around her legs before unfurling in the other direction.

"And then the hero led his lady into a tree." He tilted his head. "I don't remember that being in one of your stories."

"Then you haven't read them all." She walked backward to the orchard. Her body moved differently around Bronson when they were alone, her hips looser, more sensual, as though she was ripe with an anticipation she felt all through her.

"I can't say I've climbed many trees." He followed her to her favorite, the one with many sturdy branches that allowed her to climb nearly to the top.

"It's easy, you simply find branches to haul yourself up on." She reached up and pulled herself higher in demonstration. "Where do you go for privacy when you're at court if you have no trees?"

"We don't have privacy at court." He looked up at her from where he stood on the ground.

Court did not sound enjoyable, though she did not say as much aloud since he held it in such high regard. The whole mess of it sounded boring and crowded and full of terrible people. Ella climbed up another branch as Bronson continued to watch.

She was high enough now that he could easily see up her skirt and the idea sent an excited thrill through her. This was what she had wanted with this: to entice him, to seduce him, to finally feel what it was like to be intimate.

"Do you need help?" she goaded with a smile.

He glanced around the orchard. "Nay, I was simply worried

about the dogs."

"They'll be fine, as will Moppet." And they would. The curtain wall of the castle was extensive and stretched around even the gardens.

Bronson put his arm to the first branch and pulled himself up, then his foot on the second brought him even higher. She hadn't climbed especially high in the interest of ensuring they both kept their footing. She was glad she'd remained low enough for him to reach her easily now.

He stopped on the branch she stood on and looked about with a half-smile pulling at his lips. "It looks so different."

"It does." She gripped the branch above her head and stepped closer to him. For his part, he remained with his back pressed to the tree trunk, both his hands curled around it behind him for support.

"Isn't it incredible how you can see all around?" She touched his cheek. "But no one can see us up here?"

His eyes found hers. Dark green, lashes lowering. Oh, aye. This was what she had wanted. Craved. *Desperately*.

She lay against him, pinning him to the tree trunk, and nudged her chin to his. He kissed her, his mouth hungry with a similar need.

"We can do anything up here." She rubbed her body against him.

"I don't think 'anything.'" He chuckled nervously.

"Sit down." She guided him onto the branch with his back to the trunk, where it felt the safest. She settled in front of him, not needing the same reassurance after years of climbing trees.

She leaned forward to kiss him and put her hand to his chest where his heartbeat thundered beneath her palm. "It's my turn, Bronson."

His forehead wrinkled in confusion. "Your turn?"

She glided her hand down his flat stomach to the hem of his tunic. "To touch you."

13

Bronson stared at Ella, certain he had not heard her correctly. *She* wanted to touch *him*. Her fingers were wandering farther down his torso and she continued to flick hesitant glances in his direction.

Mayhap he had heard correctly.

He cleared his throat. "I beg your pardon?"

She scooted closer to him, wickedness teasing her lips into a sensual smile.

The branch beneath moved slightly and sent a spike of nervous energy charging through him. He gripped the trunk behind him more tightly.

"I want to touch you." Ella's fingers brushed over his groin.

Bronson sucked in a breath and tried to straighten away from her when the branch swayed under him again. He froze. "Mayhap this is not the best place—"

She kissed him, her tongue curling into his mouth with an expertise he had taught her. While her lips moved over him, so too did her hands, finding the ties of his trews and undoing them.

"Ella..."

"Shh," she whispered against his lips. "I'll be your wife soon and none of this will matter." She reached under his tunic and pressed her palm to his stiffening prick. "Do you really want to wait a fortnight?"

Nay, he did not. But it wouldn't do any good in the situation for him to say as much. Not up in a tree, not when she had lifted his tunic and was pulling free the ties of his trews. First one slipped free, then another.

He opened his mouth to protest when she wrapped her hot hand around his shaft and drew him out. She held him gently, but even the slight touch was enough to make him swell in appreciation.

She gasped. "Is it getting bigger?"

"Aye," he ground out.

She rubbed her hand down the shaft and back up, sending tingles of pleasure throughout the whole of his body. "It's growing larger still," she said in wonder. Her gaze dragged from his cock in her hands to his face. "What makes it swell like that?"

She looked so innocent sitting on a tree branch like a songbird, her hair falling loose over her shoulders, her mouth parted in amazement. And his engorged cock cradled against her dainty palm.

"You," he groaned. "The way you are holding it."

She cast an anxious glance at her hands. "Will it keep growing?"

Bronson grunted. It was hard to talk, hard to think, while she held him like that. A drop of moisture pearled on the tip. She touched it with a curious finger and spread it over the spongy head.

Sweat prickled on Bronson's brow and his hands practically scraped off the bark behind him. Her fingers stroked down him, petting him, her touch so light it nearly drove him mad.

"Your skin is so smooth here," she murmured. "And it's so hard beneath."

Bronson gave a tight nod.

Her fingertips danced over him without offering him any pressure. A blush stained her cheeks. "Tell me what to do. To bring you pleasure like you did for me."

The idea of explaining it took him aback. He'd never had to offer such details before. The ladies at court played at being innocent but were skilled as whores in the shadows. Yet having to tell Ella what to do appealed to him far more than he would have anticipated.

"Wrap your hand around it." His voice cracked as he gave the instruction.

She held him as he directed. He cleared his throat. "And squeeze gently."

The pressure of her hand increased. Such exquisite pressure. He leaned his head back against the tree trunk.

"That's it?" she asked.

"Move," he said raggedly. "Your hand. Move it. Up. And down."

The grip of her palm slid over him and a groan tore from his chest. Ella needed no further instruction as she worked her slender fingers over him, silky and hot and so, so perfect.

His bollocks went tight. He was close. Her rhythm remained too slow, too light. "Harder," he panted. "Faster."

He released the trunk in a moment of mindlessness and closed his hand over hers to show her what to do. Except as he was drawn in all directions by pleasure, he had forgotten he was up a tree.

The simple movement upset his balance and his left side dipped too low. His feet kicked out but found no purchase, and that was when he went tumbling out of the tree and onto the unforgiving ground.

He landed on his shoulder and heard a distinctive pop followed by brilliant stars of pain. His mind reeled, having gone from such pleasure to such agony, and in so short a time.

Ella dropped down beside him. "Bronson," she gasped. "Let me go get Isla."

"Cover me," he ground out.

Ella had already started to run off but stopped and turned back around. She knelt at his side, shooed away the dogs, and tied the flap of his trews with shaking fingers. "Forgive me," she whispered. "The tree was a bad idea."

"Help me up," he said tightly. "I can walk."

She carefully tugged on his good arm until he was standing. He whistled for the dogs who came trotting toward him, both brown with mud, their pink tongues long and lolling.

Fortunately, the servants were able to see to them, as well as find Moppet, while Ella showed him to a small stone room within the keep. An old woman with withered skin and bright amber-colored eyes sat at a desk filled with various jars, a pile of herbs on a metal plate in front of her.

"Is this yer Lord Calville?" She smiled, revealing brilliantly white teeth.

"Aye, Isla." Ella guided Bronson to a seat by the fire. "He fell out of a tree."

"A tree?" Isla threw her head back and gave a cackling laugh. "What was the lad doing up in a tree?"

He was grateful the agony of his shoulder had eroded any sign of arousal, lest she know exactly what they had been doing in that damn tree.

Isla pushed herself up from her desk. "I'll look him over but will need to take off his shirt to do so." She jerked her chin toward the door. "Off with ye, my lady. All the better to preserve yer innocent eyes."

Ella met Bronson's gaze and slid guiltily away. They both knew her eyes were no longer innocent.

Isla looked between them and snorted. "Off with ye anyway. If it's bad, ye'll no' want to see it."

Ella hesitated at the doorway.

"Yer sisters are looking for ye." Isla prodded her fingers into Bronson's shoulder.

He gave a hiss of pain and she pursed her lips. Whatever it was, he didn't want Ella to be there to see what this woman did to him either. "I'll be fine," he offered by way of reassurance.

Ella finally quit the room and let the door close behind her.

"Off with yer tunic, lad." Isla helped him pull the cloth over his head, as well as the linen beneath it, a difficult task when he couldn't help but cradle his wounded arm.

"Ye've got to mind yerself with that young lady." The healer narrowed her eyes and leaned in close as she examined his shoulder. She smelled of sage and several other herbs he could not identify. Her fingers pinched at the skin of his shoulder with a surprising amount of strength. "The lass has wild ideas, mind ye. Ye'll get yerself killed trying to keep up with the likes of her."

<hr />

Stars of white-hot pain danced in his vision. "So I'm learning," he said through his teeth.

"Yer arm's come away from yer shoulder."

He jerked upright. That didn't sound good. "Can it be mended?"

She waved her hand with nonchalance. "Och, aye, it's easy as sin, but painful as a hot poker in the arse."

A...what? He stared at her in horror. "'Tis only my shoulder..."

In response, she threw her head back and howled with laughter. "Hold on, lad. It's going to get worse before it gets better." She grabbed something from a small box on her desk and tossed it to him. A strap of leather. "Put that in yer mouth to protect yer fine teeth."

No sooner had he bit on the leather than she grabbed his forearm with her icy strong fingers and pulled, pulled, pulled his arm out to the side.

The pain was blinding. He growled his discomfort through the leather clenched between his teeth and found himself suddenly in agreement with the old healer.

Ella's wild ideas just might get him killed.

※

ELLA HOVERED BY ISLA'S DOOR, UNCERTAIN IF SHE OUGHT TO leave. Bronson's injury was entirely her fault. He had tried to dissuade her, but she had been too driven by lust, too eager to please him as he had done for her.

Her stomach twisted into knots over her guilt. And, truth be told, she was disappointed to have not finished their interaction. She had sensed how close he had been to his crises; how he had been swollen harder than iron in her hands, the veins straining against the thin, silky skin. He was so near to the pleasure she had experienced the night before.

"Ella." Cat's voice called to her from down the hall as she ran over, oblivious to how her skirt swirled about her ankles. "We're preparing the wedding decorations. Will you join us?"

Ella hesitated and regarded the closed door once more. No sound emerged. What was happening within?

Cat blinked. "Are you ill?"

"Nay, Bronson fell out of a tree."

Cat giggled. "We can't all be as good in trees as you, Ella. Was there much blood?"

"Nay, there was none."

Cat smiled at this. "Then he will be well. Whatever injuries he has, Isla can cure." She caught Ella's hand and pulled her. "Come, we are making the decorations for the great hall."

Ella reluctantly allowed Cat to pull her away from the closed door where Bronson was injured on the other side. Injured because of her. Cat was going on about flowers and ribbons, but Ella's mind wouldn't leave Bronson.

She was led all the way down the hall, up a flight of stairs and into the warm, sunlit solar. Leila sat on the cushioned bench between the windows, surrounded by bits of ribbons, with Moppet beside her and Hardy at her feet.

"Moppet," Ella exclaimed. The servants had sworn to locate him for her, but she hadn't been able to inquire about him yet.

"He's in a mood, I'm afraid." Leila patted his head. He jerked back from her touch, his black eyes narrowed. "Apparently he didn't want to come back inside."

"Bronson fell out of a tree." Cat giggled.

"That isn't kind," Ella admonished her younger sister.

Leila looked up from Moppet. "What was he doing up in a tree?"

Ella's cheeks burned at the very mention. "Trying something different, I suppose," she answered brusquely. "What is going on here?" She bustled to the bench and picked up a blue ribbon. "This looks sufficient."

"Sufficient?" Cat's mouth dropped open. "You are the one who is full of the most romantic notions, and you are using 'sufficient' when describing your wedding decorations?" Concern replaced her shock. "Is it not going well with him?"

"Nay, it isn't that." Ella tried to laugh off her comment, but the sound was hollow and false. "I feel awful for what happened. He was up in that tree because of me."

"You didn't do anything to make him fall, I'm sure," Cat protested. "Come, look at the flowers. We have daisies." She lifted one of the fragile green stems and twirled the white and yellow flower enticingly. "I had Drake fetch them all earlier."

Drake, Werrick's Captain of the Guard, had several sisters himself and, being the model of chivalry, was always obliging with Ella, Cat and Leila's whims.

"You made him go out to pick flowers so soon after returning back from taking Marin and Bran to Kendal Castle?" Ella asked.

Cat shrugged. "He said it was no bother." She lifted the daisy higher for Ella to see. It *was* pretty. The petals pristine white, the center wide and as brilliant a yellow as the sun.

"We can't use daisies," Leila said from where she sorted through a tangle of ribbon on the window seat.

Ella took the flower from Cat and twirled the slender stem as her sister had done. "Why not?"

Leila pieced a blue and orange ribbon together and studied them together for a moment. "Because they make Lord Calville sneeze."

Ella studied her youngest sister. "How do you know?"

"He comes to see me in the mornings when I'm going through my stock of herbs, to see Hardy." The dog at her feet perked up and Moppet slowly crept back on the cushion, closer to Leila. She chuckled and patted Moppet's head. This time, the stubborn little squirrel did not balk at her affection but nestled against her instead.

"He said they made him sneeze," Leila said. "I saw it once. His nose went twitchy and he sneezed so loudly, it frightened poor Hardy."

Hardy cocked his head.

"We could do peonies." Cat lifted a heavy pink blossom from the row of other flowers. "Does he like peonies?"

Except she wasn't asking Ella, she was asking Leila, who considered the question with earnestness.

The twist of guilt in Ella's stomach knotted with further frustration. How did she not know about the daisies? Nor any of his affinities towards flowers.

"I think he likes them well enough as he hasn't said they make him sneeze." Leila discarded the orange ribbon, then lifted a white one and matched them together. "I say we go with blue ribbons. It's his favorite color."

"How do you know that?" Ella asked.

Leila and Cat both looked at her. Even Hardy shifted his adoring gaze from Leila to Ella.

"He hasn't told me his favorite color." Leila looked at the ribbon in her hand and slowly looped it around her forefinger. "It's just that he wears blue often, and so I assumed."

"It's an excellent point." Ella smiled to cover her own oversight. She ought to have noticed such a thing as well.

Except the smile was as false as her words. She had not once noticed him wearing blue, let alone on multiple occasions. She had noticed the plumpness of the bottom lip she enjoyed suckling, she was familiar with the stroke of his fingers at her most intimate place and she knew the length of his manhood exceeded that of her hand. But she had not known his color preference, nor that her favorite flower made him sneeze.

Ella thought of Bronson often, longing to be at his side, eager for his touches and his kisses. But the preparations for the wedding made her realize one thing with certainty: she needed to learn more about who he was.

14

Bronson adjusted the sling on his good shoulder. The thing was a nuisance. Fortunately, the pain had subsided almost as soon as Isla had made it pop again.

He strode through the castle with his arm locked at an angle in the sling. It would only be for a few days, or so Isla said.

Despite the discomfort he had endured, he did not blame Ella for his injury. She had meant only to bring him pleasure. And she had, all the way up until he tried to show her how to bring him to climax. With her fingers on him, sliding, squeezing.

He paused in the hall and drew a deep breath to cool his blood. It would not do to walk into dinner with a raging cockstand. Ella rushed to his side as soon as he entered with Wolf and Bear at his heels, the beasts now clean despite their jaunt in the mud.

"How do you fare?" Her concerned gaze swept over his shoulder and widened at the sight of the sling.

"It appears arms can slip free of shoulders, as was the case with mine." He indicated the linen tied over his shoulder. "Isla was able to put it back but says I must wear this for several days."

"Are you in much pain?" Ella took his good hand. "Bronson,

I'm so sorry." She flicked a gaze around them and lowered her voice. "You had said not to, but I insisted—"

"I'm not in pain anymore, my dove." He drew his hand from hers and brought it to her face. She nestled into it, her smile one of gratitude.

"Come, eat." She drew him with her toward their chairs. "There is a troubadour tonight, so we will have a story once supper is complete."

The food was as good that eve as it had been the previous nights. Chicken with asparagus in an onion sauce, more bread than they could eat, poached pears drenched in honey. As with all evenings when he ate such decadent fare, his thoughts drifted to Brigid and Lark. They would surely arrive within the next several days.

He was grateful they would be in Werrick Castle with him, where they would have a comfortable place to sleep and good food such as the trenchers heaped before him.

"Lord Calville," the Earl of Werrick called to him from the head of the table. He indicated the sling with his eating dagger. "You took a tumble from the tree today, did you?" He chuckled. "Need I even ask how it happened?"

Bronson's mouth opened and closed, his voice locked somewhere between the unspeakable truth and an unprepared lie.

The earl chuckled and waved a hand at Bronson. "You needn't tell me, lad. 'Twas only a jest. We already know Ella doubtlessly lured you up there. Mind you watch her." The earl winked at his daughter. "She's part sprite, I tell you."

Several people at the table laughed, including Ella. When Bronson gave her an incredulous look, she simply pressed her lips together and shrugged despite her reddened cheeks.

She lifted her goblet of wine and let it hover in front of her mouth. "Their assumptions are innocent," she whispered before taking a delicate sip. She set the cup aside. "And I intend to make it up to you."

"Hopefully not in a tree," he said in a low voice.

She laughed and shook her head. But the brush of her foot against his under the table told him she already had something planned. Only this time, he knew that if his life might be in any form of danger, he would allay her intent.

After they had finished eating, an awkward venture for him with only one hand, and after several more jesting remarks about Bronson's fall from the tree, the benches were moved toward the great yawning hearth where a merry fire crackled. The troubadour stood before the fireplace, atop a stool to add a bit more height to his short frame.

Though slight in stature, his large voice made up for the smallness of his body, and his story carried throughout the great hall. The story was one of a woman who never thought she would find love, and a noble knight who sought only to perform one act of heroism for his lord. Though it was inevitable that the woman and knight should meet and fall in love, Ella still emitted soft, wistful sighs with each predictable turn.

The hour was late when the troubadour finished the last of his long poem. The crowd broke apart, each going about his or her own business. And so, it was that no one thought to question if Bronson would see Ella to her chamber that night.

He guided her in the darkened hallway with his good arm. "You are better at reading than he was at sharing his story."

Ella gave a little laugh. "You shouldn't say such things."

"'Tis true." He leaned close to her. "And your stories are far better as well."

Her laugh was throatier this time. "I'm pleased you enjoy them so."

He stopped in front of her door, the correct one this time. Ella gazed up at him, the skin around her eyes tight as though she was assessing him.

He lifted a brow with curiosity.

"What color do you prefer above all others?" she queried.

"Blue." He smiled. "Why do you ask such a question?"

She shook her head. "'Tis not important."

He touched her cheek and her lashes swept down. This was his favorite part of the night, above the fine meals and the troubadour and even any dessert Nan could put together. He loved this time with Ella best, when she was soft and warm and as eager to kiss him as he was her.

Their lips touched, gently, softly, and then the tips of their tongues brushed one another. Ella nuzzled his neck with her nose, then his ear.

"Leave your door unlatched tonight," she whispered, her breath sweet and hot against his ear.

He straightened and gazed down at her. She smiled and slipped into her room.

❧

Ella's heart threatened to pound through her chest with nervous excitement. She lifted the small hand mirror once more and glanced at her reflection. Had she put on too much rouge? Not enough?

Was she being overly critical?

Aye, that was definitely it. She had spent the last hour in her private chambers readying herself as the castle quieted for the night. Bronson's room was only a short way down the hall from hers. A brisk walk would have her to his door in moments. She pulled a cloak over her shoulders and secured it at her throat. If nothing else, the voluminous fabric would cover her simple night rail beneath, and the hood would hide her identity if someone should happen upon her.

She put her hand to the latch of her door and paused with reverence. This would be it. The night she would give herself to Bronson. The night she would tell him she loved him, and when she would show him as much. Her body was already burning with the need for release.

She pulled her door open and went out into the dark hall. Her feet were bare on the cool stone floor, but more importantly, her steps were silent. She moved like a shadow to the door she knew was Bronson's and quietly entered.

He sat before the fire, the elbow of his good arm propped on his knee as he stared into the flames. At the quiet click of his door closing, he lifted his head and grinned at her. "Does the evening require a cloak?" He got to his feet to approach her. He still wore his blue and gold doublet and leather trews from supper.

She was not so overdressed. With her gaze locked on his, she pulled the hood back and unclipped the fastening. In a quiet rustle of costly fabric, the heavy cloak fell from her shoulders, leaving her in nothing but her night rail.

Bronson paused mid-step as his gaze combed over the length of her.

She walked toward him with the slow saunter she'd seen tavern ladies use, her hips swaying with promise. "It's warm enough to not require a cloak for anything other than concealment." She stopped in front of him, so close her bosom nearly touched his chest. "I don't imagine I'll need this night rail either."

Bronson's gaze swept down her once more and lingered on her breasts. Her nipples prickled at the attention and she felt them growing taut. He swallowed. "Ella, you are a maiden and I am not yet your husband."

"You will be my husband soon." She stroked a hand over his sling. "Your poor arm. Does it pain you?"

"Nay."

"Let me make it up to you." Her fingers slid down the sling to his stomach, over the band of his trews and down to where she'd touched him so intimately earlier. "I want you to have me, Bronson. All of me."

The bulk under her hand twitched and began to grow firm. He closed his eyes. "What you are asking cannot be undone, Ella."

She framed the thickness with her fingers and slowly moved her palm up and down. "I want you, Bronson. I can't stop thinking about how badly I want you."

He gave a strangled groan. "It isn't right for you to be here."

His manhood was now rock hard beneath her touch and it made the place between her legs grow damp, the pulse of heat insistent.

"Tell me you don't want me, and I'll leave." She squeezed the length of him the way he'd showed her.

His breath hissed through his teeth.

"Touch me and see for yourself how badly I want you." She finally released him and drew up the hem of her night rail to her upper thighs, shielding her intimate place from him while still offering herself for his caress.

His hand stretched toward her, sampling her with a single stroke. Ella whimpered as pleasure rippled through her. He clenched his jaw and fixed his gaze on his hand as he slid over her once more, then again, his finger lightly probing inside of her.

Her knees went soft and threatened to drop her from where she stood. "Tell me you don't want this," she whispered. "And I'll leave."

"That's the problem." His stare dragged back up toward her face. "I do."

"Then have me." She put a hand to his doublet and popped free the first button.

"This isn't play, Ella." There was a note of warning in his tone, even as he continued to glide his touch over her center.

She slipped another button free.

"There can be consequences." He took the hem of her night rail from her and lifted it higher.

She relinquished the flimsy cloth to him and worked even

faster on his buttons. He drew the gown up over her breasts, over her head, stopping her efforts briefly.

The night rail covered her face, then lifted her hair from her shoulders as it slid from her skin and fell silently to the floor. He drew in a hard breath and regarded her.

"Tell me to leave," she challenged.

His stare moved over her, roaming over her breasts, her legs, her thighs, her sex. He swallowed. "You're not going anywhere," he said with finality.

"I was hoping you would say that." Ella stepped toward him and gently plucked at the binding holding his arm to his body. "Can this come off?"

With a growl, he drew the sling off. He sucked in a breath that made Ella wince and moved more carefully to ease off his doublet. She helped him with the linen beneath, exceedingly mindful of his injured arm, which obviously still was causing him pain.

Even with his arm cradled to his torso, he was beautiful underneath, powerful with strength from hunting and fighting. He kept his gaze fixed on her, alternating from her face to her body, as he pulled free the ties of his trews and shoved them one-handed to the floor.

His manhood thrust out from him, pointing directly at her. He wrapped his good arm around her and the swollen length of him bumped clumsily and hot against her belly. His mouth slanted over hers, his tongue stroking as his hand played over her body, cupping her breast, curving over her bottom.

She ran her hands over his muscular back, marveling at all the raw power of him. His lips dragged down her neck to her collarbone.

She dropped her head back to give him more access to whatever he wanted to kiss, whatever he wanted to lick. The heat of his mouth closed around her nipple and needles of pleasure prickled through her. She cried out in surprise, reveling in the sensation.

He circled her with his tongue and then went to the other breast. "Do you want more?" he groaned. "Even more than this?"

"Aye," she panted. "I want everything."

He knelt on the ground and gently nudged her legs apart. She leaned her weight on a chair behind her and spread her thighs. She had been expecting his fingers, not his mouth. But that was exactly what closed over her, wet and eager as his tongue lapped decadent circles about the sensitive place of her sex.

He worked his finger inside her as he loved her with his mouth, plunging with slow care. Ella's world burst into flames, tingles in every part of her body until she could no longer handle the sensation of it all. Euphoria exploded around her and left dots of light sparkling behind her closed lids.

When she opened her eyes again, he had gotten to his feet and stood before her. He took her hand and led her on shaking legs to the large bed at the back of his chamber. She sank onto the furs and looked up at him. His arousal jutted in front of her—silky, hard temptation.

She touched him, remembering how much he had enjoyed that before. He groaned and let her explore the shaft, the spongy tip. She licked her lips and his eyes fixed on her mouth.

A wicked thought sizzled through her mind. Surely, he was not the only one who could bring pleasure with his mouth.

15

Bronson's body was tense with the need to release, still burning from Ella's touches earlier that day. She stared at his cock in front of her and cast a flirtatious little half-smirk up at him.

Her hands glided over his shaft like he'd shown her, the pressure intensifying as she neared the swollen head. His bollocks tightened at the sheer pleasure.

She watched him as she explored his cock with her hands, then licked her lips with that flash of mischief in her eyes. She parted her mouth and gently kissed the tip of his cock. He gave a strangled choke and his arousal quirked at the sensation of her mouth on him.

She glanced anxiously up at him, her eyes seeking permission. He nodded. After all, he was a man, and what right-minded man would ever say no to such an offer?

She licked him from shaft to tip, pausing periodically to kiss and brush her lips over him. An innocent's attempt to pleasure a man with her mouth. It was endearing, and sensual, and made him ready to pop.

He caught her face with his hand. She paused mid-lick and gazed up at him.

"I want you," he said in a gravelly voice.

She sucked in a breath and her tongue returned to her beautiful mouth. He lowered himself to her with his good arm, stretching his nakedness over the soft warmth of hers. Lust pounded painfully at his groin and echoed in his ears with a desperation to release.

He didn't ask if she knew what they were to do. Clearly, they'd had enough play that she could deduce as much, especially for a woman with desires as intense as Ella's.

He ran his hands over her legs. First her delicate ankles, then up to those shapely calves that had haunted his nights since he arrived at Werrick Castle. Her skin was smooth and warm under his touch, her breath shaky. He traced his fingers up her pretty knees and down the delicate path of her inner thighs.

"Part your legs for me," he whispered.

She did as he asked, revealing the glistening, swollen folds of her sex, flushed pink with longing. His mouth found hers, his kisses languid and gentle. Lusty though she might be, it didn't mean the act wouldn't frighten her.

He rose on top of her and nudged the head of himself against her, a feat not easily done with only one damn arm. Fortunately, he was so hard, and she so wet, her center slightly stretched from his efforts when he licked her to climax earlier. He sank in slightly and stopped.

He kissed her once more and raised his head to see her reaction. Her forehead puckered, as if in concentration.

"Are you all right, my dove?" he asked.

She blinked, nodding. "Aye."

He thrust forward, inching deeper. She stiffened.

"Relax into it," he said softly. "It will only be uncomfortable this one time." Or so he hoped, if all the rumors he had heard were true.

The arm he had pressed to his side was more of an inconvenience than he'd anticipated. He wanted to touch her breasts, her sex, to bring her to release while they coupled.

He kissed her and slowly eased out before nudging back in again. "Touch yourself, Ella."

She leaned back on the pillow to regard him.

"Do you know how to do that?" He nuzzled her neck, speaking into her ear. "To touch yourself and bring on your own crises?"

She nodded against his cheek.

He groaned. Of course, she did, a woman with such deep sexual need as she. "Do it."

Her fingers slid between their bodies, brushing his shaft just above where they were joined as she did so. He moved carefully to ensure he didn't hurt her, pumping in and out, letting himself go deeper and deeper each time. She was slick with need and her breath came out in short, excited pants.

He bent to capture her breast in his mouth. "Aye, like that," he said against her sweet skin. One final plunge and he was fully buried within her.

He swirled his tongue around her nipple, and he felt her finger over her sex increase its speed. She was moving with him now, rocking her hips to meet his thrust, her thighs squeezing at his waist. They moaned with each joining, the clamp of her sex around him getting tighter until he could scarcely bear it any longer.

She removed her hand from touching herself and instead clung to him. Her hips worked under him, seeking the necessary friction she needed.

Sensing her climax soon upon her, Bronson captured her mouth with his, just as she gave a scream of pleasure. Her sheath clenched rhythmically, pulling at him and pushing him over the edge. He grunted with the force of his crises and finally, after days of fantasizing about this very moment, poured his seed into Ella.

He collapsed on his side, his good arm shaking from the incredible effort of having held himself up on it for so long. "Did I hurt you?" he asked once he finally had breath enough in his lungs to do so.

Ella turned her face toward him. A dreamy expression played on her lips and her face was glowing with a light sheen. She shook her head. "You pleased me. As much as I had anticipated you would."

Her words brought on a swell of pride. He was glad to have brought her such bliss.

"And did I...?" Ella gave a sheepish smile. "Did I please you?"

Bronson lay his head back on the bed and groaned. His body was still warm from the euphoria she had wrought. "Aye, even more than I imagined you would."

"Had you thought about it?" She rolled over so she was laying partially atop him. "About me?"

"Every waking moment and even many while I slept," he said earnestly. "You're incredibly beautiful. Ever since that day you teased me with your naked leg..."

She lowered her head, her expression incredulous. "I teased you with a leg?"

He nodded. "Oh, aye, when it's as perfectly shaped as yours." He ran his good hand over her calf in demonstration. "You dropped it right in front of my face and swung it back and forth."

Ella's lips pressed together as though trying to quell a smile and slid her gaze from his.

"What is it?" he asked.

She shook her head, her mouth still pressed closed.

"Tell me, or I shall have to find alternate means to get the information from you." He lifted his brows suggestively.

"Now I really don't want to tell you." Ella laughed, a low, intimate sound. "I think my father's plan has worked out."

"Oh? Pray tell what you mean by that."

"This time we've had together." Ella lifted her shoulder in a delicate shrug.

Bronson wanted to kiss that shoulder. And then the whole rest of her. He knew she would have to return to her own chambers soon, but he wished she could stay with him, for them to pleasure each other again and again throughout the night.

She had been a maiden, however, and her body would need to recover from what they had done. The stain of blood on the sheets was proof enough of that. Despite her enjoyment, blood did not come without pain.

"We have had an enjoyable time together," Bronson agreed.

"Mmmhmm..." Ella lay her head on his chest while her fingers played idly through the sprinkle of dark hair. "I wasn't sure until tonight, until this."

She drew herself up on her elbow and met his gaze. "I love you, Bronson."

She loved him?

Victory soared through him.

He crooked a smile up at her and trailed his finger over her narrow chin. "And I love you, sweet dove."

Their union promised to be mutually enjoyable, for the feelings blossoming between them, everything seemed to be absolutely perfect. With growing love and passion such as theirs, nothing could possibly go wrong.

❦

ELLA WAS IN LOVE WITH BRONSON. IN EVERY DECENT, PURE and utterly wicked way it was possible to be in love with someone.

Over the next several days, they could not keep their distance from one another. They met in alcoves and snuck out on rides without a soldier to guard over them. They slipped into empty rooms and went to one another at night. They did not, however, climb anymore trees.

Each time they were together, they touched and loved one another's bodies, bringing the other incredible pleasure.

She could scarcely go through a minute of her day without the idea of him inside her, or tasting her, or touching her. They didn't even speak when they came together, their bodies saying all that needed to be said.

The wedding planning was coming along nicely for having been done in such a short period of time. Ella stared out the window of the solar several afternoons later and wished she was naked in such beautiful light with Bronson there to stroke her.

"Oh, Ella, you're so in love." Cat laughed and snapped at the air.

Ella jumped slightly and regarded her sister in surprise. "Did you ask me something?"

"Aye, several times." Cat smothered a giggle behind her hand and slid a glance to Leila, who did likewise. "What sort of food do you think ought to be served at supper? What is his favorite meat?"

Ella thought for a moment. She didn't know what his favorite meat was. He had commented on food often as well, and yet for the life of her, she couldn't recall what he'd said at any of those moments. "Venison," she lied. After all, he had eaten it. And what man didn't appreciate a good cut of venison?

Besides, if she chose everything, he would love it all because she had selected it for him.

Cat's eyes sparkled. "Oh, I love venison too. This feast will be wonderful. What sort of drink is his favorite?"

"Wine." Ella replied this time with confidence. He drank wine at every meal.

"Aye, but what kind?" Cat pressed.

Ella blinked. If he had even bothered to comment on the wine, she hadn't paid it a single thought. "Bordeaux claret," she replied. It was her favorite wine, and one was as good as the other, wasn't it?

She'd meant to ask him more questions about what he liked and did not. Truly, she had. Except that every time they saw one another, she fell prey to passion and forgot what she'd meant to say.

Leila tilted her head as if listening to something no one else could hear. "Lady Calville and Lark will arrive today."

"Oh, how wonderful." Cat peered through the glass window behind Leila as though she could see the guests traveling up herself. Which she wouldn't be able to do, most likely.

Leila had a gift for knowing what was coming, though misinterpretations had left her hesitant to share her visions. She only ever said anything when she was certain an event would come to pass.

"Won't it be delightful to meet Calville's sister?" Cat spun about the room.

Ella smiled. "I can hardly wait." But in truth, she *could* wait.

Things were perfect as they were with plenty of time for her and Bronson to sneak away for romantic trysts. If he had to entertain his family once they arrived, what would happen to the stolen moments of pleasure throughout the day?

"Is there a certain kind of tale the troubadour ought to tell?" Leila patted the bench beside her, and Hardy leapt up onto the cushion. Despite folding his long, thin legs beneath him, he still took up most of the seat.

"Father will not like that if he sees it," Ella warned her.

"Then he mustn't find out." Leila slid her a glance. "As he doesn't find out how often you slip away with Lord Calville."

"Leila, we said we wouldn't mention it," Cat hissed.

Heat warmed Ella's cheeks. Apparently, the moments of privacy she'd taken with Bronson had been noticed. She would need to refrain going forward. After the one they had planned that afternoon, of course, for it was far too late now to cancel.

"Well, I suppose I've seen nothing." Ella winked and her sisters laughed.

"Then we are back to my original question about the troubadour." Leila bent her head toward Hardy, giving him a scratch under his collar. The sunlight coming in played over her dark hair and made it gleam like polished onyx. "You said he reads your books, correct? What story does he seem to like best?"

Ella hesitated. He had not mentioned reading her books in several days and she had not seen him in the solar. Had he stopped? Rather than confess this to her sisters, she lied again. "I believe he likes the story of the female knight and the prince the best."

"That's Geordie's favorite too." Leila grinned at Cat.

"How do you know?" Ella asked.

Leila hopped off the bench and Hardy followed behind her. "It was in his letter. I need to take Hardy outside, but I have everything necessary for putting together the wedding." Leila paused and pressed a kiss to Ella's cheek.

Ella sagged back after Leila's affection. Geordie's letter. Ella had forgotten. Cat had meant to read it to her the night Ella changed to the mistress of the castle's chambers.

"Oh, Cat." Ella opened her arms to her sister. "I'm so sorry."

Cat waved off the embrace as well as the apology. "You have been busy falling in love." She caught Ella's hand and squeezed it. "I'm so impressed that you know him so well that you can answer these questions so thoroughly."

Heat rose in Ella's cheeks. She nodded her thanks, as speaking it seemed nearly impossible at that exact moment.

"I'll leave you to your afternoon while I settle the arrangements with Nan." Cat embraced her, pressed a sweet kiss to her cheek and was gone.

Bronson entered the room only a few moments later. His green eyes lit up when they found hers. "Good afternoon, my dove." He glanced about the room. "Are we alone?"

He no longer had to wear his sling, but still favored his right arm over his left.

Ella nodded. It was on the tip of her tongue to ask if he still read her books, if he still enjoyed the stories, but his arms were around her in an instant and all thoughts and concerns flitted away.

His lips brushed over her jawline. "I haven't been able to stop thinking of you," he growled.

She tilted her head to the side to allow him better access to her neck, her breasts, craving the heat of his mouth. "And I you."

"I need you." He took her hand and put it to flap of his trews, where he was already hard and hot.

Ella moaned in anticipation. She jerked free his ties and drew out his hardness as he carefully walked her backward, toward the door to the solar. While the door didn't lock, it could be held shut with their bodies, especially if they leaned against it. With the privacy and golden warmth of the small solar, it had become one of their favorite rooms to meet.

Bronson lifted her skirt, his fingers immediately finding her center. His arm had healed properly enough for full use of it again, and the pleasure he gave with two arms was intensely wonderful.

He lifted her leg against the wall, spreading her open for him, as he grabbed his cock in his free hand and positioned it at her core. The heat of the swollen tip blazed against her sex.

Ella wriggled in his hold, desperate for him to plunge inside of her.

A knock sounded at the door. They both straightened immediately. Ella's dress dropped down while Bronson's hands disappeared under his tunic to tie shut the closure to his trews.

"What is it?" Ella asked in a sweet tone.

"My lady," Drake's voice came through the door. "The Countess of Calville and Lady Lark have arrived."

"Oh, how wonderful," Ella stammered. "I shall be down in a moment."

"As will I," Bronson declared from behind her.

She shot him a chastising look and he shrugged. "We are reading in here." He pulled a book out, opened it up and tossed another in her direction.

Ella stretched her hands out and snapped the book from the air before it could hit the ground. "Are you mad? You can't handle books like that."

She cradled it to her chest as though it were a baby. Surely, Bronson knew better than to handle books so callously.

Once Drake's rhythmic footsteps faded away, Ella set her book back on the shelf. Bronson offered her his arm and led her down toward the bailey to meet his stepmother and half-sister.

16

Bronson stood proudly with Ella on his arm as he waited for the retinue traveling with Brigid and Lark to arrive. The small wooden cart with their trunks rattled behind them as they rode up on fine brown horses alongside several of Werrick's soldiers, sent with them to ensure their safe passage.

The Earl of Werrick had given them good horses to ride, as well as protection, and for that, Bronson could not have been more grateful. Lark stared up in awe at the castle as they approached while Brigid smiled kindly at Bronson and Ella.

"Your stepmother is b...b...beautiful," William stuttered from where he stood beside Bronson, his gaze locked on Brigid. "Beautiful," he said again, this time under his breath, in a whisper and without the stammer.

Bronson turned a curious eye to William, who watched the procession come to a halt like a man seeing a work of art being unveiled.

"I will introduce you." Bronson hid a smile at the man's reaction.

William's expression became quickly shuttered. He shook his head. "Nay. That is n...n...not necessary."

It was a surprising response when his reaction had been so strong upon seeing Brigid for the first time. Bronson stepped forward to help her from her mount while Peter assisted Lark. Both ladies were dressed in fine clothes that suited their station and, in Lark's case, her size.

The coin he had given them when he left, as well as additional funds he'd had sent from items he'd sold, had gone to improving their appearances considerably. Both women practically gleamed with good health, and it warmed his heart to see it.

"Brigid." Bronson bowed to her. "You and Lark look lovely. I do hope your journey was an easy one."

"Oh, it was wonderful." Brigid's gaze wandered up to the castle. She touched a hand first to her chest, then to her mouth as her eyes filled with tears. "The castle is beautiful." She reached a hand for Bronson's. "You have done so much for us," she said softly. "Thank you."

"You needn't mention it," Bronson said quickly. He hoped she would not mention it again lest Ella hear.

After he'd worked so hard to get Ella to want to marry him, he could not lose her affections. Not now when they were so close to the wedding. Not when Brigid and Lark looked to be thriving once more.

"Ella, this is my stepmother, Brigid Berkley, the fifth Countess of Calville." He regarded Ella and saw her as Brigid must, with tumbling locks, a beautiful smile and fine silk clothing. "And this is my bride to be, Lady Ella Barrington, third daughter to the Earl of Werrick."

Ella curtsied. "Well met, Lady Calville. Welcome to Werrick."

Brigid reached out a hand to stop Ella. "Oh please, that isn't necessary. Do call me Brigid. We never fell on formality in my home, and I think the title of Lady Calville will be far lovelier on you."

Lark shifted closer with shy steps, her long brown hair pulled back in a simple braid. The green kirtle she wore was of fine cotton and such a deep shade of green, it made her eyes appear startling in her fair face.

"And is this Lady Lark?" Ella asked.

Lark nodded and glanced up sheepishly at Bronson. Reticence wouldn't do among brother and sister though, not for him. He caught her in a hug that lifted her feet from the ground and had her laughing before he set her back down.

Leila came forward with two handfuls of small purple and white flowers, which she handed to Brigid and Lark. "If you set them by your bed, they will not only look beautiful, but will also help you sleep well."

"How kind of you," Brigid said. But it was Lark that Leila was watching with quiet hope. No doubt a friend for little Leila to play with. They were about the same age, he wagered.

"This is Lady Leila," Bronson said by way of introduction. "Leila, will you be so kind as to show Lark where she'll be sleeping? Mayhap introduce her to Lady Catriona and Nan and Bixby? But mind her around Moppet." He lowered his voice with warning and widened his eyes dramatically. "She won't want to be left alone...with Moppet."

"Oh, he isn't that bad," Ella offered in reassurance.

But Leila and Lark were both already laughing and running into the castle, hand in hand, with Hardy dashing behind them. Bronson watched the two go and a sense of lightness filled him. This was the life Lark should have had from the onset. One of wealth and happiness, filled with friendship.

He was glad to finally offer it to her.

Brigid was introduced to the Earl of Werrick and Drake. William, however, had gone missing. Once introductions were done, Brigid was shown to her chamber along with Jane, her remaining servant, to refresh from her journey before supper.

No sooner had Bronson's stepmother left the room than he felt himself being pulled into a shaded alcove. Ella arched her body against him. "We have unfinished business, my lord."

"Later, my dove." He pressed a kiss to her brow. "I must ensure their trunks are delivered properly to their rooms."

"Rohesia will see to that." Ella locked her hold on him more tightly. "Touch me."

Bronson glanced behind him to ensure no one was nearby. Especially not his stepmother or Lark. They would be terribly disappointed to find him in such a compromising position. He shook his head. "Later," he promised.

Ella gave him a coy smile and slid her leg between his, nudging at his cock with her thigh.

"Ella, cease this at once." His tone was sharper than intended, but it had the desired result. She released her hold on him. He plucked at the fabric of his doublet to ensure no wrinkles were visible.

"We cannot always go about like this," he said more gently. "Later, my dove." He placed a kiss on her smooth cheek and left to see to Lark while Brigid freshened up. Children seldom needed the time to gather themselves after a long journey as their elders did.

Sure enough, he found his half-sister in the hut with Leila as they bundled herbs together to string along the rafters.

"That one is chamomile," Leila said. "You can use it in teas and many other things."

Both girls and one wayward hunting dog lifted their heads as he entered the small space. Lark and Leila both smiled and Hardy's tail began to thump with enthusiasm.

"Lady Leila is showing me how to use herbs for healing." Lark hurried over to him and held out the small white flowers that were in the bundles Leila had given to them upon their arrival. "These are chamomile. Won't this be so wonderful to know when we return to Berkley Manor?"

Bronson's chest went tight with his sister's excitement to learn about herbs. She was not thinking of this finer life as permanent, but as an opportunity to glean what she could to better her life with her mother at Berkley Manor. It was obvious she was anticipating returning to the life they had led before, once this was over.

"Aye, my little Lark, it will be most helpful." He rubbed a hand over her head and bent to offer greetings to Hardy. The dog leaned his head back until it was nearly upside down, watching him with soul-deep brown eyes, while his long pink tongue dangled out of the corner of his mouth.

Now Hardy could watch over Lark in addition to Leila, keeping both girls safe.

Bronson straightened. "Thank you for making Lark feel so welcome."

Leila gave him her shy smile and nodded. "'Tis my pleasure."

And no doubt it was. Leila's sisters were all older than her. He imagined having Lark visit was a wonderful opportunity for her to befriend someone her own age.

"Hardy, keep these two out of trouble," he commanded.

The dog tilted his head in confusion and the girls both laughed.

"We'll be good," Leila reassured him.

Certain they would get on well, Bronson left to ensure all preparations for their stay had been handled accordingly. After the hard life that his stepmother and half-sister had lived, he wanted them to have only the best.

For the first time in far too long, his life was going well. Not the kind of well he'd enjoyed with his father where his days were filled with a perception of carefree enjoyment, for now he knew the sacrifices others made for such pleasures. Nay, this was going well in a way that had his family cared for with a beautiful, lusty betrothed.

He needed only handle several more tasks and would meet Ella after supper, and after they'd eaten...

He grinned in anticipation and set about his duties.

Ella had not seen Bronson all day, except in passing. The man ran around as though he were mistress of the house, seeing to preparations for his stepmother and half-sister to ensure that they were comfortable. While it was considerate of him to do so, Ella could not help but miss their many clandestine meetings.

In the time she had been spending with Bronson the prior few days, however, she had been neglecting her sisters. She sought to make that right in her time away from him now. She found Cat in the room they once had all shared together, sitting before the fire with her head bent over Geordie's missive.

She looked up with a smile. "Did you think of something more to add to your wedding preparations?"

The mere mention of the wedding preparations rankled Ella. It was supposed to be a wonderfully romantic event to plan, but in reality, it was tedious and full of far too many things she was not certain of, like, everything Bronson preferred.

She set Moppet's bag on the dressing table and Moppet peered out from beneath the flap.

"Nay, I just thought I would like to ready for supper in our room, like I did before." Ella indicated the letter. "And you could read me Geordie's letter."

Cat's eyes sparkled. "I would like that very much."

"Where is Leila?" Ella glanced about the room.

"With Lark." Cat rose from the chair and settled her letter from Geordie on the bed, then went to the clothes trunk. "The two of them were immediate friends. I think it's wonderful for Leila to have someone her own age, and I am glad that we will be getting a new sister."

Moppet hopped down from the table and raced over to the parchment. Ella lifted it before he could touch it. "Then this is the perfect time for me to hear about Geordie's letter."

Cat happily obliged and read on and on, with giggles and a wide smile, about Geordie's adventures on campaign with the king. Cat and Geordie had been inseparable since they were children and although Cat was truly happy for him, his absence had struck her hard.

The door to their room opened and Leila entered with Lark, Hardy trotting at their heels. Moppet raced back into the bag with an irate chattering that caused them all to break out in a fit of giggles. Together, they all readied for supper, helping each other while chatting. Lark, though somewhat timid, appeared to fit right in with the Werrick sisters, and Ella was only too happy to welcome her into the family. As they were making their way to the great hall later, Lark strode along beside Ella.

"I'm so pleased you will be marrying Bronson." Lark's cheeks went pink. "I can't imagine a family more wonderful than yours to belong to."

There was something about the young girl that made Ella want to curl her arms around Lark protectively. Mayhap it was how painfully thin the child was, or mayhap it was her wondrous expression as she gazed around Werrick Castle, as if she had never seen such finery.

"We are happy to have you join us," she replied earnestly. "And I know Leila is pleased to have someone her own age to talk to."

They walked into the great hall and Lark stopped abruptly, her mouth falling open in awe.

"Have you not been inside the great hall of a castle before?" Ella asked.

Lark shook her head.

Ella regarded the girl curiously. "Have you never gone to court then?"

Lark shook her head again. "Does it look like this?"

"Far grander, with many meals served and stiff kirtles laced far too tight so you can scarcely move." Ella walked rigidly for two steps, her arms locked out at her sides.

Lark laughed.

"But there are troubadours who tell the most wonderful tales." Ella led Lark down the side of the great hall, past the many rows of trestles.

Lark's attention fixed on a mountain of rolls in the center of one table. "What is a troubadour?" she asked distractedly.

Ella blinked in surprise. It was a strange thing for the girl to have not gone to court by the age of fourteen, but entirely another for her to have never been exposed to a troubadour. Even in the country, the traveling story tellers often made appearances in villages between visits to wealthier homes.

"They tell the most wonderful tales of love." Ella put her hand over her chest and sighed with happiness. "We have written several of their stories down if you would like to read them."

"Oh, I cannot read." Lark made the admission as if it were nothing, as if it were simply a declaration to have a second helping of food or a bland comment upon the weather.

Ella frowned at such a horrible fate as not being able to read. They arrived at their table and there was no more time for her to discuss the matter.

Bronson rose as Ella approached. She smiled at him, but the action felt forced. Was he aware his sister was unable to read? And what of all the books he'd said his stepmother and Lark most likely possessed?

Not only was he not aware of his sister's affinities, he had actively hindered her life. First by not taking her to court while he had spent years living there, and then by not teaching the girl to read. It was appalling.

His stepmother, Lady Calville, was at Ella's right. A woman who was nearly as thin as her daughter. Threads of silver gleamed in brown hair the same color as Lark's. The woman glanced affectionately at Ella with the kind of smile one gives someone they have known all of their life, unguarded and warm.

It made Ella immediately like the woman, and twinged Ella's

guilt at her selfish reaction earlier that day after Bronson had left to see to his stepmother and Lark.

Ella took her seat and tried as best she could to return the warmth of the sentiment. "I trust you had as comfortable a journey as is possible for such a long distance," she said.

Lady Calville dipped her slender fingers into the bowl of water at her side and held them out to a servant to wipe clean for her. "Aye, it was pleasant. Your father went to great expense to see to our comfort with such fine horses. It was considerate of him."

Ella went about her own ablutions while she took in what Lady Calville had said. She had assumed Bronson had taken the financial burden of his stepmother and Lark's journey. It was interesting that her father had taken care of it all.

"Actually, I believe it was William who made the preparations." Bronson indicated where William sat several places down.

Having heard his name, the steward ceased speaking to one of the servants and turned his attention to Bronson.

Lady Calville leaned forward to better see him. "Thank you for all your efforts in arranging our travel. It was a smooth and pleasant journey."

William's face went red. He nodded. "Y...y...y...you're very w... w...w...welcome, m...m...my l...l...l..." He grimaced. "My lady." Once he finally finished speaking, he lowered his head.

Ella tried not to let the puzzlement show on her face at William's odd behavior. His stammer was more pronounced than usual, and his shyness was almost painful to witness. Whatever had gotten into him?

"Are you eager to attend court after the wedding?" Lady Calville asked.

It took a moment for Ella to realize Lady Calville was addressing her. She pursed her brows. "I beg your pardon?"

Lady Calville darted a glance to Bronson, seeming suddenly uncertain of herself. "Are you eager to attend court after the wedding?" Lady Calville repeated. "Of course, you are always welcome to come to Berkley Manor. We would love the company."

The servants laid out two trenchers of steaming meat, venison as well as pheasant, in front of them. Nan had gone through considerable effort to make the new guests feel welcome.

"That is kind of you, Brigid." Bronson sliced off a bit of pheasant and deposited it on Ella's plate. "But we'll be returning to court as soon as the wedding has completed."

Ella stared at him, stunned by this news. Foolish though it might be, in the entire time of their courtship, never once had she considered where they would live. She'd only been focused on Bronson, on how he made her feel.

He then sliced off a bit of pheasant for himself and did not take any of the venison. Ella's stomach soured. Clearly, she did not know this man she would wed at all.

17

Supper lasted the better part of a lifetime. For truly, there was nothing worse than having to play at being joyful when one felt anything but within.

Court.

The word swelled in Ella's mind until it consumed her. She wanted to turn to Bronson and demand to know why they must go to court. Surely there must be somewhere else they might live.

"I hear there is a village nearby," Lady Calville said.

Ella's smile was beginning to strain her face and her cheeks trembled with the effort to maintain the pleasant demeanor. "Aye, there is."

"I should like to go at some point." Lady Calville took a bite of her food.

Her plate had been laden with food two times over and now only several pieces of roasted turnips remained. Strange that a woman as thin as she could eat with such vigor.

"William goes often," Bronson offered suddenly. He nodded at Ella as though wanting her to add more.

"Aye, he does," Ella continued. "He is well-liked there, as he offers aid to many of the families and always has marzipan for the children."

Lady Calville appeared taken aback by this information. "That is exceptionally kind of him."

"Aye, and we can go together on market day some time if you wish," Ella said.

Lady Calville nodded. "Aye, I would like that very much."

The servants came around to clear the plates. Lady Calville gave a regretful stare as her plate with the remaining bits of turnip was taken.

Ella leaned closer to Lady Calville. "They can leave it if you like."

Lady Calville waved her hand with a little laugh. "Nay, 'tis nothing left."

With supper having finished, Ella anticipated some indication from Bronson, either an offer to walk her to her chamber, or even a silent nudge to indicate he wanted her to visit him later.

Berry pastries were served with fluffs of cream, followed by the pouring of more wine, and still Bronson did not offer any sign of wishing to be alone with Ella. The bewilderment and frustration she'd felt earlier compounded into hurt.

At last, Lady Calville finally declared herself exhausted from the journey and was shown to her room. Once she had left, the remainder of the supper party began to make their departure.

Bronson caught Ella's hand as she was beginning to leave and ran a finger down her palm. Pleasant chills prickled over her skin.

"I'd like to come to your room tonight," he whispered. "I believe we have unfinished business, as you put it."

Her mind shoved into the forefront memories of the pleasure they so often shared. The irritation she'd felt earlier slowly waned as her breath hitched. Before she realized what she was doing, she was nodding in ready agreement to see him.

As she waited for him later that night, her body warred with her mind, craving physical release as much as it did answers.

When at last the latch to her door clicked open, she was met with a rush of bittersweet anticipation.

Bronson strode in wearing the same tunic and trews he had at supper, his intense gaze locked on her. A shiver of excitement ran through her.

"I see you left more clothing for me to remove." He closed the distance between them and gently nudged her back against the wall. His pelvis met hers with an eager flex, his arousal already evident through the layers of clothing. "I'd hoped you'd be naked on the bed, waiting for me with that little smile you give me."

He ran his finger over her breast, teasing the nipple hard through the silk.

Though simple, the caress made her go damp with arousal. "What smile?"

"The one you give me when you do wicked things." He tilted her face up and leaned close for a kiss, when Ella put a hand to his chest.

"Stop."

He froze and lifted a brow in question.

"You never informed me we were going to court," she said.

He leaned an arm against the wall, casual and intimate all at once. "I didn't think it warranted saying. Where else would we go?" His finger toyed free the bow of her sark from beneath her kirtle.

Ella leaned her head back to see him better in the low light. "To Berkley Manor."

He frowned, as if the idea had never occurred to him. "That is Brigid and Lark's home."

"It could be ours too," Ella said hopefully. "Or we could go to my dower lands." The last suggestion was more ridiculous than logical, but he did not laugh.

"My home has always been at court." He lowered his face once more and bit the ribbon to pull it free. "And it will be your home as well."

She put her hand to his chest and again, he stopped. "I don't enjoy court."

He was daft if he had not gathered as much through the many conversations they'd had on the topic. She had languished over the pomp of it all and how terribly uncomfortable the clothes were. How could he not know?

"You could go to Berkley Manor." He traced his finger down the side of her jaw and ran the tip over her lips.

Mayhap he was taking her idea into consideration after all. Ella relaxed somewhat.

"Although, I would want to visit with you often." Bronson tilted her face up to his. "I cannot imagine going long without this. Without you."

He bent to kiss her neck, but she pushed her hand to his chest a final time.

"You would be at court without me?" she asked.

"It's where I belong, Ella."

"I don't want to go to court." Tears burned in her eyes and she slid away from beneath his arm, turning her face so he would not see them.

"It's your place as my wife to go with me." Though he spoke gently, the words still struck deep within her. "But I will not force you." He came behind her and caressed the side of her neck. "Get on the bed. I want to taste you."

His words might have swayed her from this conversation moments before, but not now. Not when the hurt of realization echoed through her like something hollow and barren.

She shook her head, beyond any lustful temptations. "I need time to think."

There was a moment of hesitation before he spoke again. "Take all the time you need, my dove."

And with that, he was gone. But his tenderness lingered behind. He wanted to be with her. Because he loved her.

How often had he shown her the depth of his affection for her?

Enough for her to believe it. Enough for her to feel as though she was in love with him. Only now she was beginning to realize mayhap she did not know him at all. For if a man truly loved a woman, how could he allow himself to be separated from her?

And if she truly loved him, would she doubt this marriage so much?

※

The following day, Bronson did not see Ella when he broke his fast. Eager as Bronson was to hunt with the Earl of Werrick, he'd wanted the opportunity to speak to Ella before their departure.

He paused in the sunlit solar and cast a guilty glance at the neat row of books. He had stopped reading Ella's stories. Based on her reaction to him the prior evening, he had stopped being her hero as well. The thought left an unpleasant sting in his chest.

She did not wish to go to court, and yet he could not imagine his life without it. The merriment, the brilliance of life, the hope that the king might one day seek his counsel. Bronson was an earl. It was his duty to be at court, to be with his king.

He stood before the row of books and reached for a red one with no markings to be seen upon its creased leather spine. One Ella had written.

The sound of laughter trickled up from outside. A glance out the glass window showed Leila and Lark darting about on a stretch of grass with Hardy tearing ahead of them in a gray blur. A smile stretched over Bronson's lips.

"Bronson," Brigid's familiar voice pulled his attention from the window.

"Good morrow, Brigid. I trust you slept well."

"Aye." Her eyes swept around the sunny room and flicked up

toward the colorfully painted rafters. "How could I not amid such beauty?"

Her awe struck Bronson in a tender place. This was not how her life should have been. Brigid was a countess, a woman who should not be impressed by a leaded glass window and a bit of paint.

"My father should have taken you to court," Bronson said.

Brigid lowered her gaze from the brightly colored ceiling. "I don't know that I would have liked it."

"You would have had fine clothes, costly furnishings such as these, food to eat." Bronson glanced at the book in his hand. Mayhap Brigid and Lark might even have learned to read. "He didn't give you the option to go, did he?"

"Nay." Brigid strode toward the shelves of books and her fingers hovered over the neatly lined spines. As if reconsidering, she withdrew her hand.

"And you never asked him?" Bronson pressed. He drew a book from the row, one with gold leaf layered over the soft leather, and handed it to her.

Brigid opened her mouth, as if to protest, but she closed her fingers around the book. "I did not."

"Why did he leave you there at Berkley Manor, Brigid?" Bronson clenched his jaw in frustration. "We had wealth enough at court, and he always told me we should care for women, but then the way he treated you and Lark..." The whole mess of it was too baffling.

"I should like not to speak ill of the dead." Brigid opened the book and ran her finger along a painting of a woman peering through a castle window, the blues and reds vibrant against the parchment.

Bronson fisted his hand at his side. "I have plenty ill to say of the dead when it comes to my father, and the whole of it centers on you and Lark."

"It was my fault." Brigid kept her gaze fixed on the book,

wandering over letters she could not read. "I got with child immediately after we were wed. I was ill through most of it and when Lark came, it was too soon. Your father…" Brigid paused, as though collecting her thoughts. "He did not believe Lark to be his child."

"That's preposterous," Bronson growled. "One need only look at the child—"

"He did not." Brigid closed the book. "He would not."

"And so, he left you in the country with nothing." Bronson's stomach churned with disgust for the man he had once regarded so highly. The life they led had been a good one, filled with feasts and hunting and carousing. Aye, his father had had his share of mistresses, as did most men at court. While it never sat well with Bronson, he overlooked it. Everyone did.

It sickened him now to think of the fine lodgings those women had been kept in, the silks they wore, the gems glittering at their throats and fingers.

All while Brigid and Lark were nearly starving.

"We had Berkley Manor." Brigid placed the book back on the shelf. "The land provided. And we've had each other, and even wonderful Jane, who has stayed on for so many years."

"You will have far more going forward," Bronson vowed. "With this marriage, I will become a wealthy man. I intend to use that to see your life set to rights, starting with Berkley Manor."

It was the first time he'd said the words aloud, that he'd be wealthy once he wed Ella. That he was poor with nothing to his name now. The announcement rang hollow within him.

"Do not simply marry for fortune." Brigid turned to him, her face relaxing into a smile. "Though I think you do not. Lady Ella has a way of lighting up the room. And your face." Brigid reached out and took his hand with a gentle squeeze. "I hope you find happiness with your new bride."

The sting in Bronson's chest was back. He nodded slowly. "As do I." He glanced out the window to find the topic of their conversation slowly walking through the garden. Her hair was unbound and blowing in a gentle breeze. Moppet darted about behind her like a loyal dog, one with a foul disposition.

"My lord." Rafe appeared in the doorway and gave a polite bow. "Your horse is being brought around."

Bronson backed away from the window. "If you'll excuse me."

Brigid inclined her head respectfully. "By all means."

He exited the room but did not head toward the stables. Nay, he walked in the opposite direction, toward the gardens. "I will be but a moment," he said to Rafe. "There is something I must do before our departure."

Rafe bowed again with acknowledgment. "Aye, my lord. I'll inform the Earl of Werrick of your slight delay."

Bronson nodded his thanks and quickened his pace, away from the solar and Brigid and even hunting, and raced to where he knew Ella to be.

❧ 18 ☙

Ella braced her fingertips on a thick tree branch for balance and tiptoed closer to peer through a crisscrossing of twigs to where a nest lay, snug in a cradle of rough bark and leaves. Fuzzy gray bodies writhed and wriggled against one another; their protestations of hunger sharp in the spring air.

Ella held her breath, as though that might somehow keep them unaware of her presence and counted the small nest of birds. Three.

Her heart dipped low into her stomach.

Only yesterday, there had been five.

The realization made her feel even more miserable than she already did. Tears welled in her eyes.

Court.

And if she chose not to go, she would never see Bronson. What was even worse still, he appeared to be fine with such an arrangement.

She ground her teeth and returned her stare to the small nest.

Ella had been tracking the progress of the birds since she first found the eggs, noting how large the nest had become, what materials were gathered to put into it, when the first shells had begun to crack. If only counting had not been part of her inquisitive observation.

Initially there had been eight eggs, each as small as a thimble and brilliantly blue. After several days, an egg had gone missing. When the birds hatched, one had never opened. Shortly after their birth, she had found another one, cold and still below the shallow nest.

Ella sighed. Mayhap she ought to close the door on her curiosity regarding the functionality of nature. It was uncaring and cruel.

Or mayhap one day she would simply stop counting.

She glanced once more at the nest and found the new threads of color running through the uppermost portion of its walls. Bits of blue in various shades with flecks of gold showed against the natural dun.

A twig snapped and she jerked her head in that direction, her hand going for her dagger. Her gaze did not search far before landing on the handsome face of Bronson. He stood out like a beacon with his berry red cloak and bright blue doublet.

He nodded to her. "Good morrow."

She returned the gesture and the reply.

"You shouldn't be out here alone." He spoke with a jocular confidence that rankled her.

Ella turned away from him, putting her attention back to the birds. "I can handle myself."

"Aye, I've seen that. Which is what gives me cause to worry."

Suddenly the openness of the garden felt too small. She did not want to be out here with him, breathing in his warm, expensively spiced scent that reminded her of stolen moments of passion.

Her nipples tingled at the memory. Those days had been so simple, so perfect. So lacking in reality that she ought to have known better. She looked down upon him with a ready excuse on her tongue, eager to flee, but paused at his expression.

He stared at the bird's nest with a frown creasing his brow.

"What is it?" She glanced anxiously at the birds once more to confirm that they were still safe.

His confident grin faltered to something sheepish. "You'll think it's foolish."

If he'd meant to rouse her genuine interest, he had succeeded. She motioned for him to continue.

"There are only three." His voice was low with solemnity.

Her heart gave a little skip. Had he truly noticed? "And yesterday there were five," she said.

He started at this, as though he was surprised to learn of her awareness. "Aye."

"Mayhap we should stop counting."

"Is such a thing possible?" he asked.

Ella stared up at him, seeing a different side of him. "I think not."

"Come, let us go back to the castle." He offered her his arm.

She hesitated.

He lifted his elbow higher in offering. "I wish to speak with you before I go out hunting with your father. About attending court."

She slipped her arm into the crook of Bronson's elbow, which was warm and more comforting than she wanted to admit. He angled himself so his body blocked the cool wind for her.

Before they strode off, his other hand moved discreetly, drawing something from the pocket of his doublet. As they walked forward, his arm shifted backward. It took only a furtive glance for Ella to realize he carried an unspooled bit of blue thread. His fingers brushed against one another, depositing the lone bit of woven wool into the nest.

Bronson had been the cause of the nest's colorful hues. No doubt it was warm and without issue from the weather with such quality materials. She might not know Bronson fully, but there were parts of him that were certainly good. And that was what made this all the harder.

"I understand you do not wish to go to court." Bronson led her to the garden. "And I am required to attend."

She glanced up at him and found him watching her.

He stopped and stroked his thumb over her jaw. "I do not like the idea of being there without you."

Her heart fluttered. Her stupid, hopeful, foolish heart.

He gazed at her as though he were memorizing her face, the way she envisioned a man ought to stare down at a woman he cared for. "Ella, my dove, come with me to court and I promise you we will get away from time to time."

She exhaled her disappointment. "I am not meant for court, Bronson." She indicated the large garden. "I am meant for this, for being outside, for climbing trees, for reading the day away." She shook her head. "I cannot be the woman quietly standing at your side in uncomfortable clothing, and—"

"There you are." Ella's father waved and strode from the castle toward them.

Bronson stood further back from Ella, at a more respectful distance. Lord Werrick grinned at them. "I'm pleased to see the two of you getting on so well. Daughter, may I take your betrothed away before all the good game hides in the brush?"

Indeed, her father did look pleased. But then, it had been his intention from the first for her to fall in love. "Aye, but only if I don't have to hear of your victories later." She shuddered.

Her father chuckled and ruffled her hair.

Bronson, however, cast a long, lingering look at her that made her breath lock in her chest. "Think on what I said."

Ella nodded, agreeing only to think on it. For how could she ever truly agree to go to court? How could such a life ever be happy?

THE DAY WAS GOOD FOR HUNTING. THE SKY OVERHEAD WAS clear, the sun bright enough to warm them all despite a chilly wind. It was far different from the courtly hunts Bronson was used to: less people, less wine, less gossip.

He drew in a deep breath of crisp air and had to admit there was a certain appeal to the wildness of the land, the freedom of not being perpetually surrounded by people. In a sense, he could understand Ella's hesitation.

Bear trotted alongside Bronson's horse, his remaining hunting dog as Wolf was back at Werrick with a belly swollen with pups to be born in a sennight or so, and Hardy was at Leila and Lark's sides. While Bronson ought to be upset at having lost his fastest hunting dog, Hardy was far happier with the girls than he'd ever been chasing game about.

"Ella seems taken with you." Lord Werrick scanned the nearby forest for any signs of movement.

Bronson lowered his head in acknowledgment. "But she had not anticipated going to court."

The earl gave a hum of understanding. "There are many rules at court, and my Ella has never been one for rules. It's my fault, I'm afraid."

They urged their horses on through the forest, but all around them remained still.

"Ella did not take it well when Lady Werrick died, God rest her soul." The earl released his reins with one hand to cross himself. "It was not a kind death, as those from childbirth seldom are. After Leila was born, Ella seemed to…" the earl glanced up at the sky as though searching for the right word before shrugging. "She seemed to fall into herself. As if she intended to replace the world around her with the one that she made up in her head. But it seemed to make her less distraught to do so and I did not stop her."

A conversation with Ella rose in Bronson's mind, how she had mentioned her mother dying after delivering a babe. She'd never answered his question when he'd asked if the babe lived. He now understood that babe to be Leila. Suddenly the difference of the girl's appearance made more sense, as did her need for a companion who was not one of her sisters.

Movement rustled one of the bushes, but Lord Werrick did not bother looking in that direction. "I confess I was too consumed in my own grief to raise Ella as a girl ought to be raised. And now she is the lady you know today. One who balks at rules, does as she likes, and runs wild." A gleam of affection showed in his eyes. "There is not another girl like my Ella."

"Do you think I can convince her to join me at court?" Bronson watched the bushes and reached a hand out to Rafe to grab his bow and arrow.

"Aye, she'll go, but you'll need to make it her idea to do so." Werrick's gaze slid in the direction of Bronson's attention.

Bronson took the bow and arrow, nocked an arrow and drew the bow back. He gave a little hiss at Bear, who tore off into the foliage to make the inhabitant flee out into the open. A small brown bird darted into the air. Nothing worth bothering to shoot.

Bronson lowered his weapon. "Might you offer a suggestion on how to make her want to go?"

"My daughter has an impetuous heart. Tell her of the aspects of court you think she will enjoy and don't make her change who she is." The earl sat forward in his saddle and peered into a copse of nearby trees.

Bronson remained quiet, for Ella could not remain who she was at court. There were no trees to climb, no quiet, warm rooms to slip away into for reading. Her fair hair, which she loved to wear unbound, would need to be braided and coiled about her head, secured with gilded nets and gauzy veils.

"There's another thing about Ella you should bear in mind." Werrick motioned for his servant to hand him his own bow and arrow. "She's different from other lasses. You know that already, I presume."

Bronson nodded, his gaze fixed on the trees.

"Love her for who she is." Werrick clicked his tongue and one of his dogs ran forward.

A beast barreled from its hiding place, coarse black hair, yellowed tusks and snorting with rage. A boar.

Bronson's body fired with energy and together they raced forward. The hunt was on.

19

Market days were always crowded in the village. Vendors called out as Ella strode past with Brigid, William and the guard behind them. Ella had not liked market days as a child. After the attack, she found them overwhelming.

There had been too many people she did not know and did not trust, and far too much noise. So, while her sisters had gone to market for honey pastries and woven ribbons, she had stayed in the quiet solar, curled up in the window seat with a book.

Now that Marin and Anice were gone, the task of going to market day periodically had fallen upon Ella. Admittedly, she was not particularly good at it. Not like her elder sisters were.

"How are the market days in London?" Ella asked Brigid. "Surely they must be quite large."

"Aye." Brigid looked over a bin of parsnips with an assessing gaze. "London is so large that there are several market squares within the city."

Several market squares? Ella had not gone to shops while at court. At least not that she remembered.

"You wouldn't go." Brigid rested a hand on Ella's forearm with tender reassurance. "Servants attend market for you in a place such as London. You would need only to remain at court."

Ella's shoulders relaxed with gratitude. She was fortunate to have Brigid's counsel in matters such as court life. Mayhap knowing more would help her not dread it so much.

They moved on to a small booth with various colors of thread. When the ladies approached, the shopkeeper drew out a small box of fine silk that gleamed in the sunlight.

"Is there much work to organizing household affairs when one is at court?" Ella asked, hopeful for the response. She had never been one to enjoy running a castle as Marin and Anice had. Not having to manage a household would be a grand benefit.

Brigid flushed. "I'm afraid I did not attend court as a wife."

Ella blinked in surprise. "Forgive me, I thought you had been at court with the late earl."

"Nay." Brigid flashed a smile at her, one that was too quick and too bright.

Ella had evidently made her uncomfortable with such questioning. The idea of putting such a kind and gentle woman in a state of unease left Ella's own cheeks growing warm.

"I should like to see Berkley Manor," Ella said to change the topic. "I imagine it is quite lovely."

Brigid bit her lip. "Aye." Her reply was slow and filled with obvious hesitation.

The conversation was not going well. Was there something amiss at Berkley Manor? Did Brigid think she would be losing her home?

If Brigid did not wish her at Berkley Manor, then surely there was no place for Ella but at court.

"You are always welcome, of course." Brigid gave another unconvincing smile and selected a bit of blue thread. Before she could draw out her coin purse to pay, William placed a coin in the man's hand.

Brigid looked up, startled. "Thank you."

"'Tis my job as steward t...to see you ladies well cared for." He winked at her then. Winked!

Ella had always known William to be a happy man despite the sorrow he had suffered. But never had she seen this flirtatious side of him. There was something endearing about it, especially when Brigid lowered her eyes with the demure shyness of a maiden.

A little boy with dark hair stopped in front of them and gazed up at William. "Are ye Lord Werrick's steward?"

"Aye, lad. I am he." William crouched down to the boy's level and smiled.

The boy shook the hair from his eyes. "My da is Edmund. If ye have the time, might ye come to his shop?"

"Aye, I'll be by in a moment." William fished out a small coin and set it in the boy's hand to pay him for the message. The boy scampered off and William straightened. "You ladies enjoy the rest of the market while I see to the butcher."

"Nay, we can join you," Ella said. Her blunders at conversation with Brigid left her uncertain what to say. The distraction would be welcome. She turned left and began to walk. "After all, I have yet to meet him." Marin had always said it was important to know every supplier to Werrick Castle personally. Yet another thing Ella hadn't done.

William strode quickly to Ella's side. "Forgive me, my lady, b... but you must be thinking of the prior butcher." He turned and indicated a shop several doors down in the opposite direction. A wooden sign hung down from iron scrollwork with what appeared to be a pig etched on it.

Ella cringed at her own oversight. William was being polite as the shop was in the same place.

The former butcher, Old Betsy, had put up all her wares for sale to move to southern England to be near her daughter. Edmund the Strong had come from a village on the Scotland border when his house was burned down in a raid. He'd offered

Old Betsy a good sum and there he'd been for the last several months.

William led the way, holding the door open as they entered the shop to find a large man in a leather apron. His long, dark hair was thick and lined through with strands of silver. The breadth of his shoulders and the gray blue of his eyes gave him the appearance of a smith rather than a butcher.

"Good morrow, sir." The butcher lowered his head respectfully to each of them in turn. "My lady. My lady."

"Good morrow, Edmund." William grinned at the man in the congenial manner he always bore. "This is Lady Ella. She wished to meet you."

Edmund bowed. "Thank ye, my lady. Ye give me great honor with yer presence."

Ella nodded, unsure of what to say. Nan had groused about the man ever since Old Betsy left. But then, Nan wasn't one for change and Ella suspected her dislike of the man had more to do with that than his meat. "Well met, Edmund."

"Your lad said you wished to see me," William said.

"Aye." The large man glanced to Ella and Brigid. "I dinna mean to interrupt the ladies from their perusal of the market day goods."

"'Tis fine," Brigid offered. "We were preparing to leave soon."

"Then I dinna want to delay ye any further." He procured a wrapped parcel from the shelf. "Would ye mind delivering this to Nan for me?"

Ella reached for the parcel, but the man looked to William, clearly having meant to give it to him.

"I'm going to the kitchen when I get back." Ella kept her hand out. "I do not mind delivering it."

"Thank ye, my lady." Edmund placed the wrapped meat in Ella's palm with obvious hesitation. "Please tell her it's a gift for her."

"I will." And with that they made their way back to the keep.

Ella was silent as they rode back, her thoughts on court, her future, Bronson, everything but the pleasant conversation going on between William and Brigid. As kind as Brigid was, and as open and honest, it was clear she did not want Ella and Bronson to go to Berkley Manor. That thought was in the forefront of Ella's mind.

She had not even wed yet and already she felt as though she did not belong anywhere.

❦

THE HUNT HAD BEEN A GOOD ONE. THEY HAD SUCCESSFULLY taken down the boar and three stags, a meager amount by court standards, but a great accomplishment for two men with bow and arrows and a handful of hunting dogs.

There had been something natural and honest about how it had been done that appealed to Bronson. Far better to have nature everywhere rather than an army of horses, a mass of drunken courtiers and more dogs than there were beasts in the brush.

They entered the bailey to find Ella, Brigid and William having only just arrived from the village. Ella allowed Peter to assist her from the horse and smiled her thanks before looking up and seeing him. Her cheeks flushed in a way Bronson found immensely appealing. He missed the way he could make her cheeks go pink when they were alone together, fumbling in alcoves or loving the night away.

"What did you get in the village?" He indicated the parcel in her hand.

"Something for Nan from the butcher." She lifted the wrapped item and tilted her head coyly. "He means to sweeten her toward him."

He led her from the stables and into the castle. "Will it work?"

"You're welcome to join me to find out."

He held out his hand for the gift. "It would be my honor, my lady."

She passed it in his direction, letting him heft the slight weight of it. The clean scent of outdoors and sunshine wafted from Ella's hair and made Bronson's blood go hot with longing.

A quick glance confirmed they were alone. "I've missed spending time together."

Ella drew a soft intake of breath. Evidently, she had missed it too. He could practically hear her heartbeat quickening.

"When we are at court, we will be with one another every night." He brushed his hand against hers.

"You were right about Brigid," Ella said abruptly. "She does not want us to join her at Berkley Manor."

They made their way down the hall and shifted slightly to allow a servant to pass. The savory scents of the kitchen grew stronger as they got closer.

Bronson frowned. *He* didn't want Ella at Berkley Manor. At least, not until he was able to get it repaired and in good order. As it was, the place was nearly ready to collapse in on itself. "You asked her?"

"Nay, I implied I wished to visit with them there." Ella hesitated in front of the kitchen door. "I do not think she wishes me to go. She became very quiet. I believe I may have caused offense." Ella swallowed and looked at her feet.

"You did not offend." Bronson lifted her chin with his fingertips. "Berkley Manor is ancient. I am sure she expects you would prefer something more comfortable."

He ran his thumb over her sensual lower lip and Ella's gaze softened in a way he knew all too well.

"More comfortable?" The corner of her mouth lifted. "Like court?"

"Exactly." He leaned closer and nudged his chin against hers. "I will not force you to wed me, Ella. Tell me when you are ready and that is when we will wed."

She drew in a soft breath. "Truly?" she asked against his lips.

"I want you to be happy with this union," he murmured. "The king did not tell us when we must be wed, only that it had to be done."

Their lips brushed lightly, just enough to set his heart pounding. He wanted to cup the back of her head and capture her mouth in a searing kiss. But, nay.

It was better to let her desire burn. To make her want him enough to do anything—even attend court of her own volition. To make the choice to marry him.

He eased back. "Shall we deliver this parcel?"

Ella blinked in surprise. She gave a knowing smile. "Trying to tease me to win my favor?"

"Is it so evident?" He pushed the door open for her.

She went through while giving him a long, slow stare that sizzled through him. The lady knew exactly what she was doing.

Ella's demeanor immediately shifted from one of a sensual temptress to that of a good friend as she smiled at Nan. For as much as Ella had said she was not a court lady, Bronson anticipated she would do exceptionally well.

"And what are the two of you doing down here, aside from crowding my kitchen?" The twinkle in Nan's eye took the admonishment from her question.

"I've just come from the village." Ella indicated the package Bronson carried. "Edmund the Strong said to give this to you."

Nan gave an exasperated sigh. "The man is impossible." She wiped her hands on her apron and accepted the gift from Bronson. "I don't know why Old Betsy couldn't have stayed on."

Ella raised her brows at Bronson while Nan unwrapped her present.

"Mutton," Nan pronounced. "And not nearly enough to feed more than one person. Mayhap two if eaten sparingly."

Bronson nodded his approval. Mutton was the finest bit of

meat to be found in England and Scotland. The butcher was working hard for Nan's approval.

"I think he means for you to eat it, as it was a gift." Ella peered at the raw meat. "It was a very kind gesture."

Nan huffed and folded the parcel once more. "Mutton's too fine for the likes of me."

Ella folded her arms over her chest. "In that case, I order you to do it."

Nan put her fists on her hips. "Ach, you are a saucy lass." She waved at Ella and Bronson with both hands. "Go on with you. Out of my kitchen so I can finish your supper."

Ella laughed and scooted toward the door, grabbing Bronson's arm as she did so. "Enjoy the mutton, Nan. No one deserves it more than you."

"It didn't work," Bronson whispered to Ella once they were in the hall.

"Didn't it?" She smirked with a sly expression that made Bronson's blood heat.

He led Ella to the stairs as they both needed to return to their rooms to ready for supper. "Do *you* think it did?"

Ella went up the stairs slowly. "Of course. I've never seen Nan so upset about a gift before."

Bronson matched Ella's pace, enjoying the time alone with her before people surrounded them once more at supper. "And that will win her over?"

"Aye." Ella gave a secretive smile. "I believe our new butcher has captured Nan's attention."

Bronson nodded slowly. "And she doesn't want him to."

Ella paused at the top of the stairs. "I must ready for supper, but I shall see you down in the great hall soon."

Though no one was around, Bronson did not kiss her. He took her hand and gently turned her wrist before pressing his lips to the warmth of her palm. Her fingers curled over the kiss, holding it.

"I shall see you in a moment's time." With that, he bowed and departed. The book he'd taken from the solar sat heavy in his pouch still. He intended to read it, to discover more secrets to Ella's heart.

Movement outside caught his attention. He peered through the open window to where three figures ran about below with a slender gray dog at their side. Bronson couldn't help but smile as Leila took Lark's hand and pulled her along toward Cat.

Except then, Cat put a bow into Lark's hands. And an arrow. Then, little Lark shot at a target some distance away.

The smile lifting at Bronson's lips now tugged downward. Regret suddenly nipped at him. Lark was expected to become a lady, one who would fetch a fine husband at court. She was not meant to learn to wield bows and fight like a man when there was no true need for her to do it.

He would speak with her on the morrow and put a stop to such wild play.

20

Bronson stayed up through most of the night, not in Ella's bed, but reading her book. The story had been one of great love, in which the hero had been a knight who swept his lady off her horse to kiss her.

While he was not certain how easy it would be to sweep Ella from her horse, especially when Kipper appeared to be jealous, he was still skilled at courtly love. Chivalry was encouraged at court, and Bronson happened to be one of the best. Surely, the aspect of being wooed romantically in front of the whole court would appeal to Ella.

He made his way to the great hall to break his fast and found her already there. She looked up at him and then cast her attention demurely to her lap, the action flirtatious. It made him want to lift her chin and kiss her soft mouth.

Lark sat with Leila and Catriona, the three excitedly chattering together, with Hardy at their feet. The dog stared up at them in eager expectation, pausing to glance at one before shifting to the other.

Bronson took his seat beside Ella. He had not mentioned Lark's prior activities at supper the evening before. Well, save for a brief comment to Brigid, who had simply gazed affectionately at Lark and said she was pleased to see her daughter so happy. And while Bronson was pleased to see her happy as well, Lark was supposed to behave like a true lady.

She would be married off at some point, as all women were. Bronson wanted her to have a good future, with a man who could afford to give her a quality life where she would never wear ill-fitting clothes. Where she would never be forced to go hungry again. In order to do that, she would have to do what was expected of an earl's daughter.

Bronson broke open an oatcake and drizzled a bit of honey over it. "I trust you slept well, Lady Ella?"

She stirred at the pottage in front of her. "Aye." She turned her head in his direction.

Bronson bit into the oatcake and washed it down with a bit of ale. "I hear you and your sisters have been planning the wedding feast."

"I...we...are nearly done." Ella gave him a strained smile and pushed around her pottage.

"Did I ever tell you how many books there are at court?" He waved over a servant to refill his ale.

Ella turned slowly toward him. "Books?"

"Aye, many more than what you have in your solar here."

A servant eased a flagon between them and filled Bronson's goblet. Bronson waited until the boy departed. "And we shall have new gowns made for you."

The bright interest in her eyes dulled. Her father's words came back to Bronson. *Don't make her change who she is.*

"You can keep them simple if you like," Bronson suggested. "More comfortable. I cannot have my lovely wife unable to breathe."

Her face relaxed somewhat, and the tension eased from Bronson's chest. This was where he excelled. At knowing what people wanted and giving it to them.

"Fine silks that compliment your beautiful skin." The back of his hand gently brushed hers. A purposeful accident.

Color rose in her cheeks.

"The softest of wool for winter, edged with sable." He leaned toward her. "You'll be the loveliest woman at court, the most well-read of all the courtiers in attendance. And you'll be my wife."

Excitement danced in her eyes.

Bronson pulled her hand into his despite the witnesses present at the table. "When shall it be then, my dove? On the morrow? Two days hence?"

Ella cast him a coquettish glance and opened her mouth to speak. It was at that exact moment Lark reached for her drink and the sleeve of her gown rose on her arm to reveal skin that was black and blue with terrible bruising.

Bronson straightened. "Lark, your arm."

His sister slunk back in her chair and eased the sleeve back into place at her wrist.

"Push your sleeve up," he demanded.

Lark stared miserably at her lap. Even the blue ribbons threaded through her braids and tied at the ends seemed to droop. Dear God, was someone abusing her? Surely, it was not one of the Lord Werrick's daughters. And yet, that bruising.

Someone would die for this.

"Your sleeve, Lark," he said in as gentle a tone as he could muster.

"It was my fault." Cat sat forward and put a hand to Lark's shoulder.

Bronson turned to the young woman in horror. "What did you do to my sister?"

Cat lifted a shoulder. "I taught her a bit of archery."

"Cat." Ella said her name in a warning tone. "What happened?"

"My wrist guard was too big for her." Cat's voice quavered and her eyes filled with tears. "I don't use it as I never bruise anymore.

It's been so long since I have that I forgot..." She hunched her shoulders forward and looked down. Several tears fell from her eyes and into her lap. "Forgive me."

If nothing else, Cat's sorrow did serve to dampen Bronson's rage. "She should never have been shooting arrows in the first place," he said. "She is a lady, one who will attend court with us. There is no need for her to learn to use a weapon."

"It is always good for a woman to know how to defend herself," Ella countered. "Cat did not intend to hurt her."

"Lark will have a husband to care for her." Bronson tried to keep his patience intact. "And in order to attract a man of sufficient title and wealth, she will need to be appealing."

"And engaging in archery, or knowing how to defend oneself, is not appealing?" Ella tilted her chin.

A slight warning tapped in the back of Bronson's mind. "Nay, it is not," he answered regardless.

"The woman ought to be at the mercy of men to better attract one," Ella surmised. "By being vulnerable. How romantic."

The warning in Bronson's mind grew louder.

"You are not her protector." He indicated where Lark still sat with her head lowered.

Ella considered him. "Neither are you." Her brow lifted in such a way as to suggest her words were meant to be a barb.

And indeed, they were. Her words sank deep into his chest. Because all this time, he had not protected Lark. All this time, he had been carousing at court, oblivious to her suffering, and that of Brigid. He wanted to safeguard them both now and this was the best way he knew how, damn it.

He shifted his focus onto Lark and found her chair empty, as well as those of Cat and Leila. Even Hardy was nowhere to be found.

Ella got to her feet, her movements calm despite the brilliant color showing in her cheeks. "Excuse me."

Bronson rose from his chair. "Allow me to escort you where you—"

"That is not necessary." Her eyes flashed. "Because even if it is unladylike to do so, I can defend myself if need be."

With that, she spun away from him and quit the great hall. It was then Bronson realized she had never given him the answer regarding their marriage. And after what had transpired between them, he might not get his answer any time soon.

※

ELLA STARED DOWN AT THE OPEN BOOK IN FRONT OF HER. THE courtier in her new story was the worst kind of evil. One who sold women off into marriage at a whim.

She lay down her quill. Even though hours had passed, her heart still thundered in her chest every time she thought of Bronson's response to Lark learning to fight, of his intent to wed her to someone at court. Some nobleman, of course, one dripping with wealth.

Her stomach twisted at how any man could be so devoid of caring. And this was who sought her own hand in marriage? "It's disgusting, Moppet."

The squirrel twitched his head toward her and scrunched up one eye.

Ella huffed out a breath of anger, but it did little to quell the rage knocking about inside her. Still, he did not deserve to be the enemy in her book. A nip of guilt entered her conscience and she slapped the cover closed.

Restlessness prickled at her nerves. She got to her feet and paced the room. It was not enough. She had tried being alone, writing, even climbing a tree. Nothing would allay the anxiety racing through her veins.

What she needed was a ride through the countryside. The endless blue sky overhead, the swell of rolling hills beneath

Kipper's galloping hooves, and the wind blowing through her hair as though she were soaring. Aye, that was what she needed.

Decision made, Ella pushed the book beneath the window seat cushion and made for the stables to have Peter saddle her horse.

He was changing the straw in a stall when she entered.

"Peter, please ready Kipper."

He straightened from his task and peered behind her through the door. "I don't see your guard."

She indicated the dagger at her waist. "I don't need a guard."

Peter resumed his task, scooping the dirty hay from the empty stall. "Even if you had your axe, I'd have to deny you."

"Please, Peter." She went to him and stood before the stall he was working on. "I have to get away. I can't stay here another moment."

He paused from his work to regard her. "Lady Ella, you know I cannot do that. We've all been informed that no one should ride outside the castle walls without a guard." His brows furrowed with the sincere look he always gave, the one which had buried deep in her heart for so many years. "Not even you."

She dragged in a deep breath. "I cannot stay here. I have to get out, to ride, to think." She clenched her fists. "I just need to be free, Peter. Please."

Tenderness shone in his hazel green eyes. "I cannot."

Freedom slipped between her fingers and entrapment closed in around her. It echoed in her ears and radiated within her chest.

"I thought you were happy." There was a softness to his voice, as though he was afraid of speaking too loudly.

It plucked at the sorrow in Ella's heart and tears prickled in her eyes. "I'm not."

Somewhere in the stables, a horse neighed, and the heavy clop of its hooves sounded against the floor. Most likely Kipper.

"I *thought* I was happy." She hated that her voice quivered, but she couldn't stop it. "I thought I was in love. But he is just like every other nobleman out there, wanting a woman to be vulnerable, believing she needs him to take care of her."

Peter leaned against the handle of his pitchfork. "Part of your beauty has always been your independence. I'm certain Lord Calville feels that as well."

Ella blinked against her tears. "I doubt it."

"Mayhap it's because you don't see him look at you the way I do." Peter raised his brows and grinned at her.

His wonderful, charming grin that somehow did not affect her anymore. In a way, it bothered her to be so unaffected. Because it meant her interest had shifted from Peter and to Bronson, which meant she cared for Bronson enough for him to hurt her as deeply as he had.

"He wants to take me to court." The tears were coming now, too fast to stop. "I do not want to go." She looked away, ashamed of her tears.

"Lady Ella, please don't cry." Peter moved closer and opened his arms.

For her?

Even as she wondered if she ought to accept his comfort, her body decided it would, and she was stepping into his embrace. His arms folded around her, strong and firm, his scent so much like she had expected: hay and sweat and something masculine.

"You'll be fine, Lady Ella." His voice rumbled in his chest against her ear. "You'll be happy."

His warmth surrounded her, his strength, and suddenly she was sobbing against his shirt. Her arms curled around him, drawing him closer to her, not with lust as she had the first time she'd gone to him nearly three weeks prior, but with the need for comfort.

"I love him," she whispered.

"I know." Peter hugged her closer. "I had hoped this would happen. I only want the best for you, Lady Ella."

"It was why you rejected me." Ella lifted her head and

regarded Peter. "Is that why you wouldn't become my lover? Not because you didn't think I'm beautiful?"

Peter flushed, his embarrassment endearing. "I've always found you lovely. But I'm the Master of the Horse, and you're the earl's daughter. And even if we were not..." He shook his head. "I am not a man for marriage. My heart will never focus on only one woman. My ma was the same way and I saw what she did to my father." He shifted his eyes away. "I would never do that to a woman."

Ella stared up at him, this man who she had been fascinated by for so long, and yet who she never really knew. Apparently, this was a recurring problem in her life. Cat might trust too readily, but apparently Ella loved too quickly.

"I'm sorry," Ella said.

He gave a lazy little half-smile. "Don't be. I just wanted you to know why I couldn't be your lover."

A soft thump came from outside the stables and before Ella and Peter could pull away from one another, the door flew open.

21

Bronson shoved his way into the stables, hoping he had heard wrong. After all, it had been difficult to listen from his vantage point and he'd only just made out the words "your lover."

He stopped short, halted by the slap of the image before him with Ella held in Peter's arms, the same way Bronson had so often embraced her. She jerked away, but it was too late. Bronson had seen enough.

With a roar, he launched at Peter and slammed his fist into the servant's face. Pain shot up Bronson's arm at the force of his hit and Peter staggered back, his hands going to his cheek.

"Stop this." Ella put herself between the two men, even as Bronson was drawing back his arm once more.

"You do not wish me to beat your lover?" Bronson asked bitterly, his muscles flexed to strike again.

"He is *not* my lover." Ella stared at him as she spoke with conviction. Her nose was pink and her eyes red-rimmed. As though she had been crying.

Why would she be crying?

Bronson glared at the man behind Ella. Though Bronson's fist still ached, he longed to drive it into the Master of the Horse several more times. "I heard him say something about being 'your lover.'"

Ella sidestepped slightly to put herself in front of Bronson's gaze once more. "Then if you were listening to the entire conversation, I wager you heard why he had turned down my offer to seduce him."

Bronson narrowed his eyes. "Your offer to seduce him?"

"Aye." She crossed her arms over her chest. "When I first found out I would have to marry an Englishman I had never met. I decided to enjoy my own life before having to accept what was being forced upon me. I went to Peter to give myself to him, and he rejected me."

Bronson flexed and clenched his sore hand. "Then why were you in his arms now?"

"Because I wanted to go for a ride, and he wouldn't let me without a guard." Ella's eyes flashed. "Because I cannot stand the idea of remaining in this castle one more moment with all the anger and frustration building within these walls. It was more than I could bear. Peter was comforting me. Nothing more."

Bronson shifted his glance toward Peter once more.

The man nodded and dropped his hand from his cheek. "I have far too much respect for my lord's daughters to ever sully any of their reputations. And I enjoy my employment far too much to do anything to jeopardize it."

The Master of the Horse spoke without hesitation, his back straight and his expression earnest. Either the pair were exceptional liars, or they were indeed telling the truth. Then there was Ella's face, red and puffy, the way it happened when ladies cried. Bronson had seen her face in passion many times, and never once had it resulted in a reddened nose or eyes.

"What angers and frustrates you so within the castle?" Bronson asked Ella, more softly this time.

For the first time, she looked guiltily away. "You."

"Me?"

"You want to sell Lark off to someone at court, to make her appealing to the men who might take advantage of the vulnerability you force on her." She widened her stance on the dirt floor and met his gaze. "You have never taken her to court for an introduction, nor has Brigid been at court since becoming a countess. The women are nearly starved, and neither can read. Is this what you want in a woman? Is this to be my future? And what of our daughters?"

The vehemence of her words pummeled into him in sharp strikes. She had seen so much more than he had realized. Except she had assumed it had all been his fault.

"Ella—"

"You said I could marry you when I decided I was ready." She lifted her chin. "How can I be ready any time soon when you have so little care for the women in your life? And I did not throw myself into Peter's arms just now. I was truly upset, and he sought only to help allay my tears."

Bronson frowned. What the hell had he been thinking in allowing Ella to make the decision when to wed him? What had been meant as a romantic gesture might just have become his greatest obstacle.

"Then I apologize, Peter." He spoke slowly, carefully, knowing that every word would be weighed by this woman whose opinion of him would dictate his future, as well as that of Lark and Brigid.

The Master of the Horse shrugged with indifference. "It's not the first time it's happened. It's only been the first time I've been innocent."

"Lady Ella, will you join me in the solar?" Bronson dug deep into his courtier's charms and bowed low to her. "I believe there is much to discuss." He straightened and offered her his arm.

Ella accepted his proffered arm. "Aye, there is."

Then, without a backward glance at Peter, she allowed Bronson to take her from the stables. The tension in his shoulders began to ebb. He need only talk to Ella, to explain how his father had been. Even as he thought of such a discussion, he cringed with self-disgust. For how could he confess that he had enjoyed life as Lark and Brigid had suffered? How could he offer such an ugly truth, to pull away his mask and let her see how he had once been? After a lifetime of keeping his secrets guarded, it was hard to imagine them so bared.

"It is not as it appears," Bronson said under his breath. It was all he could bring himself to say until they were alone, but it would have to be enough. For now.

Rafe appeared in the castle entrance and raced in their direction.

"My lord." Rafe offered a sloppy bow in his haste. "You must come quickly."

Bronson opened his mouth to decline when Rafe spoke over him, "And Lady Ella as well." The servant's chest rose and fell with the frenzy of his breath. Clearly the lad had been running about in his search for them.

"Surely this can wait," Bronson began.

"Forgive me, my lord, but it cannot." Rafe clamped his hands in front of his waist as he often did when overly concerned with a bit of news he intended to share. "Lady Lark and Lady Leila have gone missing."

ELLA GOT THE RIDE SHE HAD BEEN WANTING, ONLY UNDER circumstances that left her bereft. She and Bronson rode alongside one another, alternating between calling for Lark and Leila.

Everyone at the castle had scattered through the surrounding land, seeking out the girls. No soldiers had seen them depart, and yet they were not within the castle. It had been impossible to discern what had happened to them. At least until Ella's father had thought to look at the box in Cat and Leila's room, which held the key to the secret exit at the rear of the castle. He'd found it empty.

Lark and Leila were somewhere outside of the castle. Alone. With only Hardy to protect them. Chills chased up Ella's spine.

When she had intended to ride earlier, the prospect of being alone outside the castle walls with marauders nearby had not seemed dangerous. But two young women on their own turned the idea into one of certain death.

"Lark," Ella cried into the wind. "Leila!" Her throat was raw, and her heart stung with each unanswered cry.

"Why would they leave the castle?" Bronson growled in his frustration.

"Do you truly have to ask?" Ella encouraged Kipper over a hill and toward a heavily wooded area that might provide the perfect shelter for two girls to hide within.

Bronson stared into the distance, his expression hard. "Mayhap I was too hard on her."

Ella said nothing as she peered through the dense foliage.

"Mayhap my expectations were too harsh," he continued.

Something moved in the depth of the brush. Ella's heart stopped. She put up a hand to silence Bronson.

He sighed. "Aye, I know you already knew as much, but—"

Ella put her finger to her lips to shush him. She slid from Kipper's back and pulled her battle axe free of its holster on the saddle. Bronson joined at her side with his sword drawn.

A twig snapped, followed by a distinctive rustling in the bushes. Ella jerked her head in the direction and Bronson nodded. Together they made their way to the sound, weapons drawn and ready.

Ella's heart thundered in her chest even as her feet were silent. Step by careful, quiet step they made their way to the bushes. A soft whimper sounded within.

A gray whip of a tail poked from the leaves and lashed back and forth.

"Hardy." Bronson dropped to the ground and shoved aside the branches. "He's been tied up here." His fingers worked at a loop of blue ribbon attached from the dog's collar to the strong base of the bush. "These are the ribbons Lark wore in her hair."

No sooner had the knot slipped free, Hardy bounded out of captivity in a single leap that nearly dropped Ella to the wet forest floor.

"Why would they have tied him up?" Bronson straightened to his feet.

Ella reached a hand down to stroke Hardy's fur to calm the poor, frantic dog. Her fingers caught something cold and hard. She shushed him quietly and reached for the collar once more. Carefully, she dislodged the item, on yet another blue ribbon.

A key.

And not just any key—the one to the secret entrance.

Her heart stopped. "I think I know exactly why they would do this." She held out the key. "They knew Hardy would die to protect them."

Bronson studied the key and uttered a low, uncourtier-like curse. "Hardy, do you know where the girls are?"

The gray dog whimpered and curled his skinny body forward, his tail flickering in a nervous wag. Bronson held the blue ribbon to the dog. "Go to Leila and Lark!"

Hardy sniffed it and then took off to the right. Ella and Bronson raced through the forest until Hardy stopped abruptly on the outskirts where he grumbled and snuffled at the ground. He took several steps in one direction, then the other and sniffed again. Another pitched whimper told Ella and Bronson all they needed to know: Hardy could not find their trail.

The girls were gone.

"We need to return to the castle to inform Papa," Ella said. "They may have been taken for ransom." Even as she spoke, Bronson was already making his way to the horses.

Hardy led the way back home, keeping so many paces ahead

of the horses Ella worried he might become lost and lose his way. But each time they crested a hill, a visible gray streak showed across the landscape. At last they arrived at the keep and left their horses with Peter. Any suspicion or animosity on Bronson's part toward the Master of the Horse had completely disappeared in light of his concern for his sister.

"There has been a missive." Peter took their horse's reins. "The earl awaits you in the great hall."

Ella's heart sank as her suspicions were proven correct, for a missive could only mean one thing: Ransom.

Bronson's hand found Ella's and together they hastened to the great hall. Papa looked up as soon as they entered and quickly approached. In the distance, Brigid wept softly into a square of linen with her servant, Jane, at her side.

"Have they asked for a ransom?" Ella asked her father.

He nodded, his face ashen. "It's the Armstrongs. They've requested an exorbitant sum."

Ella looked to Bronson, expecting him to lift his chin and claim it would be paid, no matter the cost. Except he did not speak up. In fact, his face had gone as gray as her father's.

"What is the demand?" She pressed. "We must pay it." She dug in her pocket for the key to the secret entrance and displayed it for her father. "We found this on Hardy's collar. He'd been tied to a bush by a blue ribbon, one Lark had been wearing earlier."

Her father took the key from Ella and slowly curled it into his fist. He closed his eyes as one did when they bore a great pain. "Then it is true. They knew they were being pursued."

Ella's heart squeezed. "They saved Hardy and kept us all safe."

"But at what cost?" Bronson asked quietly. "We cannot allow anything to happen to them."

William rushed into the room. His gaze found Brigid and his steps faltered for only a moment before continuing his path to Ella's father.

"My lord, we can give the funds requested, but it would take a good portion from the amount set aside to cover the grain for this winter." William held out a ledger. "I do not even know how we could transport so much coin safely."

Ella's father scrubbed a hand over his face. "And so, I must choose between my daughter, or my people?"

Shock and fear rocked through Ella. Her father was a wealthy man, more so than most nobles. If they were requesting a sum that would cut into the means for their winter store, surely the request was indeed staggering. And yet, how could they sacrifice Lark and Leila, girls who were only just beginning to become women, barely starting to live their lives?

How could this be happening?

Ella turned to Bronson. "Can you not do something?"

He swallowed and shook his head.

"You have great wealth," she whispered. "You speak of it often. Can you not spare some to aid our sisters? To keep them safe?" She clutched at his sleeves. "Bronson, please. They will be tortured. Killed. Or God knows what."

Her words choked off. For God knew exactly what. And so did Ella.

He lowered his head. "I cannot help, Ella."

"But—"

He stared down at his toes. "I do not have the means."

Ella blinked. "I...I don't understand." She took his face in her hands and turned him toward her. "What are you saying?"

"I have no fortune." He lifted his gaze to hers as if his eyes weighed more than stone. "I have nothing."

22

Ella nearly staggered beneath Bronson's confession.
I have no fortune.
She took his arm and pulled him away from where her father and William spoke in muttered whispers.

"I don't understand," she said again, her voice low to protect the discretion of their conversation. "You always speak of great wealth, of purchasing fine items and having enough coin to toss about freely."

"I did have coin," he agreed. "Or I thought I did. Until my father died, and I realized he had spent it all. Berkley Manor owes more taxes than I can possibly afford, and creditors have begun to hunt me down. I have no wealth. Only debt."

"Your garments," she argued. "The fine silk, the quality leather, the jewels…"

"All remaining from when my father controlled the purse strings without prudence." His jaw clenched. "There is nothing left."

Sudden understanding dawned on her. "Why did you agree to wed me?"

"Our king requested it of me." His answer was quick, simple. Too ready and obedient. A courtier's reply.

"The king is questioning my father's loyalty due to Marin and Anice both wedding Scotsmen," Ella said. "My marriage to you, an Englishman, is meant to prove my father's fealty to the English crown. What do you get from your union with me?"

Bronson's gaze slid from hers and lowered.

"What do you get from your union with me?" she asked again, her voice louder, sharper.

William and her father stopped speaking for only a moment to regard them before resuming their quiet conversation.

"The taxes I owe will be dismissed," Bronson said finally. "I'll be given a stipend for a year to aid me in getting the lands in order to generate income once more, and I also will get your considerable dowry."

"You came here because you were desperate for this marriage." Her mind was racing, and her heart was keeping pace.

"You required a little winning over." He winked in that charming way he did when he wanted something. No doubt what he wanted was for their discussion to be over, to refocus his efforts on what to do for Lark and Leila.

Ever the courtier. The man used charm to smooth over all aspects of his life that became rough.

A sudden thought slammed into her like a war hammer.

"I imagine you would do anything to get me to wed you." Something deep and painful constricted in her chest as she unveiled her fears. "Even read a lady's books to understand her heart. To know how you ought to behave to win her over. You didn't do that to be romantic— you did it to be who you thought I wanted long enough to win my favor."

Bronson did not deny her claim. He did not rail against the absurdity of it or declare his eternal love for her in protest. In fact, he said nothing at all.

And that silence said more than any protest he might ever try to offer.

She was correct in her brutal assessment. He had become the man she had wanted in an effort to win her over. For her wealth.

Her stomach roiled with acid. "Who are you, Bronson Berkley?"

The proud lift of his shoulders sagged. "I am a courtier, Ella. I am the man I am required to be when the need calls for it."

"And your offer for me to decide when to allow the marriage." She scoffed. "You thought you had already won me."

The skin around his eyes tightened. She knew not what to make of the expression but was beyond caring. "You do not know me anymore than I know you."

There was no time to deal with any of this. They needed to get the girls free.

Before he could offer some paltry excuse, or attempt some charming facade, she strode toward her father. "What can we do to save Leila and Lark?"

Papa did not appear surprised by her interruption. "We will send out several parties of soldiers to see if any Armstrongs might be found that we can use to counter their demands. Mayhap they might be on the English side. If we can locate them beforehand, we can use them to barter and save the girls. Otherwise, we will have to conceive a plan to manage our winter grain stores." His blue eyes went watery with a father's sorrow. "We cannot allow them to remain with the Armstrongs."

"I wish to join the search," Ella insisted.

"Nay," her father said. "'Tis too dangerous. I will not have two daughters placed in harm's way."

"I will keep her safe." Bronson appeared at her side. "We will go together."

The earl regarded Bronson and chewed the inside of his lip. "You may join the search party with my soldiers, Ella, but you are not to go on your own."

Ella nodded.

"I would l...like to g...go as well," William said.

Papa shook his head. "Nay, you'll need to see about gathering the funds. You are right, the amount is considerable and will require a good amount of effort to get in order."

William looked over his shoulder to where Brigid cried against her servant's shoulder. "Aye, my lord."

"Go to her," the earl said. "Let me speak with my daughter."

William did not hesitate and strode quickly to Brigid, opening his arms for her to fall into as she sobbed with a pain William no doubt understood far too well.

The earl regarded her once more. "You will wear your armor and you will not make any foolish decisions that will put you in harm's way."

Ella nodded. "Aye, Papa."

"Calville, I task you with her safety." Her father narrowed his eyes. "If anything should happen to her, I will put the blame at your feet."

"She will not be harmed," Bronson swore.

The earl's face relaxed and he nodded. "Very well, then I will allow you to help with the search. In the meantime, I will send missives to the other wardens for their assistance in discovering Lark and Leila's whereabouts. We will see them rescued."

There was steel in his voice, the kind that told Ella he would not stop until Leila and Lark were found.

After a final nod of her father's head, Ella and Bronson were dismissed to prepare for departure.

"I will not let you down," Bronson said to her.

"I do not need you to join me." She slid him a hard look, this man who had read her stories to become someone she would want. The gesture of reading her books had been romantic when she'd thought he'd wanted a glimpse inside her heart. It was entirely another thing when he used it as a guide to change who he was.

"Regardless, I am by your side." He touched his hand to his sword.

She did not reply. There were more important things to focus on now.

Instead, she marched on to her chamber to ready for the search and tried to block out the hurt radiating from her chest. For as much as she tried to ignore the stark pain, his betrayal had cut her deep.

※

Things could not be going any worse for Bronson. Lark, whom he had brought to Werrick Castle to protect, was at the mercy of reivers. He only hoped they could get her and Leila back quickly.

Then there was Ella, and the impending marriage he had ruined. Her cool demeanor told him enough even if he hadn't seen the tightening of her jaw, or the flush of her face. But he had seen them. Hell, he'd felt them, like daggers digging into raw wounds. And could he blame her? He had presented a fake part of himself to her. After he'd been so long at court, he scarcely knew who he was at his core anymore.

He waited for her to depart the hall before leaving for his own chamber. Rafe immediately joined him.

"Will you be going with the guards to try to find Lady Lark, my lord?" Rafe asked.

Bronson nodded.

Rafe pushed open the door to Bronson's apartments and held it open for him. "I will pack the belongings you may need and get a bag of food for you from the kitchen."

Bronson entered the room and the door clicked closed behind him. "Rafe."

The servant paused in his frantic race across the room. "Aye, my lord?"

"What would you say are my..." Bronson paused, feeling suddenly like the court fool. "What would you say are some of my best qualities?"

The question was vain and insipid, but Rafe's face didn't reflect any judgment. Instead he pursed his lips in genuine consideration. "You're generous, my lord. You are the most charming of all the courtiers and always know what to say to the ladies."

The servant nodded with his own satisfaction at his answer and resumed the task of gathering the provisions for Bronson's journey to find Lark.

But Bronson was not as pleased by the answers. Charming and generous. Was that really all that made him up? His ability to please? To charm? To pay?

In none of Ella's stories had the men been courtiers who could shift to please everyone around them. Nay, they were men, sure in who they were, filled to the brim with conviction and purpose.

"Is that all?" Bronson asked.

Rafe paused once more and slowly lifted his head from the hauberk he was laying out.

"Do I have purpose in life?" Bronson pressed. "Am I perhaps poetic? Or...?"

Or what? God in heaven, why had he even bothered with this terrible conversation?

Rafe's fingers nervously plucked over the chainmail. "You are kind," the servant answered slowly. "You often consider other's feelings, and you care for Lady Calville and Lady Lark. I believe that to be your best quality."

Bronson ran a hand through his hair, and for once didn't bother to smooth it back down. Aye, he was trying to save Brigid and Lark and was doing a poor job of it. Lark was now missing because he'd brought her to the border.

"Is this about Lady Ella, my lord?" Rafe carried over the padded underclothes that went beneath the chainmail.

Bronson held still to be dressed. "Aye," he conceded.

"She is an intelligent woman." Rafe stepped onto a small stool and raised the gambeson over Bronson's head.

"I'm aware."

"Mayhap charming her will not be as effective."

The gambeson fell over Bronson's face, momentarily blinding him before it settled over his shoulders. "I'm aware," he repeated grimly.

"Then might I suggest the truth?" Rafe met his gaze. "Whatever it may be, however difficult it might be to dislodge. She's not from our world. She is her own person, without worry to the thoughts of others. I think she would like you to be the same."

Bronson gritted his teeth. "Aye."

Rafe worked at the ties on the gambeson, securing it. If the servant was right and Ella did crave the truth about Bronson, the time of their search would be perfect for telling her about his father. Pathetic though it might be, he even needed to explain how he had been convinced to wed her.

And he needed to be himself.

Except after a lifetime of being a courtier, such a prospect was not as easily achieved as one might assume.

Once he was fully dressed by Rafe, Bronson was finally prepared not only for the search party and battle, but for handling Ella as well. The armor was heavy and awkward, practically sparkling in its newness, as it had all only been worn for ceremony rather than its true purpose.

Bronson made his way in clanks and clinks down to the stables, his own clanging steps reverberating off the walls around him. Ella was there already, speaking in soothing tones to Kipper. Both the horse and the lady appeared comfortable in their armor. Her battle axe was slung on one side of the saddle with another weapon on the other. Good God, was that a mace?

He turned his attention to her, taking in the fitted chainmail shirt and plated tunic belted over it. Greaves covered her legs and she held a helm propped against one hip. Her normally loose, flowing hair had been braided back, out of her way.

She looked every bit of a soldier as any man he had ever seen.

As if sensing his assessment, she cocked her chin up at him. "I told you I'm not meant for court, my lord." With that, she lowered her helmet onto her head and swung easily onto her horse.

Except she was wrong. She was exactly meant for court. It was women like her—

people like her—who set tongues wagging, who provided salacious gossip to those salivating for more. She was the kind of woman who would fracture the doldrums of those many interminable days of feasts and troubadours.

The kind of wife most men would not want, except Bronson could not imagine being with anyone else.

He made his way to his own large destrier. The beast looked the part with crisp red and white livery, the gleaming plate strapped to his large, flat brow. Except getting onto the back of the large animal was not as smoothly done in the weighty armor, certainly not as easy as Ella had made it appear.

Lark and Leila, he reminded himself. He was doing this for them. To find them and bring them home safe.

With great determination and difficulty, but hopefully less floundering than it felt like, he managed to get himself onto the horse with the aid of a stool. No sooner had he climbed successfully atop his steed than the search officially began. He edged his horse closer to Ella, hopeful of getting her far enough away from the others to finally have a true talk to explain his father, and Lark and Brigid. The thought of Lark pinched at his chest.

He bided his time, focusing on scouring the surrounding area for any reivers they could find. It was a wild hope that an Armstrong might linger about, but it was the best outcome, if such a thing were possible.

He caught sight of Ella alone, edging toward the outskirts of the search party, and pointed his horse in her direction. Where did she plan to go?

Wherever it was, it wouldn't be without him.

23

Ella bristled at being with the group of soldiers. There was no stealth to a band of men, especially when the lot of them wore chainmail and plate. No doubt the Armstrongs would hear them coming and have ample time to flee.

Not that any of it mattered. The Armstrongs would be fools to stay on the English side of the border, and if the band of English guards went traipsing into Scotland, it would likely start a war.

Nay, they were relegated to English soil. And her father knew that.

One lone woman, however, could easily pass over the Scottish border. The Armstrongs resided in the debatable lands. The area was dangerous, but she knew well how to take care of herself.

Overhead, the clouds had begun to darken, and the air took on wet chill that clung to her skin and sank into her bones. A storm would be upon them soon and would allow an ideal opportunity to slip away.

Ella edged further to the outskirts of the group. No one seemed to notice the gradual way she'd eased away from them.

No one except one particular man in a set of armor so new, it sparkled even against the overcast sky. Bronson rode toward her, his face solemn with determination. There would be no getting away from him.

Ella reigned in her patience as he approached.

"I need to speak with you," he said.

She would have no choice but to listen. If nothing else, to bide her time while she waited for those who had noticed him crossing through the group to lose interest in them.

A low growl of thunder came from overhead. He squinted up toward the sky before returning his attention to her. "It isn't as you think with Brigid and Lark."

Ella shifted in her saddle. "This is not a discussion we need to have now."

"I disagree." Bronson edged his mount closer to Kipper. "You need to know I am not the man you think I am."

Lightning forked through the darkening clouds.

"I don't know who you are." She remained back when the rest of the guards pushed onward. "Only the man you were pretending to be. But I do see how your stepmother has lived, as well as dear Lark." Her voice caught on Lark's name.

It was too painful to consider Lark and Leila in their situation. To imagine them frightened. Possibly hurt.

Nay, she could not think on it.

"I'm not my father." Bronson's jaw set beneath his new helm. "That much I can tell you. It was not me who did not see them cared for. I did not know that they lived without, while my father and I spent lavishly at court. Nor did I know all that was bought was on credit."

The men had not noticed her hanging back. Yet. They would, though. She need only hide in the nearby patch forest for a while.

A memory nipped at the back of her mind, when Bronson had said he did not want to be a husband like his father had been. She'd wondered about the statement at the time.

Even now curious questions rolled about in her mind. But

questions could come later. Once Leila and Lark were safe. When there would be time for such luxurious things as apologies and conversation.

A rumble of thunder sounded with such depth that the ground shuddered beneath them. The impending storm would be violent.

The group had begun to move onward in their haste to complete their search of the countryside. The search that would be fruitless while they remained on the English side of the border.

"We are falling behind." Bronson nodded for her to proceed ahead of him.

Ella fisted her hands at her reins to hide her immense irritation at his courtly ways. If he led the way, she could disappear into the nearby forest. But with her in front, he would easily see her if she left the party.

The wind snapped the cloaks of the soldiers before her and sent a billow of leaves rolling across the grass. Ella encouraged Kipper to walk slowly forward. Bronson did, likewise, following at her side.

There had to be some way to get him to leave her be. She bit her lip in contemplation. If she was too placating, he would know she was lying. If she was too curt, he might try to allay her concern and then she would never be free.

"I know you do not wish me to travel at your side," he confessed.

She slid him a slow glance. Could it be this easy? Could she simply ask him to leave?

"Then you needn't remain at my side." She said the words softly, so as to remove as much sting from their meaning as possible. After all, she did not wish to be cruel. She merely wanted to be free, now and for the rest of her life.

He gazed at the group of Werrick's soldiers who continued to get farther ahead. "You do realize if you turn me down, there will be another suitor. The king will want you wed to an Englishman, regardless."

Ella gritted her teeth. He was right, of course. Except she had already given her maidenhead to Bronson, as well as her word to her father.

A lock of stubborn hair slipped from the plait down her back. Before she could brush it aside, Bronson reached out and tucked the strand of wild blonde hair over her shoulder.

It was a romantic gesture, delicate in its quiet intimacy. Exactly the kind of thing she would have written into one of her stories. Exactly the kind of thing he would have read and assumed she wanted in a man.

He shifted his hand closer to her face and let his gauntlets caress her cheek. "Not all men will care if they make you happy, Ella." His eyes were a darker shade, the same as when he was aroused.

Her body reacted in spite of her anger and warmth hummed through her.

"And you would?" she asked. "Care to make me happy?"

"Aye." He slid his hand away and took his reins once more. "I want nothing more than to make you happy."

He said it so earnestly, Ella wished to believe him. Just as she wished to believe everything that he'd told her in the time they'd known one another.

Lies. They were all lies. A courtier with honey dripping from his lips and into her ears. Into her heart.

Tears burned in her eyes. She hated the freshness of her wounded heart and how fiercely such cuts still stung.

His brows lowered in his helm and furrowed over his handsome green gaze. "Ella."

"Please, leave me be." It was the excuse she had been looking for to make him go. Only she had not anticipated having to sacrifice so much of herself to get it.

Bronson hesitated, as though he meant to try to discourage

her request. Instead, he politely inclined his head. "As my lady wishes."

And then he was gone. As simply as that. He trotted toward her father's soldiers to join in the search and leave her blessedly alone.

Thunder cracked once more overhead, so loud and sudden it caused many of the men to leap in surprise.

Now. The time was now.

While the men rushed onward to get out of the storm, Ella steered Kipper toward the nearby forest they had searched earlier. There had not been any reivers within, but there had been a cave sufficient for hiding.

With a final glance behind her, she slipped between the tightly spaced trees and was gone.

BRONSON HAD NOT BEEN STARTLED BY THE CRACK OF THUNDER overhead. After the constant rain and storms of his journey to Werrick Castle, no amount of weather could frighten him.

He turned behind him to ensure Ella was well. After all, he had promised her father he would keep her safe. He'd promised himself as much too.

However, Ella was not directly behind him as he'd anticipated. She was slipping into the forest they had recently searched through. Had she seen something?

He almost called the rest of the guards to follow him, but then thought better of it. They were still farther ahead and if he rode to catch them first, he might lose Ella in the thickness of the woods.

He turned his steed and followed her into the forest. Rain pattered on the leaves around him in soft pops and slaps. He pushed his horse faster to ensure Ella did not slip from his view.

She turned suddenly in her saddle and stared at him from over her shoulder.

"Leave me," she said sharply.

"Not out here," he called back. "Not on your own."

She picked up speed and his horse matched the pace, keeping her in his line of sight. The rain fell harder now. It ran down his helm and into the neck of his armor, trickling icy water down his back.

Together they raced through the woods as the rain pelted down on them. The wet cold chilled Bronson's hands within his gauntlets and though he could not feel his grip on the reins any longer, he still held tight. Finally, Ella stopped in front of a cave and leapt from her horse.

"Leave me be." She jerked a bag from the back of her horse and left her horse beneath the lip of the cave to keep it from the rain.

Bronson pulled his steed to a stop. "You know I cannot do that." He tied his horse beside hers and followed her into the cave.

She'd tugged off her helm already and the hair that had come loose from her braid fell in wet waves around her face. "Why did you follow me?"

"Why did you leave?" He drew his helm off as well and tucked it under his arm. "To get away from me?"

She studied him and the hardness of her gaze softened somewhat. "To get away from them. We'll never find anything in a group. Not on this side of the border."

The roar of the rain increased and echoed off the stone around them.

"You mean to go into Scotland?" He spoke over the storm. "Are you mad?"

"I'm desperate." She lifted her chin up at him in that elegant, stubborn way she did. "To save our sisters. My father's soldiers can't go into Scotland, but a woman on her own can."

It was the perfect solution; one the earl could not have suggested. Not when he was a Border March Warden. But it was certainly something one could do on their own.

Or with someone else.

"A man and woman alone can as well," he said. "I'll join you."

"I'll do better without a courtier at my side, thank you." She turned her back to him and swept her braid aside. "Help me remove my armor."

The back of her neck was creamy white where it rose from her cowl. He had kissed her there so many times before, each one eliciting a breathless gasp of excitement. His groin tightened.

"You know I'd be helpful." He pulled the gloves off his hands and set them aside along with his helm. "The same as when we were attacked before." He reached up to stroke her warm skin at the back of her neck and stopped. "Pray tell, why am I removing your armor before we cross the border into Scotland?"

"When *I* cross the border into Scotland." She took a step backward to encourage him to remove her armor. "Because riding into the debatable lands looking like a knight is a fine way to get killed."

He unfastened her plate-lined gambeson and carefully removed it from her torso. She rolled her shoulders back, no doubt savoring the respite from the heavy armor.

"Your cowl as well?" He traced his thumb along the edge of the chainmail where it met her damp skin.

She gave a sharp intake of breath. "Aye."

He lifted the chainmail over her head. "I'm coming with you," he said when the metal had lifted from her face.

She gazed up at him with her wild, half-unbound hair. Rainwater had spiked the lashes around her large blue eyes. Beautiful. She was simply beautiful.

Without the frippery of powders and charcoal, without silk and gilding or scented oils. Natural and as she was: perfect.

Only he knew telling her as much would break the careful

moment growing between them and chill the heat growing in her eyes. For he knew that heat well.

"Will you help me with my armor?" he asked.

Her mouth curled in a slow, sensual smile that shot an arrow of lust straight into his cock. "If I do, it doesn't mean you're coming with me." She peered around him, lifted his arm and loosened the gambeson. "You wear it as though it is new."

He refrained from grunting with satisfaction as the weight was lifted off him. "It *is* new."

She cocked an eyebrow. "You aren't going to feign that it's been worn to countless victories for my benefit and regale me with stories of your military prowess?"

He held her stare. "You're not that kind of lady."

"Nay." She folded her arms over her chest. "I'm not." She perused the small cave. Light shone in from outside despite the rain, the cast gray and muted, but still sufficient to see. Sufficient even to make out the color blooming in her cheeks, her mouth.

"What kind of a lady am I?" She stepped toward him and his heartbeat tripled.

"A lady who knows what she wants. Who she is." He couldn't take his eyes from her. The chainmail rested over the length of her torso, rising over the swell of her breasts.

She stopped directly in front of his chest and slowly looked up. Her mouth was scarcely a whisper from his own, her breath sweet and warm. Her fresh scent of sunshine and flowers curled around him and held him captive.

"What do I want?" she whispered.

He had lost Ella's heart, he knew that. But it did not mean he couldn't try to still win her over with the mutual pleasures they had shared.

"Me." He ran his hands down her arms and intentionally skimmed the sides of her breasts. "This."

She gasped against his mouth.

"I've missed you, Ella." He brought one hand up to her face.

The rain and cold had chilled her skin and left it damp to the touch. He ran his thumb over her jaw. "I've missed your mouth on mine, your hands on me. I've missed those sounds of pleasure you make when I—"

She threaded her hand up the back of his neck, pushed up on her toes, and pressed her red lips to his mouth. Her kiss was hungry, desperate, and he returned it with equal vigor.

24

Everything that was wrong in the last few days suddenly went right as Ella's mouth connected with Bronson's. The spicy, heady taste of him, the way he cupped her bottom firmly in his grasp and flexed the hardness between his legs to the sensitive softness between hers. The metal plating of their leg guards clacked together.

He held her to him and gently walked her backward until she was pressed between him and the stone wall, its cold barely registering through the frenzy of her desire. His hand moved over her chainmail shirt to her breast to tease at her with a skill she hadn't spent nearly enough time appreciating.

"Take it off," she panted between kisses.

He obliged, first pulling hers away, then removing his own. She bent over and worked furiously at the straps of her leg guards. Her cold fingers fumbled with the water-swollen leather straps. It was all she could do to keep from pulling out her dagger and slicing through them. Her body was burning with longing for Bronson's touch, for the fire of his loving.

Lust pounded an impossible beat between her legs. She wanted him. More than when they'd first begun to play, more than that first night she'd gone to him. She hadn't known the extent of his affections then. Not like now when she'd spent nights alone dreaming of his strong body moving with hers, his tongue teasing and tasting, his fingers—

The straps at her greaves finally gave way and the right one fell. She gave a little grunt at her victory. So close. Only one more.

Bronson had already freed his leg guards. It was enough. She needed only one leg to wrap around his waist, to pull him deep inside of her.

With a moan, she straightened upright, into his arms. Their mouths slanted over one another's, their frenzy shared. He fumbled with the belt of his hose as she did the same with hers, so that they sagged down her thighs. He shoved the hose lower on her freed leg and lifted it to his waist, opening her to him.

His hand moved, positioning himself. Ella threw her head back, unable to take the waiting anymore.

He slid inside of her with a solid thrust that left her crying out with the most incredible pleasure. She clung to him as he pumped into her, their bodies flexing and rolling in the same desperate rhythm they'd always matched so well together.

He clung to her bottom, his face buried in her hair as he nipped and kissed her neck and drove into her again and again and oh-so-blissfully again. The bud of her sex had swollen to almost impossible sensitivity and each thrust sent promising heat radiating through her. She was close. So close. She buried her face in his chest as her body began to tighten.

"Nay," he groaned. "Look at me."

Overwhelmed by her senses, she obeyed, her eyes finding the intensity of his dark green gaze as his hips jerked into her. He clenched his teeth and gave a savage growl as her crises gripped her. She spasmed around him as waves and waves of pleasure dragged her under until she was breathless from crying out.

All at once the energy of their coupling dropped away, like a candle flame snuffed out. Bronson put his sweaty forehead to hers.

"Ella." There was a deepness to his voice, a sensuality that came only after they'd been intimate. It touched her in the most fragile, painful place of her heart. The exact spot that had once been certain she'd loved him.

She gasped for breath and leaned her head back against the hard stone behind her. She needed distance from Bronson now that their lust had been sated. He'd brought incredible release to her body, aye, but he was still the same courtier; the same fraud of a man he had been before their joining.

Her supporting leg shook with the effort of holding her upright as she uncurled her other from his waist. He held tight, as though hesitant to let her go, of sliding free from her.

Ella released a shuddering breath as she lowered her unarmored leg and the intimacy between them fell away. The heat they'd generated between one another still blazed against her skin and ran like wildfire in her veins. She had expected, nay, hoped, their passion would chill as soon as they separated. She did not want his lingering affection, lest it tear deeper into her heart.

Bronson leaned over her. "Did I hurt you?" He dragged a hand through his hair. "Was I too rough?"

Ella shook her head, unable to trust herself to speak. How could she when the ache of her loss was so great? She had loved him. *Loved* him. And he had been nothing but lies.

"Did I hurt you?" he asked again. He lifted her face with his fingertips and frowned. "I didn't mean to be so vigorous."

She shook her head with more conviction. "You didn't hurt me." At least not in the way he thought. "I wanted it as badly as you. As intensely as you. I felt only pleasure." It was true. Her body still hummed with delight at the force of their loving.

She glanced out toward the mouth of the cave where the rain appeared to have relaxed into a drizzle. "The guards will be gone by now and the rain has relented." She pulled up her hose, fastened the belt into place once more and popped the greaves off her other leg. It was a far easier task when her hands were not shaking in anticipation.

"Let us wear only our gambesons and pack the rest on our horses." She shoved her helm and chain shirt into her bag. "The reivers will not be in full dress and we should not be either. We need to appear like everyone else."

Quickly, Bronson assisted her with fastening her plated gambeson and she aided him into his. Once done, they strode from the cave to where the horses had been tied out of the rain. Ella ignored Bronson's pointed gaze on her, grateful he refrained from speaking whatever it was he clearly wanted to voice. At least for now. She was certain once they were on the road, he would continue to try.

She wished he wouldn't. For how would she ever know if he told her the truth, or simply offered another appealing lie?

She swung up into her saddle and waited for him to follow, then she urged Kipper from the woods. She didn't know when she'd made up her mind about bringing Bronson to Scotland, but he did not ask, and she did not offer an explanation. After all, she knew how much he cared for Lark, as she did for Leila.

Silently, they headed not in the direction of Werrick Castle and its safety, but to Scotland and the debatable lands filled with danger. To rescue their sisters together.

SCOTLAND WAS NOT AS TREACHEROUS AS BRONSON HAD assumed. After all the stories he'd heard, after all the wariness of the inhabitants of Werrick Castle, the lands didn't appear much different than those they had left behind on the English side.

At least until the first set of riders approached on stubby-legged ponies, wearing grimy gambesons that had seen battle. The men eyed Bronson and Ella with suspicion. In the end, they said nothing and went on their way without pause.

Ella ignored them and Bronson did the same, although he remained tense, ready to draw his blade at a moment's notice. The need never arose, thanks be to God, and the men passed by without issue, but it was enough to set Bronson on edge.

"We'll need to visit a tavern," Ella said. "I have not been to the debatable lands but I know how to get the information we need."

Bronson looked behind him to where the men had nearly disappeared in the distance. "I doubt the men here will talk."

"That's why I'm going to speak with a woman." Ella indicated a cluster of houses and steered her horse in that direction.

The only tavern in the small village, if it could even be called a village, had no name and was denoted simply by a beaten-up wooden sign with a mug of ale painted on it. There was a boy at the entrance who took several coins to see to the safety of their horses out front. Still, Ella and Bronson took their packs into the tavern with them, and Ella hesitated to leave Kipper.

Inside, the air was thick with greasy smoke that clogged in Bronson's lungs and left him swallowing down a hearty cough. Multiple candles were scattered about, emitting as much black smoke as they did light. Regardless, the room was dark, almost blindingly so, when coming in from outside.

Ella led them both to an open table near the hearth. As Bronson's vision adjusted to the darkened room, he couldn't help but notice how nearly every man stopped to stare at Ella. The gambeson hugged her fine figure and the hose extending beneath showed off her long, slender legs. The binding on her braid had slipped free at some point and her wavy blonde hair fell around her shoulders, wild and beautiful.

Bronson gritted his teeth.

Ella sat at the table, oblivious of the attention she drew. The man at the table beside her grinned, revealing a missing bottom tooth, and the reiver beside him nudged one of their companions with appreciation. Bronson hurried to take his seat opposite her.

A woman appeared before them; her clean dark hair bound back from her face. Her dress was brown and flecked with spatters of ale and grease. "What can I get for ye?"

"Ye, to warm my bed," the man missing his bottom tooth said. The table laughed and clapped their mugs on the table in appreciation.

"We've got some sheep 'round the back." The woman put her hand to her hip and turned her attention to Bronson. "What about ye?"

Ella chuckled at the woman's retort. The barmaid tossed a grin in her direction. "If those men bother ye, let me know. I'll see to them."

"I can take care of them if need be, but thank you," Ella said.

"Aye, looks that way." The woman nodded in appreciation at Ella's gambeson. "In that case, I might be calling on ye if I need help."

"My battle axe is yours." Ella smiled. "Two ales until then."

"Aye, of course." The woman nodded and slipped away.

"Everyone is staring at you," Bronson said under his breath.

"I'm not the only one." She lifted her brows at his new gambeson. It was a deep blue wool, the edges crisp where everyone else's were soft and fading. "You call quite a bit of attention yourself."

He glanced discreetly around the room and noticed the number of eyes that had settled on him. She was right. He *was* attracting a good bit of attention. Initially he had been loath to remove his armor and be left vulnerable. Now, he was grateful for her suggestion.

The barmaid appeared and set two ales in front of them. Ella gave her several coins and shook her head when the woman tried to pass some back. "For your troubles." Ella indicated the men behind her.

The woman laughed and slid the coins into a small pouch at her side. "Thank ye, m'lady. That's kind of ye."

Bronson lifted the ale, not realizing he was thirsty until that very moment. He drew a deep sip and nearly choked as the grainy liquid hit his tongue. He swallowed hard, gulping down what he wished he could spit out. A residual sourness lingered on his tongue, thick and unpleasant.

Ella drank hers without expression.

"I can appreciate a lass who likes a good battle," said a man at the table behind them.

Bronson glared toward the table.

Ella shook her head slightly. "Don't listen to it."

"I bet she can put up a fight between the sheets, eh?" Another man added.

Bronson clenched his fists under the table. "They are insulting you."

Ella glanced across the room at the barmaid. "Calm yourself. I need to speak with her a moment, and it won't do us any good if you start a fight."

Bronson frowned and glared at the men. If he were in court, he would have addressed them posthaste about their lack of consideration for a lady. If they still persisted, then he would have challenged them to a duel.

Ella got up from her seat with a warning glance in his direction. She walked across the room, much to the appreciation of almost every eye within the tavern.

The man at the table licked his lips with lewd appreciation. "I'd like to peel those hose off her legs and taste what she's got in that honeypot of hers."

"I bet the hairs there are as golden as those on her head," said another man.

It was too much. Ella had asked him not to fight, but the level of disrespect for a woman had gone too far. It was more than he could bear.

"Such thoughts ought to be kept to oneself," Bronson said in a low, dangerous tone.

At court, such a tone would have stopped most men. Here, every gaze at the table next to Bronson slowly turned toward him, shocked into silence. And then they laughed. At him.

"Is that yer woman?" The man with the missing bottom tooth asked. "Mayhap we ought to have a go at her once we knock this jackanape to the ground."

Bronson pushed up from the table. "Mind what you say."

"I see a lass in hose that need to be pulled down to bare that shapely arse." The Scotsman stood up and stalked closer. "A lass in need of a good fucking."

Before Bronson could even think about what he was doing, his fist shot out and connected with the whoreson's jaw, hopefully knocking out another tooth. His opponent's head snapped back, and the man slumped to the floor.

25

Ella knew a fight had broken out by first the shout and then the thud.

The barmaid looked to where the heavy crash sounded. "That man of yers is fighting."

Ella sighed. She had told him not to bother listening to the reivers. Apparently, he had not heeded her warning. She turned and found that the young woman wasn't entirely correct. Bronson wasn't fighting, but the Scotsmen certainly were. One lay on the ground unmoving, while two more held Bronson in place and another drew back his fist.

Before the women could rush across the room to put a stop to it, the man punched Bronson so hard in the face that he sagged back into the arms of the men holding him in place.

Ella jerked her battle axe free. "Cease this at once, or you'll feel my blade in your skull."

The men didn't so much as acknowledge her.

"And ye'll no' get another drop of ale from me." The barmaid crossed her arms over her chest.

That got their attention. The men grumbled and let Bronson go. He sat down hard on the bench and gingerly touched a hand to his cheek. The man on the floor groaned. Alive, at least.

The barmaid nodded to the rear of the room. "Take him in the back. Tell anyone who questions ye that Ceirs sent ye. I'll be there in a moment."

Ella gave her a grateful nod. Bronson, however, continued to sit. She grabbed his hand and hauled him to his feet. He opened his mouth to protest, but she cut him off. "Ceirs is willing to help us if you're done making an arse of yourself."

His strong jaw clenched. "You didn't hear the things they said about you."

Ella scoffed. He was protecting her. Again. Even though it was she who had gone to his aid with her battle axe at the ready, even though it was she who had enlisted assistance in locating the Armstrongs.

She stalked away toward the door Ceirs had indicated. If Bronson wanted to stay and be beaten for his heroism, Ella wouldn't stop him. Still, when she pushed through the door and he followed behind her, she found herself relieved.

She hadn't wanted him beaten, of course. Although God's teeth, how she craved to be free of him for a moment. His nearness seemed to cast a thinness to the air, which made it hard for her to breathe. It was the costly spices of his expensive scented oils; it was the way her heartbeat continued to trip over itself when he was around; it was how her legs nearly gave out every time she recalled what they had shared in the cave. It had been so fast, so explosively vibrant with passion and raw need.

The room was hot and humid with the savory scents of roasting meat and baking bread. A large man glowered up at them and lifted the cleaver he'd been using to hack at what appeared to be a pig. "Who are ye?"

Bronson squared his shoulders and shifted to stand in front of Ella. Ever the ready hero.

Ceirs pushed through the door. "Calm yerself, Hamish. I told them to come back here." She waved them deeper into the cramped kitchen. Once they were near the back wall, she stopped and held up a wet cloth. "For his face."

Bronson took the wadded linen with thanks and squinted his eye as he pressed it to his reddening cheek.

Ceirs studied them in contemplation. "The Armstrongs have yer sisters?"

An image flashed in Ella's mind, one of Leila and Lark huddled together, frightened, waiting to be set free. Ella closed her eyes against the pain of it. "The ransom request will deplete the coin needed to get our people through the winter."

Ceirs's mouth turned down in a frown. "The Armstrongs are a rough lot. Cruel too." She spoke softly, as though she hadn't wanted to say as much aloud. "They've attacked our village often. If ye go to rescue yer sisters, ye may no' come back alive."

Ella clenched her fists against the sliver of fear that nudged into her heart.

"It's worth the risk," Bronson said with finality, speaking the words Ella had planned to.

Ceirs's expression did not appear to be one of great confidence. "Ye'll find them past the Liddes River in the valley. There are pele towers all about, heavily fortified with reivers from what I'm told. If an alarm is raised, ye could be facing countless men." Ceirs fingered a small shell hanging from a string on her neck. "It will be verra dangerous." The graveness of her tone told Ella exactly what she feared the most for them.

Death.

But if they could save Lark and Leila first...

"Thank you for your help." Ella pulled several coins from her pocket and handed them to the woman. "If you could point us in the direction of the Liddes River."

The woman accepted the payment, then nudged through a door that opened to the rear of the tavern. The rain had begun again, falling in a steady drizzle from a gray sky. She pointed in the distance. "Ye need only go that direction for some time, ye'll find it. Ye should arrive before the sun goes down."

Ella nodded and tried to still the thudding of her pulse. She'd known it would be dangerous, but the woman's reaction had struck a new chord of terror within her. And yet, all she had to do was imagine sweet Leila and little Lark frightened and alone, hoping to be rescued or freed. Ella squared her shoulders, nodded her thanks to the woman and strode into the rain with Bronson to collect their horses.

"We ought to wait for the sun to go down so we can search for them," Bronson said when they were out of earshot.

It was a good plan. Especially in a place so dangerous. "They will have men on guard throughout the valley regardless of the time."

"Aye, but at least we'll be under the cover of darkness."

Ella hummed in agreement. Her mind spun with possibilities, ways they could try to outsmart the Armstrongs. The reivers had forces and the familiarity of the land, so Ella and Bronson would need to be cunning. But first, they would need to find somewhere to await the onset of night. Somewhere they could hide the horses, since they'd be stealthier on foot.

They definitely did not need Bronson's protective side making him careless.

"I do not want you making any reckless attempts to save me, Bronson." Ella stared pointedly at him, while he held the cloth to his cheek despite the steady rain. "Trying to look after me could get you killed, especially where we are going."

He said nothing.

"I don't need your protection." She paid the boy minding their horses and swung into her saddle. "I'll never be the helpless woman who requires saving that you find so attractive. And it would be pointless for you to get yourself killed in a needless attempt to save me."

Bronson mounted his horse. He didn't speak again until they

left the small, dismal village. "I didn't attack them because I thought you were defenseless or in need saving. I did it because they didn't respect you."

"They didn't respect me?" Ella regarded him in confusion. "They're reivers. They respect no one."

"But it was you. And you deserve respect." He removed the linen from his face finally, revealing the skin already darkening with a bruise. "They should step back as you pass, bow at your feet, be in awe of your beauty. Not hurl insults at you and leer at you like a beast in heat. I can't stand for it."

"So, you weren't trying to protect me, you were defending my honor?"

Bronson nodded. His expression was sheepish, boyish, and far more endearing than she wanted to allow herself to acknowledge. A consummate courtier. And yet, it was more appealing than she cared to admit. Charming, even.

"When we are in the debatable lands, refrain from caring so for my honor." She slid a glance in his direction. "It is not worth your life or the lives of Lark and Leila."

Because as much as she hated to admit it, she needed Bronson here. She could not save Leila and Lark on her own—if such a feat could be done at all.

※

BRONSON KNEW ELLA WAS RIGHT. TRYING TO SAVE HER WOULD put them all at risk. And yet, he could not tolerate the idea of her being injured. Or worse.

In truth, he didn't want her there. No woman should face such danger. And yet Lark did. As did Leila. His chest squeezed around the thought of them held captive by rough men.

He glanced up at the sky where the sun had begun to sink at an interminable pace into the blanket of heavy storm clouds. It would feel like a lifetime until night fell, until all was quiet enough for them to sneak into the valley.

They didn't converse as they made their way toward the debatable lands. Ella was no doubt as lost in her thoughts as he was. The only men they saw on their journey were from a distance, and none attempted to come closer.

The rain had finally ceased, and the colors of sunset were breaking through the barrier of dark clouds to turn the world to gold and red. Ella slowed her horse. "I think this might be it."

Bronson scanned the grass-covered hills swelling before them that no doubt led to the valley the barmaid had spoken of. His pulse spiked. Lark and Leila were somewhere nearby. "I think you are correct," he replied.

A stream bisected the grassland like a ragged wound. On the side opposite them was a stone structure, square in shape and lacking a door or shutters. He nodded in that direction. "That would be an ideal location to wait."

"Aye." Ella nudged her horse toward it. "Though we'll need to ensure it's uninhabited first."

They crossed the stream and Bronson slipped from his horse the same time Ella did. Their gazes met. He anticipated she would try to wave him away, but he would be damned if he let her take on the risk all by herself. If anything, she ought to wait with the horses while he went in.

Instead, they crept forward together and swept into the darkness within, weapons at the ready.

The room was empty and silent, save for the echoing huff of their breathing in the intense quiet. The roof overhead appeared to be in relatively good repair and kept out most of the rain that continued to fall steadily upon them. Quickly, they brought the horses inside to ensure their location remained discreet, and set about making the building as comfortable as possible without a fire.

They opted to leave their gambesons and gear on in the event they were attacked, though the sodden clothing against their skin left an uncomfortable chill. Ella sat in the driest corner of the structure, but Bronson found he could not sit. An image continued to rise in his mind of Lark and Leila, bound and scared, waiting to see if they would be rescued. His heart crumpled.

Seeing his sister at Berkley Manor in rags had been difficult enough, but at least there, she had been safe.

He had hated his father for having abandoned Brigid and Lark, and yet he had done something far worse by putting them in immediate danger. The desolation of the structure pressed in on him and crushed the wall he'd built up to avoid thinking of Lark. It helped him remain focused on the journey and had held his worries at bay. The wetness in the air sank a chill deep into the marrow of his bones. He shivered.

Were Lark and Leila cold? The invisible belt around his chest drew tight.

Had they been beaten? Would they be tortured? Were they scared?

That was a foolish question. Of course, they'd be scared.

He drew in a slow breath to ease the tension. There was nothing for them to do now but suffer the passing of time and the unknown.

"This waiting feels as though it will last an eternity," Ella said, as if she was reading his mind. "I've been able to push them from my mind while we were traveling. But now that we must endure the drag of time..."

"You can't stop thinking," he finished for her. "I can't either." He ran a hand through his hair. "I worry that they are hungry, terrified." He stopped himself before adding hurt, as he did not wish to shove his own nightmarish thoughts to her. Though in truth, she was probably thinking them as well.

"They're fine at the moment." Ella slid him a side glance. "Or so I believe."

He strode to where she sat in the rear corner and lowered

himself to the ground beside her. "How do you know?"

She looked down at her feet where the toes of her leather shoes were clumped with rich black soil. "I believe," she repeated, her words slow with unease.

"How?" he pressed.

When she still did not answer, he gently turned her face toward him. "Please, tell me."

"Leila." Her eyes finally met his. "She is an extraordinary girl. Not only because of her ability with herbs and with daggers, but she also has a gift. She can see things that will come to be and can sometimes even dream of the past."

Bronson utilized every drop of his courtier's experience to control his expression. He understood Ella's hesitation for speaking now. Leila was a witch.

"I can feel her," Ella whispered. "I've never been able to connect with her like this before. But now I can *feel* her on the air the way I can sense rain coming. It is difficult to explain."

Hope flickered in Bronson at this. "Mayhap it will help lead us to them." If they didn't have to comb over the whole valley, they might actually stand a chance of saving the girls and having them all come out alive.

"We can hope." The furrow of Ella's brow kept her from looking confident at the suggestion. She shivered.

Bronson put his arm around her and drew her closer. "We can keep one another warm."

She leaned away from his embrace. "I believe I had a character in one of my books who offered something similar."

"You should stop modeling men in your books after me." He grinned at her.

She did not return the gesture. He had hoped the intimacy in the cave as they waited for her father's soldiers to leave would have been enough to mend what had broken between them. But her coolness toward him indicated it had not. What they had shared had been lust. The same as what they had shared in the beginning when she thought herself in love with him.

Except through all of this, he *had* fallen in love with her. Truly in love. Not lust, or baseless desire, but love. In trying to unearth her heart to win it over, she had won *him* over. And he had lost her.

She was angry at him for having read her books, for having peered into her soul to use what he gleaned to manipulate her into loving him. He had been at fault. Egregiously so.

"I'm not one of the men in your books," he said. "If I were, I would pull a lightning sword from the depths of the earth, or befriend a dragon, or tear off my tunic and defeat them all with the virility of my powerful masculinity."

Her lips quirked at that.

He set his jaw. "I am only a man, Ella. One who learned early on at court that I had to be liked to survive. I have never had the luxury to be myself without fear my head might end up on a pike if I said the wrong thing to the wrong person. I become who I need to be." He indicated the battle axe she had on the ground on her opposite side. "The same as you."

Ella's lashes swept over her cheeks as she glanced down at her weapon.

"I confess, I do not want you to be here," Bronson continued. "There is danger at every turn, and it is torture for me knowing you could be killed. Or that I could be killed, and you would be entirely on your own, especially after I have taken your maidenhead. But I know you need to be here, just as I need to, to see our sisters saved."

Ella's gaze flicked up at him. "I wouldn't leave if you asked."

"That's the other reason I wouldn't bother trying." He smiled. "You'd just as soon go on your own rather than abandon this fight."

She pursed her lips in silent agreement.

"This is my fault." The admission tore from Bronson's soul. "I brought her here, I became angry with her for not being a proper lady. It's why she ran away. She is in this position because of me. As is Leila." He locked eyes with Ella. "I apologize for putting your sister in danger as well."

But the apology did not make him feel better any more than his confession did. Nothing would soothe his ragged soul until the girls were safe.

26

Ella could practically feel the guilt flowing from Bronson. His eyes shone with the wild hurt of it, his forehead furrowed with intensity.

But he was most likely right about Lark running off because of his outburst. And yet she didn't say as much. Not when he already knew, not when it was so heavy a burden to lay on someone's mind.

Leila's presence was all around Ella, the quiet reassurance she was safe at the moment. Ella embraced it, let it curl around her like a cloak. It eased the tension of the wait, as did Bronson's conversation.

"I only ever saw Brigid when I was a boy, soon after my father wed her," Bronson said, his voice still low to keep anyone who might pass by outside from hearing. "I did not see her again until his death. The reason for her hesitation when you mentioned going to Berkley Manor is due to its state of disrepair, as it is practically falling in on itself."

At that exact moment, a small patch of the ceiling fell and nearly landed on Kipper. The horse flicked its tail in irritation.

"Not this bad." Bronson tilted his head in consideration.

"But it requires a considerable amount of work. Although it wasn't the house that truly concerned me—it was Brigid and Lark. They were so thin. Starving. Their clothes were rags and Lark..." He drew in a pained breath. "She did not even have shoes."

Ella pressed her lips together. It explained so much now, why she could see the bones in their hands and arms, why Brigid clung to her purse so at the market.

"It is why I want a good match for Lark, a profitable one," he continued. "I can't stand the idea of her living in such conditions again."

Ella sighed at her foolishness. She had leapt to her own conclusions, expecting him to have the same reasoning as most men. And mayhap it was a safe assumption, but she had not asked for him to explain himself. Instead she had hurled insults at him and rejected him.

He had not even had a chance to defend himself. They'd been notified of Leila and Lark's disappearance soon after.

But he did not throw accusation at Ella, as she so deserved, his expression absent malice or judgment. "It was not my place to bring Brigid to court. My father questioned her loyalty to him and that is why she did not join us. I was never consulted on any of these matters and was allayed with excuses when I would ask after her. Because I did ask after her through the years. Her and Lark both. I had no idea they hadn't learned to read, that they were starving and without funds to live on."

He reached for her hand and this time she did not pull away. "It was why I worked so hard to get you to want to marry me. I needed the money, not for life at court for me, but for Brigid and for Lark. To repair their home and ensure they never went without again. Forgive me for the deception, Ella."

"It is I who should be seeking forgiveness." Guilt burned in Ella's stomach. "I have been so wrong about you."

The sky had darkened outside the open windows and she

could only make out the shadow of his profile set against the dusk.

"You weren't entirely wrong about me." Bronson lowered his head. "I was selfish too. I enjoyed court, my freedom, all the luxuries such a life affords a young man. Certainly not heroic at all. Nothing worthy of a troubadour's tale, or the ink of a lovely young woman writing a story."

But he was wrong. This was exactly the thing a hero would do in her story. He would not lay the blame of his failures at another's feet. He would admit to his wrongs and move heaven and earth to see his mistakes made right. Like trying to woo his betrothed into marriage, or even commit himself to a valley of demons to rescue two young women.

"Bronson." Her voice caught. He was not the shallow courtier who shed his skin each time there was something more to be gained. This man had depth, conviction.

He held his arm out in offering once more, almost imperceptible in the darkness now. This time, she scooted closer to him and his arm fell around her shoulders. Immediately, his body heat seeped into her chilled skin. She pressed closer, grateful to feel something other than the wet cold.

"I was so wrong about you," she whispered. "Will you ever—"

Leila's presence tugged at her mind like a nagging thought. The force of it was gentle yet unmistakable. She hadn't known Leila capable of doing such a thing.

Bronson drew back. "Is something amiss?"

Ella shook her head. "I think Leila is telling us we must go."

"It is only just growing dark. Are you certain?"

Before she could answer, the tug came once more, insistent. "Aye. We must go now."

The certainty of it gave Ella confidence. If Leila could reach her like this, perhaps she *could* direct them where to go once they were inside the valley.

Bronson got to his feet and helped Ella to hers. They required no additional preparation, as they had done it all when they had first arrived, remaining ready to go at a moment's notice. Both had agreed it was best to leave off their chainmail in the interest of stealth silence. Better to sneak about than to be well-armored and face an army.

"Now?" He asked.

"Aye."

Before he could turn away, she rose on her toes and pressed a kiss to his mouth. Quick and full of as much emotion as she could muster in only that scant fraction of a second. "God keep us all safe."

Then she rushed out of the structure ahead of him. There was no more time for additional conversation; no time to receive his return affection. Once more she shoved aside her fears to focus on the task at hand. Although this time, it was not only the fear for Leila and Lark, but also for Bronson and even herself.

They were going into dangerous territory, a place where they could easily be killed.

Bronson's footsteps swishing in the brush told her he had joined her. It was time to go rescue their sisters.

***

BRONSON'S MOUTH STILL TINGLED WHERE ELLA HAD KISSED him. He allowed his mind to linger on it briefly, relishing the tenderness, the significance of her taking the precious moment to do it. Mayhap he had not lost her, after all. There might be a chance to reclaim the heart of the woman who had claimed his own.

God keep them safe, indeed.

The rain had finally ceased. And while Bronson's garments were still damp from their earlier travels, it was a relief to not be weighed down by icy, sodden clothes anymore. But it was more than comfort that left him grateful for the clear skies. A nearly full moon shone brightly overhead, lighting the valley for them to pick through it with ease.

The closer they got, the more intensely his thoughts focused on Lark, on Leila, on being prepared for the rescue. Ella crouched behind a bit of brush and Bronson sank down beside her while they stared out at the valley before them. Only a couple men could be seen in the distance, but the area looked remarkably empty otherwise. The scent of rich food hung in the air and suddenly he understood why the timing was ideal. The men would be preoccupied with eating their supper.

Towers rose throughout the land, jutting up from the earth in powerful stone columns.

"Pele towers," Ella said quietly.

Bronson nodded. He'd heard of them before. A tall, narrow structure with at least two levels, the first of which held livestock and horses. The upper levels were where clan members slept and lived, accessed by a ladder pulled up to keep the people within safe.

Leila and Lark were no doubt in one now, held aloft and difficult to reach in such a fortress.

An impossible task that would have to be made possible.

Ella rose from her crouching position and waved for Bronson to follow as she slipped into the shadows. They moved quickly and silently, her steps confident with whatever connected her to Leila.

Ella sucked in a breath suddenly and pushed at his chest, flattening him against the wall of the tower they were beneath. She hid herself likewise beside him.

The timber of men's voices sounded nearby. The indecipherable Gaelic of Scotsman. Ella narrowed her gaze, her expression focused. It had never occurred to Bronson that she might speak the foreign tongue. Footsteps sounded and carried the Scotsman away from them.

Bronson relaxed and released his hand from the hilt of his

sword. He hadn't even realized he had reached for his weapon until then. Whatever instinct had made him do it, he was glad for it now.

Ella glanced side to side and then sprinted across the open area to the next pele tower. Bronson did the same.

Sounds of laughter came from within, mingled with the chatter of a multitude of conversations. This would most likely not be where the girls were kept. Ella glanced pointedly toward one particular tower not too far away. She nodded and his pulse leapt.

They were close.

Voices sounded nearby. Ella stiffened, but it was too late. The reivers were already rounding the corner. Quickly, Bronson pushed himself in front of her and pressed his mouth to hers with an exaggerated groan. She drew her leg up to curl around his hip, immediately catching on to what he was attempting.

A man laughed several paces behind them. Ella gasped as though in pleasure and rolled her body against his, a perfect mimic of their shared intimacy in the past. Except while it appeared that she was enjoying being taken against a wall, her hands were moving at her waist, drawing free her dagger.

One of the reivers said something Bronson couldn't understand, and Ella squeezed her leg more tightly around him. "They're coming over here," she muttered against his lips.

A hand clapped on Bronson's shoulder and tugged him away from her. Three men faced him, grinning with excitement as they stared at her. The bastards.

Ella threw a dagger into the neck of the reiver closest to him and drew up her axe. Blood poured from his wound in a great gush and he collapsed to the ground. Acting on instinct, Bronson pushed his blade into another man's throat as Ella brought her axe down on the remaining reiver's head. The three were dead before they could even cry out.

Bronson's heart raced with such force that it made his head feel too light, airy almost.

"We have to hide them." Ella glanced to a stack of barrels near a wall. "Shift those about. We'll put them behind there." She glanced around. "Hurry."

Bronson grabbed two of the men and dragged them with him. The barrels were light, nearly empty of whatever liquid was in them, and easily moved. The men were hidden quickly, and Ella resumed leading him through the maze of towers and toward the one that held Leila and Lark.

They crept over the lush grass, silent and under cover of the shadows. Finally they stopped at the tower Ella had indicated previously. The lightheadedness Bronson had experienced immediately cleared and all his focus directed on the weather-darkened stone rising above them to the glow of light at the second floor. An iron-banded door blocked their way from entering.

Ella held up her hand. Bronson froze, waiting. His pulse thundered in his temples. He wanted nothing more than to break through the damn door, to kill every man who dared to stop him, and to bring Lark and Leila to safety. Energy roared through his body and left every muscle tense and ready.

After another glance around, Ella crouched to the ground in front of the door with a long slender pick in her hand. She paused a moment and then twisted the device about. A metallic click pinged.

She waved as she pushed open the door and entered the tower. Bronson followed quickly, his feet sinking into thick black soil on the ground within. Light filtered down from the upper floor and shone on a room full of cows. The one nearest Bronson cast him a bored look as it worked at a bit of straw jutting from its mouth.

Ella grabbed his arm and pulled him with her behind a stack of hay just as a reiver came out from around a column. Bronson crouched deeper in an effort to stay hidden. But even as he kept out of sight, he gazed up at the second floor, straining to make out anything that might resemble a small face peering over at them. Nothing.

Anxiety wrestled his heart with a strangling grip. Were they in the right place? Had Ella been correct?

An item fluttered down over the edge of the upper story, a strip of something he couldn't quite make out. Not until it fell past his face and coiled onto the fouled ground where the cows had tread.

A blue ribbon.

Lark's ribbon.

The reiver shoved at a cow as he passed them. The animal lowed in protest, but still moved out of his way. With him facing the opposite direction, Bronson chanced the opportunity to stand slightly to get a better vantage on how to get to the second floor.

Several arm lengths from his left was a ladder leading up. There would be no way to climb it without the reiver alerting the others.

Which meant that he would have to die.

27

Ella held her breath as the reiver neared them once more. Sweat prickled at her brow, and the urgency pulling at her mind left her heart pattering at a frantic pace. They had to hurry. They were nearly out of time.

She pulled free the dagger, her body coiled in anticipation. Before she could launch her attack, Bronson leapt from their hiding spot and punched the blade of his sword through the man's throat, ending his life before he could make a sound.

Ella wasted no time. She gripped her dagger between her teeth for swift access and ran to the ladder. It was rickety, its rungs worn smooth by years of use. Halfway up, her foot slipped in her haste and she clattered several rungs down before catching herself.

"Hamish?" a voice asked from above.

Damn.

Footsteps thundered over the floorboards on the second floor as someone came to investigate. The slip had made Ella clench her teeth, which thankfully kept the dagger safely in place. She slipped it free with her hand now and waited for the reiver's face to appear so she could throw her blade at him.

And he did appear, but only for a blink before his face registered surprise and he pitched forward. He fell head-first and landed between two cows with a sickening crack.

Ella replaced the dagger between her teeth and climbed. One hand, one foot, one rung, until she was nearly at the top. A high pitch scream sounded, like that of a girl. Ella pulled the dagger from her mouth and scaled up the rest of the ladder to the main floor. A man stood several yards away with Leila held in his arms, his blade pointed at her throat.

He snarled at Ella. "If ye take one st—"

She didn't wait for him to finish. She sent the dagger sailing toward him. The blade sank into his eye and he staggered back, his hands going up toward his face even as his body fell in death.

Three more reivers remained that Ella could make out, all creeping toward her. Leila grasped the hilt of the dagger from the man's eye and yanked it free before setting herself protectively in front of Lark.

"Are you hurt?" Ella asked her sister as she marked the approach of the men closing in on her. A reiver with white blonde hair atop his ruddy head was nearest. More than that, he was the largest, the most intimidating, especially with the mace he hefted in his right hand.

He would need to die first.

"We're not harmed," Leila said firmly.

Ella cast a quick prayer of thanks for the girls being in good health and lunged toward the blonde-haired reiver. She did not try to aim for the center of his torso, not when he was so tall. That would be expected. Instead, she bent low and swung her axe into his knee even as his own mallet swept down at her.

The great weapon passed her head so close that the wind created by its power blew her hair off her face. The man howled in agony as the axe sank into his leg and collapsed to the floor. Ella lifted her axe to finish the fight when someone slammed into her, knocking her to the floor. She landed with such force that her teeth clacked. But she'd been hit thus before. In practice, where she'd learned how to react even as her body reeled.

She flipped over and kicked out as her attacker descended down upon her with his sword thrusting toward her neck. Her foot caught him square in the chest. He flew backward and a bloody sword exploded through his throat. His gave a choked cry of surprise, followed by a mortal gurgle.

The sword pulled free and he fell to the ground. From behind him, Bronson winked at her, and then spun about to engage their final opponent. Ella leapt to her feet and found the large reiver dragging himself across the room. Toward the window.

Not wanting to waste time running, she fell back on the ability she had spent a lifetime honing. She gripped her axe with both hands, hauled it back behind her head and sent it flying across the room. It slammed in the center of the man's back with a solid thud. The reiver jerked and collapsed into a growing pool of blood.

The clanging of swords rang out. Ella whipped her head around to find Bronson and the final Armstrong reiver locked in combat at the edge of the ladder opening. Both men swung their blades with equal power, their feet working back and forth as they parried.

Ella tugged her axe free from the fallen reiver's massive back. But before she could move to Bronson to assist with the final assailant, a hand clasped her ankle and yanked her supporting foot from beneath her. She fell with a thud onto the floor wet and warm with fresh blood.

The blonde-haired reiver dragged her closer, smearing her through the gore, his face grinning even as he lay dying. Ella didn't bother fighting him. If he was still moving after the hit to his back, doubtless only one side of him was mobile. She hefted her axe once more and brought it down on his skull.

There'd be no more attacks after a blow like that. And indeed, there was not.

Ella kicked her leg free and got to her feet.

Bronson stood alone, his opponent sprawled halfway off the ledge with a red stain across his chest.

Bronson's eyes went wide. "Ella."

"'Tis not my blood." She pulled free her axe from the reiver's body one final time.

Lark and Leila were still pressed back against the wall. Leila relaxed as Ella and Bronson approached, but Lark did not. Her small shoulders were tense, her body stiff and her eyes wide and glassy. Flecks of blood dotted her face. Most likely from the man Ella had hit in the eye with her dagger.

"Are you both well enough to run?" Ella asked.

Leila nodded. Lark simply stared.

"Lark." Bronson knelt in front of her. "I need you to look at me."

Her green eyes slid toward him.

"We need to flee. Before they come back. Can you do that for me?"

She nodded.

Ella put her hand into Leila's and squeezed. She didn't voice her gratitude for the connection Leila had somehow been able to establish but knew she would not need to. Leila looked up at her, her brows furrowed with trepidation. "I'm sorry, Ella."

Ella shook her head. Apologies and appreciation could come later. And yet there was something in how Leila looked down at her feet, in the lingering glance she cast toward Bronson after speaking, that sent a prickle of fear down Ella's spine.

"You aren't talking about this, are you?" she asked. "Leila, what—"

"I'll go down the ladder first." Bronson straightened from where he'd been speaking with Lark. "If there is someone down there, I will attack them. Ella, you go last so the girls are between us."

Ella nodded and glanced once more at Leila, who refused to

look up at her. The nip of fear grew to a gnaw. Escaping the debatable lands would be as dangerous as entering had been.

And Ella knew it would not be as uneventful.

※

Before descending the ladder, Bronson scouted the area below for reivers. No movement showed aside from the cows and no men were visible, save the two who lay dead among the trampled dirt below.

He quickly made his way to the ground floor. Once there, he drew his sword and circled the room. After reassuring himself all was safe, he waved for the others to follow. Leila climbed with the same light dexterity as Ella, their warrior training apparent in everything they did.

Lark, however, lowered herself with a jerky unease. Her face was too pale for his liking, her eyes too large and full of fear. Now more than ever, he regretted having chastised her for trying to learn how to protect herself. If she had known how to keep herself safe, the same as Ella and Leila, she would not be as traumatized.

When she finally descended, he put his arm around her narrow shoulders. "You've done well, Lark. You're a brave young lady and I need you to keep being brave just a little longer."

She looked up at him and nodded. He pulled a dagger from his boot. "Take this. If you need it, use it."

She closed her fingers around the hilt and held it awkwardly before her. "Thank you, Bronson. And thank you for rescuing us. I was so...so scared." Her eyes filled with tears.

He shook his head. "Not here. Don't think on it now. We must be brave."

Leila appeared by Lark's side and clasped their hands together. "And quiet."

Lark nodded.

Bronson's heart crushed into his ribs. Despite her obvious terror, Lark was being so strong. His precious sister, the only sibling he had in the world, the one he thought in his darkest musings he'd never see again. He resisted the urge to pull her into his arms and keep her there, so she would never be scared or threatened again. Instead, he rubbed his hand over her silky hair.

She was alive. She was uninjured.

And he would do everything in his power to ensure she remained that way.

Ella was at the door already, her head bent toward the wood as she listened intently. After a long pause, she quietly slipped the latch free and opened the door, then waved them over.

It would be far more dangerous this time running through the valley with four of them instead of two. Especially with Lark as frightened as she was. If she startled, if she screamed, it could be the death of them all.

"You must remain perfectly quiet," Bronson instructed. "Even if you get scared."

Lark pressed her lips together hard, as though she could seal them shut. He smiled his approval, trying to keep his expression easy, to prevent her from seeing the extent of his worry. With a gentle nudge to her back, he encouraged her to walk to the door and slip out.

Outside, the air was clean and fresh, a mind-clearing reprieve from the heavy odor of death. There were more reivers about now. None nearby, but their figures dotted the landscape in the distance. Ella led their party, moving swiftly in the shadows but more slowly through the lighted ground they crossed. Any abrupt movement, such as running, would call attention to them. Bronson followed at the rear of their small group to ensure the girls remained safely between he and Ella.

A reiver rounded the corner of a tower suddenly. The moment he caught sight of Ella was apparent in the stiffening of his body.

Bronson knew what he saw—a woman clad in a gambeson and drenched in blood.

Before the man could move, Leila sent a dagger flashing in the moonlight with lethal speed. He fell forward, silent and dead. A quick glance around confirmed there was no way to easily hide the body. Not like there had been with the others.

"We'll have to think of somewhere to put him," Ella whispered

"Make him appear drunk." Lark bent and retrieved the tankard the man had dropped when he fell.

It was a simple plan, but a brilliant one. Aye, someone might check on him, but a man sleeping off his ale might also be left perfectly alone. Bronson propped the body against the wall of the tower and curled his hands around the tankard. He stood back to assess the dead reiver's appearance.

Aye, he looked thoroughly sotted with the shadows hiding any visible spots of blood oozing through the dark gambeson.

They had only two more towers to pass before the most treacherous part: the run back to the abandoned stone building. After that, their passage would be easy and quick. They would be back at Werrick Castle well before dawn broke.

They made their way to the final tower without issue. However, they were met with several voices, loud and raucous. The sounds of men who had been drinking heavily.

Ella pressed herself against the wall, with the rest of them doing likewise. But there would be no other way out but beyond the tower. Lark's small chest rose and fell quickly with her rapid breath. Bronson put a hand to her shoulder and squeezed gently to convey that everything would be well.

One of the reivers spoke, something Bronson couldn't understand. If he made it out of this bloody mess alive, he swore he would have Ella teach him Gaelic the first chance they got.

A man appeared suddenly, working at his hose beneath his filthy gambeson as he staggered. He propped himself on the wall beside Ella and a steady stream of liquid splashed against the stonework. Lark crushed closer against Bronson as Leila and Ella tried to edge away.

The man grunted and gave a little bounce as he tucked himself away. He pushed off the stone and staggered back several steps. That was when he looked up, and the bleariness in his eyes from drink cleared for one awful moment as he saw all four of them against the wall.

Before even a single dagger could be thrown, the drunkard charged forward to attack and cried out.

28

Shouts of alarm came from nearby, followed by the hissing of blades being pulled from their sheaths. Bronson stood in front of Lark and ran the reiver through with his blade.

The other men all charged. Bronson tensed for battle. He and Ella had come too far to lose everything now.

"Use that dagger if you have to," Bronson hissed through his teeth at Lark. "Better their life lost than yours."

He did not see if she acknowledged his order, for the men attacked then. Six in all, four with swords, one with a mace, another with an axe. Bronson was at Ella's side when their opponents first swung their weapons.

The reivers were sloppy in their attacks. The odor of alcohol clouded around them like a fog. Ella was able to easily take down the first two while Leila and Bronson each felled a reiver. Only two remained alive.

One darted off in the opposite direction. No doubt to notify someone of the attack. Ella sprinted after him, her axe poised to strike. The final man brought his blade down on Bronson, but he blocked it before it could hit. Bronson shoved his attacker back and thrust his sword into the man's soft neck.

Ella hefted her axe and threw it at the one fleeing, the same as she had back at the tower. Her weapon hit its target perfectly and the reiver fell to the ground.

Bronson pulled his sword free and glanced at Leila and Lark. "Are either of you injured?"

"Nay," Leila said. Lark simply shook her head, her gaze fixed on the reiver whose throat lay open and spurting with blood.

A man on the ground behind Leila moved, one they had assumed dead. He drew his arm back and something glinted in the moonlight. A dagger.

Bronson rushed into action, covering Leila with his body to prevent her from being struck. Pain lanced up his side as the weapon plunged into his torso.

Bronson groaned at the injury but turned his attention to the bastard who had just thrown the weapon. He lay still once more, a hilt jutting from his bloody chest. Neither Ella nor Leila stood beside the body.

It was Lark who knelt by him, frozen in horror.

"Lark," Bronson said. Or rather, he meant to say. Her name came out in a low grunt.

"I had to," she whispered. "I had to." Her frightened stare fluttered around before settling on Bronson's side. "You're hurt."

"'Tis nothing." He looked down for the first time at his side where the dagger jutted from his body. There was a momentary disconnect with his person, as if the wounded torso he gazed down upon was not his own, but that of one belonging to someone else. The lightheadedness returned.

Rather than give into it, he gripped the hilt and yanked. Searing pain ripped through his side. Blood seeped from the wound, nearly invisible against his dark gambeson, save for the glistening wet that caught the moonlight.

"Bronson," Ella gasped. Her battle axe was tucked in her hands once more, the blade bloody with the success of her chase.

"'Tis naught but a scratch," he lied. "We need to go now." He indicated the bodies on the ground.

Ella nodded tentatively, and together they ran the most treacherous part of their escape. Every step Bronson took, a fresh stab of agony gripped him.

He gritted his teeth through the pain, shoving his hand against the wound to staunch as much of the bleeding as he could, and tried to keep up with Ella and the girls.

He would not be the cause of them slowing. Step by step, he pushed through the awfulness of the pain. They were near the stone structure now. The horses would be within, ready to ride.

Bronson cringed at the thought of being on horseback—each gallop of hooves jarring his body would be more excruciating. He was falling behind. Going too slow. He hissed hard through his breathing and urged his heavy legs to keep pace. But his body was too weary to comply. A high bit of grass caught at his shoe and sent him staggering. His steps were too clumsy and the pain too intense.

God's bones, so damn intense.

Spots of white winked in his vision and the lightheadedness returned with a vengeance. Bile rose in his throat and his mouth filled with saliva as though he was going to purge.

They were at the stone structure now. Someone was speaking, but he couldn't concentrate enough to listen, not with the white-hot blaze at his side. He caught himself on the stone wall. It was firm beneath his grip, cold and rough on his palm.

But it was not enough.

The world tipped around him until the bright stars overhead tangled with the spots in his vision. They spun about together and left his mind reeling. He pressed his hand to his side, shoving at the wound with all the strength he could muster. The action felt like he was shoving fistfuls of coals into his body, but at least it would slow the bleeding.

Suddenly there was the sweet, wonderful scent of sunshine.

And flowers. Of Ella. She was there over him, peering down and blocking out the light of the moon. Her hand was cool on his cheek.

"Bronson, can you hear me?" she asked.

He nodded.

"You'll be fine," she said. Her voice choked off, as though she meant to say more, but could not.

"We must leave," he groaned. "Now." He rolled to his good side to sit.

"Don't." Ella's hand pressed to his chest. "Let Leila—"

"Now," he ground out. "It'll help no one if we're all dead." With that, he used the force of urgency in his own tone to lunge to his knees, and from there, to his feet.

"Stay on the horse with me," he said in a low tone to Ella. If he began to fall, he knew she would be strong enough to hold him upright. He would not risk hurting one of the girls by dragging them down with him.

Ella flicked a glance behind them. The area was still empty. For now. It would not be for long. Not when the bodies were found, and surely that was only a matter of minutes. Bronson forced his body to move, walking toward the horses that were being held by Lark and Leila outside the stone building. Using the strength of his good side, he swung up onto Kipper's back. The horse shifted beneath him and whinnied, but Ella spoke in hushed, soothing tones. Finally, the beast settled and the movement of protest ceased.

Those damn stars returned. Winking and blinking. Taunting Bronson toward falling once more. He squeezed his hands into fists and breathed through his nose, steadying himself. He would not fall.

Ella settled behind him as Leila and Lark climbed onto Bronson's horse. Frantic tension hung in the air, scrabbling at them all with maddening urgency. With a flick of the reins, the horses shot forward in a full gallop.

Bronson kept his hand firmly planted against his side and clenched his eyes shut against the pain. But no matter how hard he ground his teeth to allay the torment, the damn thing burned like a hot poker had been jabbed into him.

Ella's arms tightened on either side of him. "We'll stop soon."

"Nay," Bronson said firmly. He chanced a look back where the valley was beginning to disappear. Despite the full light of the moon, it was difficult to make out if the scenery was empty, or if the reivers were chasing them.

Either way, it was not worth the risk. He would have to wait until they were safe before they stopped, to know they weren't being chased. For those reivers on their rugged little hobblers would easily catch them, and then they would surely all be dead.

THEY NEEDED TO STOP, BUT THEY ALSO NEEDED TO RIDE AND the two warred in Ella's mind as they rode onward, skirting the first village they saw. Her right sleeve was wet, presumably with Bronson's blood. The low grunts he had issued from time to time had ceased and he swayed uneasily in front of her.

Ella steered Kipper in the direction of the forest. Periodic glances behind them confirmed they had not been chased, by some miracle. Still, she would not take any chances.

They slowed their horses as they entered the forest and went in deep, where they would not be seen. With Ella and Bronson both covered in blood, they would arouse suspicion regardless of who they might cross.

Ella pulled Kipper to a stop. "Hold tight to his mane."

She guided Bronson's hands to her horse's black mane. His hands were purplish red with blood in the moonlight, but he gripped as she bade.

She slid from Kipper's back and helped Bronson to the

ground. Even with her assistance, he landed hard, wobbled, and started to pitch forward.

Ella caught him with the full weight of her body to keep from being knocked down herself. Carefully, she eased him to the ground as Leila knelt at his side.

"Is he going to die?" Lark whispered.

"I need his gambeson unfastened," Leila said, then turned to Lark. "I won't let that happen."

Lark nodded.

"He will not die on my behalf." Tears welled in Leila's eyes.

Ella worked to unfasten his gambeson. It was then she understood why Leila had looked so guilty at the tower. She had foreseen what Bronson would most likely do. Of course, it would not have been the time to mention it, not when they needed to be positive in their hopes of escape, rather than dreading one of their own falling.

Except Ella's fears were not so easily calmed as Lark's. She had seen the look on Leila's face then, and she saw the determination there now. It was not that she knew Bronson would not die, it was only that she would do all in her power to keep it from happening.

Ella pulled opened the gambeson and slid up Bronson's shirt. His entire torso was stained with blood. Her heart sank deep into her stomach. Too much blood.

"Lark," Bronson said. "We need to leave now. To go get her."

His confusion rattled at Ella's nerves. This was not normal for a man who always remembered every word of every conversation. "She's here," Ella said.

"Hold still." Leila pressed her fingers against the wound.

"Have to save her—" He gave a groan of pain.

Lark sank to Bronson's side and took his hand. "I'm here."

"Lark." His eyes closed. "Thanks be to God, you are safe."

Ella stood over them all, helpless, as one girl comforted Bronson and another saw to his wounds. His skin was pale compared to that of his sister. Far too pale. And he'd lost far too much blood. Tension knotted at the back of her throat.

"I need fabric to bind the wound." Leila pulled her dagger free even as she spoke and jerked it through the hem of her kirtle. "Help me lift him."

Ella rushed to comply, eager to assist in any way. Bronson's muscles flexed under her hands as he tried to lift his body. "I have you," Ella said.

Leila moved quickly, her dexterity on the battlefield transferring perfectly to her healing, as she bound the wound. She pulled the fabric and tied it tightly. Bronson hissed out a hard breath that cut into Ella's heart.

"To the horses now." Leila looked solemnly up at Ella. "We must return to the castle as quickly as possible. Isla needs to see to him."

Ella's chest squeezed at the implication of what was not said. If they did not return soon—if he did not see a healer—Bronson would die.

Never again would she see that charming smile of his, laugh at his attempts at poetry or be held in the safety of his arms. She would never have the opportunity to accept the marriage she had pushed away for so long.

Now, as things were falling apart, she knew their union was exactly what she wanted.

Ella helped Bronson stand. "We need to get you on the horse, but I cannot do it alone."

"'Tis fine, my beautiful Ella." Bronson gave her a lopsided smile, weaker than usual. "I'm already feeling much better."

Despite his brave words, his steps were slow and shuffling as they made their way to the horse. He pulled himself onto Kipper's back with his good side, needing almost no assistance from her. His valiant effort lifted Ella's spirits. Mayhap he would be fine.

Once more, they all mounted the horses and were again off,

heading in the direction of Werrick Castle. They emerged from the forest and rode through the Scotland border. They were nearly to the English side when a shout pulled her attention to riders behind them. Riders who were traveling at great speed.

Ella's heart lurched. *Armstrongs?*

"Faster," Ella called to Leila, who snapped her reins in response.

Their horses pushed harder, but the riders were getting closer. It was a party of men, easily two dozen of them, all on hobblers, all wearing helms and gambesons.

The wind tore at Ella's hair and stung her eyes, but she did not slow her pace. She kept her arms tucked snugly against Bronson's sides, mindful of the wound on his right.

An arrow flew past Ella and landed in the ground in front of Kipper. An overshoot. And a definite confirmation that the men were indeed chasing them.

Ella cried out for them to go even faster. But even as they pushed their horses to the limit, the beasts were growing weary, and the reivers on their sure-footed hobblers gained.

29

The English border was so close Ella could make out the familiar strip of land. Another arrow shot past, going wide as it landed somewhere to the side of them, nowhere near enough to hit.

But near enough to shoot. If they could shoot, they could easily cover the distance between them.

Kipper glided over the countryside, going as fast as he could. The thundering of hoofbeats prickled in Ella's ears and dread streaked through her.

If she could hear the riders, surely, they were far too close.

A frantic glance over her shoulder confirmed the reivers were going even faster than Ella had initially feared. There would be no escaping the Armstrongs at this rate. They cared not about borders and laws. They would follow Ella and the others into England and exact their revenge for their fallen brethren.

Ella passed over the border into England. Into her country. Where they should have been safe. But true to her suspicions, the Armstrongs paid no mind to the shift in countries as they continued their pursuit.

Bronson began to slip to the right. Ella tightened her grasp, but the galloping was too much. Tears burned in her eyes. They couldn't give up. Not when they were so close. She grasped the collar of his gambeson and tugged him upright. It was an awkward move, but she managed to seat him better on the saddle and get a stronger grip on him.

"Ye canna outrun us," an Armstrong called in Gaelic.

The taunt slid down her spine and sent fear plummeting to her stomach. He was right. They couldn't outrun them. And soon their time would be up; the distance between them closed.

They couldn't make it. Ella glanced back once more, only this time she didn't check how far away they were. This time, she counted. Going from the idea of fleeing to the idea of battle.

She lost count somewhere around ten, unable to keep her head turned for longer than a second, with the jarring of Kipper's gallop, and while holding Bronson. It didn't matter. There were far too many of them to fight. She would, of course, as would Leila, but it would be an impossible battle to win.

Her heart slid low into her stomach. They would not survive this day.

Movement showed on the horizon. A lot of movement. Ella straightened in her saddle. Men. A whole army's worth coming toward them. No doubt English.

Hope flickered to life within her once more. Mayhap all was not lost. There could be a chance to survive. Ella cried out to them. Lark and Leila did the same, waving their hands as best they could while remaining on their horse.

All at once, as though spurred by an unseen hand, the army raced toward them on a wave of horses. Tears blurred Ella's vision for only a moment as relief crashed over her in the most visceral, overwhelming, wonderful way.

"I'll get ye first." A voice said, practically behind her.

Ella didn't turn to look at the man. She simply rode and prayed the English could make it to them first. An Armstrong appeared to her right, large and with a face that looked like he'd had a fall or two in his life. He held his horse's reins with one hand and swirled a mace with the other.

Ella edged Kipper away. He followed.

She couldn't lift a blade to defend herself. Not when she had to hold Bronson upright. She would take the hit and hope she lived. Better that than to drop Bronson and leave him for certain death.

An arrow punched through the man's chest. He jerked at the impact and fell behind. The arrow had a white fletching.

Catriona.

Ella snapped her gaze to the army, only yards in front of them now. The moon glowed down, illuminating tunics with the fierce black hawk standing out against the green tincture field, and a stripe of yellow running down its center. She cried out.

The Werrick livery.

These were her soldiers.

Cat rode at the head of them in full armor, another arrow nocked, then flying, then nocked again. The wave of soldiers rushed forward and fell around them in a curtain of protection.

"Lady Ella." Drake leapt from his horse and ran to her.

"Bronson," Ella said raggedly. "Lord Calville. He's been struck. I fear I cannot hold him much longer."

Drake was at her side in a moment, helping to pull Bronson from Kipper's back. She relinquished her hold on him, allowing Drake to take his weight from where she'd clutched him to her. Immediately, the heat from his body against her skin cooled, and her arms ached with heavy stiffness.

Drake set to work, summoning soldiers with the fastest horses to see Bronson to the castle, while Ella, Lark and Leila were escorted back with the protection of an army. Werrick Castle came into view just as the sky began to lighten with the promise of a new day.

Cat pulled her horse alongside Ella's. "You had us all worried."

"Do you think Papa will forgive me?" Ella asked.

Cat glanced to Bronson's horse with Leila and Lark on the back, and her mouth curled up into the optimistic smile Ella knew so well. "Aye. But I don't know that I'll ever forgive you for going without me. I'm glad we were scouring the lands through the night trying to find you. We were about to return to the keep when we caught sight of you."

Ella would ordinarily have had a quick reply for her sister, but this time any quip she might have uttered was rendered silent by the weight of her concern. They'd made it to England, to Werrick Castle and Lark and Leila were now safe.

But what of Bronson? He hadn't even grunted as he was hefted into the saddle in front of Drake. She glanced up and found Leila watching her with a solemn expression.

Ella's youngest sister dropped her head in apology, as though it had been her fault. It was not. Ella knew this.

Ella's throat grew tight.

Bronson was a hero of the truest kind.

He'd saved Leila's life by throwing himself in front of that reiver's blade.

They stopped at the castle as the portcullis rose. Her father waited on the other side in a hastily donned tunic and trews. Once the gate opening was waist-high, he ducked beneath and ran toward them. It was a sprint of desperation, one born of fear and love brought together in a powerful tangle.

Leila jumped down from her horse as their father arrived. He pulled her into his arms, and she tucked her dark head to his chest while he murmured the reassurances of a father who cared immeasurably for his daughter. A moment behind him was Brigid, racing toward Lark with her night rail billowing out from beneath a cloak. They fell into one another, weeping, while William regarded the reunion from a distance with a relieved smile.

The earl released Leila and turned his attention to Ella. His eyes were still glassy with tears, his weathered face lined with tension. She cringed and met his gaze. The sun was just beginning to stain the sky with red and turned the blue of his eyes to an ethereal purple.

"Ella." His voice was firm and low with warning. The way he'd spoken when she was a girl and disobeyed him.

She lowered her head at the gentle chastisement. The toes of her shoes were still dark with the dirt from the hut floor where she and Bronson had waited to rescue Lark and Leila. That had been a lifetime ago. Or so it felt. Certainly, it did not seem to have been mere hours. "Forgive me, Papa."

"You could have been taken as well," he said sternly.

She nodded and continued to stare at the black dirt embedded in the creases of leather.

"I could have lost two daughters at once." Her father's voice broke off, causing her to lift her gaze.

His eyes were red-rimmed and glossy. "It was so risky, Ella. Too risky."

Several months back, Ella would have run into his arms, as much to allay his tears as her own. She'd blinked them back, unwilling to allow emotion to carry her away.

"Bronson," she choked. "I may have lost him."

The hard clench of her father's jaw told her exactly what his assessment of Bronson's injuries were. "He is with Isla."

Ella nodded her gratitude and ran in the direction of the keep.

"Ella." Her father's voice gave her pause. "Do not go."

She didn't turn back. "I wasn't there for Mother. I will be there for him." Her voice quavered. She had not been strong enough to face her mother's death when she had been a girl. But she was strong enough now and made stronger by Bronson.

Ella wound through the familiar passage to where Isla kept a small room of her goods and curatives. Images of Bronson flitted through her mind unbidden with each step. The way he'd stepped in front of the dagger, saving Leila, how he'd run without complaint until he dropped from the intensity of his wound.

But him being a hero had always been there. Even in his

charm, when he'd caught her as she fell from the tree that first day, the choicest cuts of meat he put on her plate, the little smile he gave when he talked about reading the stories she had written.

He had been a hero all along and she had been too stubborn to see it, too locked on the idea of a couple falling in love first and then becoming betrothed. Then later, too blinded by lust.

But now she was in love. Not through desire as before when he'd made her breathless with his kisses and the way he touched her, but true, heart-pounding, soul-clenching, all-the-world consuming love.

She loved him and she *had* to tell him.

Her pace quickened down the hall all the way to Isla's healing room. The door was closed. Ella didn't ask if she could enter, for she might be told she could not. She wouldn't be put off again, not like she had been with her mother. Then she'd been too young, grateful for the barrier of a heavy door, for Cat hugging her and chanting that their mother would be fine.

Ella pushed into the room and stopped short. Bronson lay on the table, still and pale, blood smeared over his torso. The room was quiet. So quiet, it pressed on her soul and made a deep ache echo within her chest.

Isla glanced up and the sober expression on her face made Ella's stomach drop.

Bronson was so damnably tired. Exhaustion tugged at him, luring him to sleep, but he fought against it.

Ella. Where was she?

She had been at his back, holding him in the saddle. Or was it, she had been running at his side in the debatable lands? Or mayhap, she was on the upper level of the tower amid sounds of battle, while he'd been desperately climbing the ladder?

The harder he tried to concentrate on what had last

happened, the more the events pushed away from him. Where was Ella? Lark and Leila. They had rescued them, hadn't they?

He groaned and the sound of it resonated with the grinding pain in his head. Why couldn't he think?

And where was he, for that matter?

He dragged his eyes open with great effort. The walls were stone, several shelves laden with various pots and bottles. He needed to sit up, but his body would not comply with the thought, his limbs too heavy. His efforts slipped beneath a wave of fatigue and he succumbed, his eyes closing.

"Bronson, you needn't move." A woman's voice sounded at his side.

"Ella." Her name rasped from his throat.

This time, it was easier to open his eyes, especially when he knew she would be there. A reward for his efforts.

And indeed, she was. Her hair was bound back with several loose tendrils falling around her face. She blinked down at him.

"Bronson?" She leaned over and graced him with the sweet smell of sunshine and freshness.

He breathed her in with reverence. "Ella."

She held his face in her cool hands, her blue eyes wide and desperate as they searched his. "I'll marry you, Bronson. Even if it means going to court, I will marry you."

"I don't know where I am, or how I got here. But I like the words you're saying." His voice was weak, his speech clumsy and difficult to manage. He grinned, regardless, in an attempt to set her at ease. "Are we in the tower?"

Ella shook her head. "We're at Werrick Castle."

His mind clouded over. The memories of Scotland... Had those been a dream? "Lark," he said. "Leila."

"Safe." Ella stroked her hand over Bronson's brow with tenderness.

His memories jumbled against one another. "We saved them?"

Concern darkened the brightness of Ella's gaze. "Aye, we did." She straightened. "Isla, I think something is amiss."

The healer's puckered face loomed over him. She touched his cheeks where Ella's hands had been only moments before, her fingers dry and warm. Her amber eyes bored into his. "He's fine."

"But he doesn't remember," Ella protested.

Bronson wanted to argue that he did remember. But he didn't. At least not all of it. Nothing more than snatches of images fluttering through his brain like birds taking flight on a hunt.

Isla lifted her shoulder in a shrug and withdrew from his line of sight. "The lad has bled heavily. It can leave them addled."

Bronson scoffed. "I assure you, I am not addled."

"Where are ye then? Do ye remember?" Isla asked.

More images flitted in his mind. A reiver lying dead on a floor among the hooves of cows, a blue ribbon on the earth beside him. A drunk man propped against the stone wall of a tower. The stars overhead, bright and blinking down at him. He had known where he was but couldn't remember.

"Aye," Isla confirmed. "Ye're addled."

"For how long?" Ella put her hand to his chest.

The healer peered down at him, her mouth grim. "May be a day or two. He'll be weak for several months is my guess, with how near he was to death."

Several months? Bronson tried to sit up, but his body would not cooperate. Not when he was so damn tired.

"But he'll live?" Ella asked, her voice pitched.

Isla did not immediately answer. Her prolonged silence jabbed a blade of fear into his heart and shoved aside his exhaustion for one sharp moment. Was it truly so bad that he might die? That he might never get to hold Ella in his arms again? Or tell her...or tell her...

"I love you, Ella," he said raggedly.

She shifted her gaze back to him. Tears swam in her eyes and the muscles of her neck strained against her flushed skin. "Bronson." His name was a soft whisper on her lips.

"He may yet make it," Isla said quietly. "Hope isna lost yet, aye?"

There was a hesitation to the woman's words. The tiredness was back, tugging at him like a strong current, threatening to drag him below into the darkness of oblivion.

"Bronson, please, stay awake." Ella grasped his hand in hers and held onto him firmly.

Mayhap that grip could keep him from the desire to sleep. He squeezed her hand as much as was possible, holding on to her as though his life depended on it.

"You said you would wed me." His words were a tired groan. "Did I imagine that?"

"Nay," she replied. "I promised to marry you. Because I want to. Because you have always been the true hero of my story. I thought you were pretending to be someone you weren't for so long, but I've learned the truth about you. You're brave and loving and you'll sacrifice everything for those you care about. I want to marry you for the man you are, and I want to marry you because I love you."

A knot lodged itself in the back of his throat and warmth filled his eyes. She loved him. Truly loved him.

"Ella." The warmth spilled over the corners of his eyes. He clung onto her hand, determined to ward off the pull of death.

No matter how long he had to resist the temptation to close his eyes and give in to the pull of oblivion. He would fight, he would win, he would *live*.

30

O*ne month later*

BRONSON STOOD IN FRONT OF THE CROWDED CASTLE CHAPEL. Bernard, the twitchy little chaplain, was behind him, a bible splayed open in his palm. Not that Bronson paid him much mind.

Nay, his gaze was fixed on the door Ella would come through.

His heart pounded in his chest and the lightheadedness left him feeling dizzy. It was not an uncommon feeling these days as he still recovered from his injury—or rather, from the blood lost during his injury. He could swear he'd consumed every animal in all of England with the amount of red meat and bone broth shoved in his face in the last month while he recovered.

And though he'd done as he was told, and eaten as he was told, his body had been slow in its recovery. Even now, he leaned the bulk of his weight on a cane. But he was not willing to prolong this moment any longer.

Brigid sat in one of the pews at the front with William at her side. Her eyes were bright with unshed tears, her mouth curled in a broad smile. In the last month, she had become the mother he'd been so long without. She and Ella had alternated visiting times to ensure he was never alone. Ella had taught both her and Lark how to read, and all three had relished keeping his countless hours of healing filled with stories and adventure.

Lark had a mind for stories, as it turned out. In fact, she and Leila had assisted him in completing his wedding present to Ella. It had taken the entire month, most of it written in Bronson's own hand, but some of it in Leila's when he grew too weary. It was finally complete, and the book rested against Bronson's heart beneath his doublet.

The story was about two unlikely lovers forced into an arranged marriage neither thought would work. After a month, Bronson considered himself an expert on romantic stories and this was one for the ages. If he did say so himself.

The doors to the chapel rattled and his heart skipped in his chest. It was time.

They opened and revealed the silhouette of a woman whose shape his hands and heart knew well. Ella stepped into the chapel, a vision in midnight blue with her long blonde tresses unbound. Her cheeks were rosy, and her eyes sparkled. She clutched a bunch of flowers in her hands, but he could not pull his gaze from the joy on her face long enough to even consider what type they might be.

Anice and Marin had arrived several days prior for the wedding. They were at either side of her, as well as Cat, Leila and Lark who all giggled to one another and rushed to their seats as Ella strode down the aisle toward him. The stained glass windows flickered various colors over her as she walked, casting her in ethereal gold, brilliant green, sensual red, each even more appealing than the last. The lightheadedness returned with a powerful jolt that nearly knocked him to the ground at the beauty of the woman he loved.

He tightened his grip on his cane and forced his breath to remain even. He would not allow his body's weakness to ruin the most incredible moment of his life. She kept her eyes locked on his down the entire length of the aisle until she was at his side.

He breathed her in, her sunshine, her happiness. His heart swelled to the point of bursting in his chest.

"You look beautiful," he said reverently. Someone in the nearest pew gave a quiet, wistful sigh.

Ella put her hand over his on the cane. "And you are as handsome as ever, Bronson Berkley." She bit her lip.

"I can scarcely wait to give you my wedding present," he whispered as they both looked forward.

"You aren't alone in that." She slid him a glance from the corner of her eye.

Bernard thinned his mouth in obvious disapproval of their long conversation. They both immediately fell silent and the wedding proceeded.

It was a short ceremony, thanks be to God. Standing for such a long period of time was difficult for Bronson, but it was more than that. He had waited far too long for Ella to become his wife. His lovely Ella, who was intelligent and kind and brave enough to stand behind her own convictions.

She had given him a second chance when he had not deserved it, and they were all the better for it. He would spend his life devoted to her, to her continued happiness, even if they were pulled to court.

They had spoken of it, and they would return to Berkley Manor to oversee the land and its repairs. With the king on a military campaign, Bronson's immediate return was unnecessary.

All at once, Bernard was uttering the final words of marriage that tied them both together. Ella smiled at him, a beaming, beautiful smile that shot straight into his heart and lit up his soul. Bronson stepped toward her, cupped her face with his free hand and lowered his mouth to hers.

Cheers erupted all around them.

"I love you, my dove," Bronson said against her mouth before releasing her.

"And I love you." She gave him a coy look. "I can't wait any longer to share my wedding present with you."

Even as she spoke, their families were rising from their seats to follow them from the chapel.

He led her down the aisle. "If you can't wait, then neither can I." His hand lifted for the breast of his doublet.

She tugged on his arm, dragging him to a brief stop. Her brilliant blue eyes danced with excitement, her cheeks and lips flushed. She was practically glowing with her joy. "I'm with child."

He would be a father. A better father than his own had been.

A rush of emotions slammed into him. Joy. Immense, overwhelming joy. Eagerness for the future they would all share together. And fear. Cold as ice and gripping. For they had not lain together since their early days of courtship, due to his injuries. Which meant she had been in a delicate way when they went to the debatable lands.

"I did not know then." She nudged him forward.

"Is my face so telling?" He asked. "I used to be so much better at masking my emotions."

"I like you better this way." She nestled closer to him. Her hand brushed his chest and she paused. "What is this?"

He grinned down at her. "My gift to you. For later."

Because as much as he was looking forward to giving her the present, now was for celebrating her gift.

ELLA HAD NEVER BEEN HAPPIER THAN SHE WAS THE DAY OF HER wedding. Her story had taken such a wonderful turn: an unwanted union with the most incredible man, their unexpected love, and the beauty of life growing within her even as they said their vows.

For all the times she had worried over how wrong it all was, it was now so perfectly right.

And it would continue to be so.

They made their way into the great hall where the silver had been polished and Nan had laid out a feast worthy of a king. Bronson led her to the dais. Though he tried to hide it, the day had exhausted him. His steps were slower, more measured. Despite the joy lighting his handsome green eyes, his face was still an unhealthy pallor.

She had been hesitant to accept his idea to wed before he was fully recovered, but he had been insistent, and she had been so eager. It had been all too easy for him to convince her. They would not leave Werrick Castle until his health was restored and would see to Berkley Manor being prepared in the meantime.

Ella sank into her chair beside Bronson and linked her fingers through his. A small plate of various nuts caught her eye. She would have to save several of them to give to Moppet and his newfound lady squirrel later. Ella's darling pet had taken to a smaller squirrel in a tree in the gardens—his own happy ending.

While she missed having Moppet's comforting weight at her side in the bag she used to wear, she was grateful for him finding his own way. It was, after all, why she worked so hard to heal animals. To give them the life they had before once more.

Bronson's gaze on her stomach pulled her attention from the plate of nuts. "Are you pleased?" she asked in a quiet voice.

He stretched his fingers to gently brush over her stomach. "I couldn't be more so."

It was all the conversation they were able to have for the moment, as their family and friends came forward to offer their felicitations. Marin and Bran were the first, wishing them the same bliss that they had found in their union, followed by Anice and James with their small son and Piquette. It was good to see her sisters so content in their marriages.

Next came Cat who made Ella promise to allow her to visit,

followed by Leila who had recovered from the guilt of Bronson having taken the dagger meant for her. After all, he had saved her life in doing so, but she had saved his by tightly binding his wound. After her sisters came Brigid with Lark, followed closely by William and Hardy. The dog had not left Lark's side since her rescue, as though sensing her need for protection.

William had agreed to oversee the running of Harlick Castle, the property included in Ella's dowry, in addition to his duties at Werrick Castle. But Werrick Castle would have to find a new steward eventually to allow William the opportunity to have a new life. That Brigid and Lark had eagerly agreed to reside at Harlick Castle might have had some impact on his decision.

Last of all came Ella's father. He regarded them both with a wistful smile. "Your mother was a romantic like you, Ella. I can feel her here in this room, beaming with pride for you." He reached over the table and squeezed Ella's hand. "I will always love you, daughter."

He nodded to Bronson. "I know you'll take good care of her."

Bronson inclined his head in agreement. And with that, the feast began. The food was cooked to perfection, the wine ran without limit, and on and on the musicians played, filling the great hall with merriment.

The food and drink restored some of the color in Bronson's face. He looked at her now, his expression tender. "I have yet to give you your wedding present," he said.

She lifted her brow. "Oh?"

He made a show of pulling open the breast of his doublet, concealing what was within as he slowly drew it out. She craned her neck with curiosity and saw the edge of a book between his fingers.

"Is it *Roman de la Rose*?" she asked excitedly.

He shook his head as that lazy smile tugged at his mouth. "You'll not have heard of this book." Before she could ask any more questions, he held it out for her.

The cover was smooth, worn leather, the kind that appeared to have been well handled. It did not appear like other books with their ornate impressions and gilding. Nay, it looked like one she might write herself.

Her interest piqued further, she drew it from his hand and opened it. A slanted script filled the page. But not of her own writing.

She lifted her head in question. "Is this a story?"

"Aye." He took a sip of wine. His knee bounced under the table. Was he nervous?

"Who wrote it?" she asked.

He set his goblet on the table and fingered the stem. "Someone who most likely has no business attempting to write."

She glanced down at the pages and read the first line.

The betrothal was unwelcome, both for the arrogant courtier who had spent his life only worrying about himself, and for the golden-haired beauty in a faraway land.

She gasped and snapped her head up. "Did you write this?"

He shrugged, his unease making him reticent. It was endearing, this shy side of her husband.

Warmth filled her chest. "You wrote it for me."

"You said there were no stories on arranged marriages." He indicated the book. "Now there is one."

"For me," she repeated.

He grinned unabashedly. "Aye. For you."

She turned the page to see where the lady fell from the tree. Then to another section where the man tried to woo her. "And how does it end?" she asked.

"Happily, my beautiful wife." He closed the book and put his hand over hers. "Happily ever after."

Ella's cheeks hurt from smiling so broadly. Bronson, who had claimed to hate books when he met her, had taken the time to write one for her. To give her the very story she had deemed impossible. "Have you given it a title?"

He gave her a little smirk before answering. *"Ella's Desire."*

EPILOGUE

Palace of Westminster
March 1341

Court life was not as difficult as Ella had anticipated. In fact, she found she rather enjoyed it. While there were often complaints from others, that the food took so long to arrive at mealtimes, that it was cold, or that the apartments were cramped and fit little more than a bed. Ella and Bronson had experienced no such inconveniences.

William had done well in his management of Harlick Castle and its surrounding land and had trained the new steward at Berkley Manor to apply the same knowledge. As a result, both lands benefitted considerably. This had left William in the wonderful position to finally wed Brigid in a lovely ceremony Ella and Bronson had been fortunate enough to attend. The profitable lands also left Ella and Bronson exceptionally wealthy.

In a court where the king had run his coffers dry with war and conquering, being a wealthy noble put them in a high position. Their food arrived at the great hall plenty warm and their apartments were large enough to even offer a spare room for Catriona to visit.

Despite the constant strings of gossip that threatened to entangle those bold enough to incite it, there were many moments of peace. Like the one now in the garden. Some of the plants were beginning to show green once more after being dormant for winter, though there wasn't a substantial tree in sight to climb. But it was an enchanting place one could bundle up warmly to enjoy, especially when one would rather spend time with their child than be indoors.

A shadow fell over Ella. "I thought I might find you out here." Bronson sank down onto the blanket she had laid out.

Their daughter, Blanche, squealed in delight at his arrival and pulled from Ella's grasp to race over to her father. He caught her and lifted her into the air. The sweetmeat she'd been eating fell onto his chin with a plop.

Ella pushed her hands to her mouth to suppress a laugh. One she was unable to contain as Bronson carefully lowered their daughter and turned his scrunched-up face in Ella's direction. "I don't suppose you have a bit of cloth handy?"

Of course, he knew she always had a bit of cloth handy. "Here." She handed it to him as she quickly snatched up the sweetmeat to prevent Blanche from putting it back into her mouth.

Bronson gratefully swabbed his face. "It would appear I have been defeated yet again." He winked at Ella and pulled Blanche back toward him, this time keeping her on the ground. He propped her on his legs and bounced her up and down, much to their little girl's great delight.

"Again," Blanche cried. "Again."

And again and again Bronson complied with a laugh.

Blanche's nurse, Bess, sat nearby, idly working on a bit of

mending. They'd hired the kind older woman to look after Blanche while at court, where children were often unwelcome. Indeed, most did not bring their families to court at all. But Ella and Bronson could no sooner leave their child at Berkley Manor than they could their own hearts. It was in these moments in the garden, away from prying eyes and the gossip which abounded, mostly about their decision to bring Blanche, that Ella was most happy.

"Where is Cat?" Bronson stopped bouncing Blanche and surveyed the surrounding area.

Ella nodded in the direction of several courtiers gathered around a lutist who plucked out a slow, romantic tune. "With her new friends."

There, Cat sat upon a stone bench by the young, handsome knight, Sir Gawain, a man who had only recently arrived. He was nearly a head taller than Cat, with shoulders as broad as Bronson's and a face that had the eye of nearly every lady at court. Including Cat's.

Bronson narrowed his gaze. "I don't like how she looks at him."

"Under our careful watch." Ella waved her hand dismissively. "Next week, we return to Berkley Manor and she to Werrick Castle. Let the girl enjoy the appeal of courtly romance."

"Oh, so courtly romance is something to be enjoyed then?" Bronson set Blanche on the blanket. The child immediately tried to dart away. He pinched the back of their daughter's coat, holding her in place as her feet worked in a determined march. "I remember a young lady who was immune to my courtly charm."

Ella sniffed. "Mayhap I was merely stubborn in my admission of its effectiveness."

Bronson shifted closer, bringing Blanche a step back with him. She found it to be a great game and began leaping forward with bursts of laughter.

Bronson held fast to little Blanche. "So, you like the courtly love?"

"Sometimes," Ella replied coyly. "Depends on the man."

He smirked. "And which man might that be?"

"A true hero, someone wonderful enough to inspire stories of love."

He nodded in consideration. Blanche threw her arms and legs up as though flying, and indeed she was as Bronson kept her lifted by the back of her coat. "He sounds like a noble and chivalrous man. Is he handsome as well?" Even as he spoke, he lifted his chin to the side to display his sharp-jawed profile.

"Oh, aye. Except he knows it all too well." With a laugh, she turned his face toward her and met his gaze. She wanted to kiss him, to have a moment alone with him to show how very much she loved him.

Soon they would be at Berkley Manor once more with its fine furnishings and the repairs that had taken it from ruin to luxury. There, they would have their privacy to truly show their affection without having prying eyes.

With the state of turmoil court was in over the king's return from campaign several months prior, the entire court seemed on edge. He'd let go many ministers and judges on account of how affairs had been run in his absence. It had made for an unhappy king and a lackluster court.

"Mayhap it's a lady who lets the man know it so well," Bronson said.

Ella scooted closer to him with a smile. "What a lucky lady."

"Indeed." And with that, he lifted Blanche into his arms and used their daughter to block their faces for a quick moment, long enough to press his lips quickly to Ella's lips.

Blanche clapped her hands as he set her down then distributed her own kisses to her parents and charged after something unseen. This time, it was Ella who caught their daughter and pressed a kiss to the girl's silky blonde hair.

"And lucky for the man as well." Bronson settled back and gave Ella a smug little smile.

She raised her brows in silent question.

"Lucky him for being everything his lady desires."

* * *

Thank you for reading ELLA'S DESIRE! I read all of my reviews and would love to know how you enjoyed the story, so please do leave a review.

Up next is CATRIONA'S SECRET

Geordie has always been in love with Catriona, and after finally securing his knighthood, he's nearly ready to do what he's always dreamed of: propose marriage to Cat.

Are these two destined to be star-crossed lovers? Or will their love be stronger than the treachery of court and the secrets that threaten to tear them apart?

Keep reading for a first chapter preview of CATRIONA'S SECRET

If you'd like to stay up to date on all my new releases, as well as get bonus scenes and info before anyone else, please sign up for my newsletter:
www.MadelineMartin.com

CATRIONA'S SECRET
Chapter 1 Preview

May 1341
Brampton, England

Lady Catriona Barrington awoke to a familiar clenching of her stomach. She squeezed her eyes shut against the discomfort in the hopes it would pass. It did sometimes.

She hated this queasiness. It reminded her of the sensation of being drunk, of having too much wine. Of that regrettable night with too many bad decisions. She hadn't had a sip of wine since.

That had been nearly two months ago, and still the memory was so strong in her mind. The wine, the poor decisions, Sir Gawain, that resonating hollowness within her.

She shuddered under a fresh wave of nausea. Sweat prickled at her brow. She was losing her battle with the strange illness that had plagued her since her return to Werrick Castle.

Isla thought it might be the switch from English fare to the more rustic food of the border. Cat had accepted the explanation and hadn't bothered to seek further counsel, even though she continued to be ill. Eventually, she would readjust to the food at home. Wouldn't she?

Cat's mouth filled with a flood of saliva. She clenched her hands into the sheets, inundated by thoughts of Sir Gawain's whispered promises and flattery.

All of court had been thus: promises and flattery. Resplendent with costly fabric and sparkling gems that lay like a fine veneer over all the cultured courtiers.

Her older sister, Ella, had always been the one to sway toward romance, but even Cat had fallen prey to the seduction of court. There she was not merely a younger sister, but a woman in the prime of her life, ripe for wooing. She had felt beautiful, special.

She did not feel either such thing on the last night of her time at court, when she'd accompanied Sir Gawain into the rose-laden alcove. What had followed had been over quickly enough to send her reeling, leaving her with a sticky mess and regret.

He had not mentioned marriage, but she could not help but think of it. She *ought* to marry him after what they had done.

Cat lurched upright, yanked crudely from her unpleasant thoughts. Her attempt to put off her illness had left her with scarcely enough time to reach the ewer before her stomach divested itself of any remaining food in her stomach from the night before.

When she'd first returned to Werrick Castle and found her effects moved to her mother's former room, Cat's reaction had been a blend of emotions. Disappointment to no longer share a room with her youngest sister, Leila, after eighteen years of having done so. But there was also an appreciation for her own maturity in now occupying her mother's room, as all her older sisters had before her. Now, Cat was simply grateful.

She was able to keep everyone from worrying unnecessarily over her while she readjusted to food on the border.

After she'd cleaned herself, she made her way down to the great hall. A familiar voice among the conversations floated toward her.

Marin.

The realization that Cat's eldest sister was visiting sent her speeding through the stone archway and into the wide expanse of the great hall. She'd always loved this room best in all the castle. It was where life happened, dances and weddings and feasts. Troubadours' voices echoed in the great space as they spun their tales and added their own spice of magic to the room already filled with colorful tapestries.

And now this room brought her a reunion with Marin, whom she had not seen in more than a year. Marin got to her feet as soon as her gaze landed on Catriona.

Women as tall as Marin often wore their height like an ill-fitting mantle. But not Marin. Nay, she rose like a queen, her slender frame regal and beautiful.

"My precious Cat." She opened her arms and drew Cat into her embrace.

Cat remained cradled against Marin for a long moment. Perhaps too long, but Cat didn't care. She could stay forever hugged against Marin, breathing in the comforting scent of lavender that always surrounded her sister. Cat had been only six when their mother had died, thus Marin had been more mother to her than their own.

"I hear you've been unwell." Marin released Cat and examined her with a concerned eye.

Cat waved her off and smiled brightly. "'Tis naught to concern yourself with. I simply need to get accustomed to border food again after all the rich fare at court."

"I hear you had a lovely time at court." Marin tilted her head in suspicion. "You attracted the attention of quite a few eligible nobles."

She simply shrugged as the heat blazed in her cheeks. Sir Gawain would likely propose marriage soon and they would all know exactly which noble's attention she had caught.

Marin laughed. "If you are being quiet, then what I heard must be true." She withdrew a missive from her bag. "I was visiting with Ella and she asked me to give you this."

"That was so kind of you to bring it all the way here to me." It was all Cat could do to remain calm as she took the note. It was even more difficult to keep from tearing it open to read what Ella had written. No doubt it contained the requested information on Sir Gawain, exactly as Cat had asked.

"Of course, I was already planning to visit." Marin peered at the entrance of the hall. Not once, but several times. Cat turned to regard the empty corridor behind her to see what pulled at Marin's attention.

"Forgive me." Marin flushed. "I confess, I'm also here to see Isla, in the hopes she might offer some advice on what I can do to encourage my ability to conceive."

"Oh, Marin." Cat's heart flinched for her sister's barrenness. It was so unfair that the one who had been mother to them all for the last eighteen years would now be without her own children.

"I'm not unhappy with my life," Marin said quickly. Her face softened. "I'm incredibly happy at Kendal with Bran. It is quiet and peaceful. Mayhap a little too peaceful now that his sister and her family have moved to their own home." The familiar, wistful smile tugged at the corners of her lips, the same as it always did when she spoke of her Bran. He'd been an unlikely husband when he'd threatened to kill Cat in order to breach Werrick Castle's walls seven years prior.

She'd forgiven him almost immediately when she realized he'd managed to take the castle with only one single death. *Eversham.* The brave soldier's name would forever be emblazoned on her heart. He had fought valiantly to keep Cat from being used as bait to force open the castle gates.

Cat fingered her letter, prodding her fingertips with the corners as she listened to Marin, who always took the time to give everyone her full attention.

"Regardless of what I try, of how much I pray, I continue to get my courses." Marin glanced at the hall again. "Ella suggested I see Isla."

Something tickled at Cat's mind. She hadn't had her courses since just before going to court and hadn't had them again since she'd returned. Cold prickled all over her.

"Ah, there she is." Marin reached for Cat's hand. "Say a prayer for me."

Cat simply nodded, mute with the force of the sudden realization. How could she still be sensitive to food she'd spent a lifetime eating? Especially when Nan was such an exceptional cook.

Cat had heard women with child were often ill. One of her sisters, Anice, had mentioned as much before. Typically, the illness occurred in the morning. Cat's pulse thundered in her ears with the very real possibility that had not dawned on her until that very moment.

She could be with child.

With shaking hands, she wrenched open the letter from Ella, tearing through the Countess of Ellingsworth's carefully stamped seal without ceremony. In desperation. Had Sir Gawain asked after her? Sought to see her again? Asked for her hand in marriage?

They would have to be wed soon, of course. Immediately. The thought sent a shudder racing down her spine. But she could not think now on if she wanted to wed him or not.

She unfolded her sister's missive with haste and skimmed over the carefully curling letters looping across the parchment. There were several noblemen asking about Catriona after she'd left; one in particular, Lord Loughton, wanted to see her again so that she might meet his son who would be a wonderful match. Ella strongly encouraged the introduction. Cat drew her brows at that and read on. Why was Ella not mentioning Sir Gawain?

More details on men who had showed interest, then a bit of information on Ella's daughter, Blanche.

Nearly panting in her frenzy for any news about Gawain, Cat flipped to the back of the page where one short paragraph was written. One awful, damning paragraph.

You asked after Sir Gawain, and I tell you that you need not waste another breath on him. I learned that not only has he been married for some time, but that his wife is soon to bear their first child.

Whatever strength had been holding Cat upright drained from her. She put her hand to the table to brace herself and carefully lowered herself to the bench.

She touched her hand to her stomach as another wave of nausea rolled through her.

Cat's gaze went to the empty hall where Marin had departed with such hope, so desperate for what Cat did not want and irony's cruel twist had most likely delivered upon her.

For there was a very strong possibility that Cat was carrying a married man's child.

※

Four years had passed since Geordie Strafford left Werrick Castle. Now it rose before him, larger and far grander than even he remembered. The king's coffers ran low from the war campaign and he'd sent the vast majority of his force home, including Geordie, who had no real home.

With parents who had abandoned him, leaving him to be slain for their sins, and no wife, Geordie returned to the closest thing to a home he had: Werrick Castle. To Cat.

His heart pounded in a collision of excitement, anticipation and nerves. He hadn't seen Cat in four years, though they had exchanged missives when he was somewhere long enough to receive one. His gaze skimmed the top of the castle wall, seeking out a woman with ribbons of gold hair dancing in the sunlight, her bow drawn back to track his approach.

But there were only Werrick guards. And no white-fledged arrow sank into the ground when he got within an archer's range. She was still at Werrick Castle, was she not?

But then, he had not received a letter in several months. Had she been married off, as Lady Ella had? The thought churned his stomach. If Cat was not at Werrick castle, was it still home?

He did not ask after Cat when a soldier called down for him to announce himself, nor did he see her in the bailey. Lord Werrick emerged from the keep and gave him a hearty embrace as soon as Geordie disembarked from his steed.

"My boy," the older man said fondly. "Has the campaign finally run its course?"

"For now," Geordie confirmed. "Until the king can secure more coin, from what I understand."

"And you, a knight." The Earl of Werrick nodded in approval.

Geordie's chest swelled with the praise. Lord Werrick was as close to a father as he'd ever had, and Geordie had spent his entire life in the pursuit of the honor of becoming a knight. A profession of the most noble, to compensate for his true father's notorious perfidy. It was an accomplishment Geordie was proud of. One he could not wait to share with Cat.

He glanced about the courtyard but did not see her.

Lady Leila, the youngest of the Earl of Werrick's five daughters, welcomed him next. The little girl had grown into a lovely young woman. His fellow knights would have tripped over themselves to bestow her with trite endearments of affection and nonsensical sonnets. She gave him a huge smile and embraced him. The scent of dried herbs told him she was still dabbling in the art of healing.

"It's good to have you back." Lady Leila released him and stepped back. "Cat will be overjoyed to see you again."

"Is she—"

Before he could finish the question, Drake, Werrick Castle's Captain of the Guard, clasped arms with him in greeting. "Sir Georgie." He flashed a wide grin at him and emphasized the word "Sir."

"You'll be in these ranks soon," Geordie promised. If it weren't for the constant training from Drake, Geordie might never have succeeded in becoming a knight at all. Or lived through battle, for that matter.

"Being half-Scottish doesna recommend me." Drake spoke stoically, as though it didn't matter, but Geordie knew it did. They had always shared their hopes of becoming knights.

A howl of delight turned Geordie's head. A large woman with gray hair peeking beneath a floppy mob cap bustled toward him and stopped abruptly. "Surely, this isn't my Geordie." Nan, the castle cook, cast a playfully shrewd look up at him. "He was a stick of a lad, as tall as he was thin."

Geordie offered a helpless shrug.

"Always the quiet one." She leaned close and offered a saucy wink. "You just wait 'til Cat sets her eyes on you."

Geordie's pulse spiked. "Is she here?"

Nan's kindly face split into a wide smile. "That she is, but she's only been home for a bit of time since her jaunt at court. You've got excellent timing."

"How is she?" Geordie asked the simple question, rather than the storm of the ones assaulting his mind. Was she healthy? Was she happy? Had she missed him? Had she become betrothed?

It was the last question that left a gnawing at his gut.

Nans lips pulled downward. "She's been ill since returning from court. The food there might have been too much for her. Aside from that, she's been as bright as the sun, the same as she's always been." Nan winked at him. "And always eager to get a letter from you."

Warmth touched his cheeks at Nan's last comment. "She is well now?"

Geordie had only been to court once for a sennight, but he knew how rich the food could be, and how vastly different than the fare Nan dished out.

"I've not heard of any more complaints of her illness, and she looks bonny as ever." Nan clasped her hands to her chest. "I'm so delighted to have you home. I'll make some roast pheasant in honor of your arrival." She hesitated. "If you still care for pheasant…"

It was all too easy to recall Nan's roasted pheasant, baked within a wall of bread and rising from a sea of roasted vegetables. After nothing but cold cheese, murky ale and the tough bit of grain they called bread at taverns, the idea of getting such a meal was nearly more than he could bear.

"Oh, aye," he confirmed. "I very much like pheasant still, especially if you already have some on hand. You needn't go out of your way on my behalf."

"I don't." Nan swept at a dusting of flour on her apron. "But, I'm on fine terms with the butcher." A flush colored her cheeks.

Geordie stared at Nan with curious assessment. Was she actually blushing? "Surely, this isn't the butcher you hated when he first bought old Betsy's business?"

Nan gave a girlish giggle. "Edmund is not so bad once you get to know him."

Any other questions Geordie might have asked died away on his tongue as the slender figure of a young woman filled the entrance to the keep. She strode outside, into a beam of sunlight that lit her hair like rare gold and made the deep sapphire blue of her eyes glow. If Cat had been ill, she did not look it now. She radiated with good health, her cheeks and lips a becoming shade of pink.

She stopped abruptly, then gave a squeal of delight and rushed toward him, not stopping until she had thrown herself into his arms. He embraced her gently despite her firm grip around him and breathed in her delicate floral scent. She still smelled the same, like summer roses fresh in bloom on a sunny day.

"Geordie." She eased back and looked up at him, no longer a girl, but very much a woman.

The most beautiful woman in all the world.

High cheekbones showed where once her cheeks had been apple round, and he noticed for the first time how full her lips were, how supple. But it was more than just her face, it was her body as well. Her waist nipped in at the middle, then flared out with a swell of womanly hips, and her narrow chest had blossomed into firm, rounded breasts. He was staring. He knew it and yet he could not stop himself.

But he was not the only one.

She gazed at him, lost in her own observation. Her mouth parted. "Geordie," she said his name again.

Even her voice had lost its childish softness and was now stronger, with confidence and sensual femininity.

All at once, those four years of separation, the hollow loneliness, the letters having to make do for her absence, they all faded away. Catriona. Cat. *His* Cat.

She was all that mattered. And with her, he was finally, truly home.

http://www.madelinemartin.com/book/catrionas-secret/

AUTHOR'S NOTE

I did a lot of research on books while writing Ella's story. I found it all so fascinating, I wanted it to be in my author's note for those of you might be enjoy learning about them as well. Books in the 14th century were actually referred to as 'manuscripts' (meaning written by hand). However, I took the creative liberty to refer to them simply as 'books' for the ease of reading.

Pages of a manuscript were of either parchment of vellum which were made of animal skins, generally from a sheep, calf or goat. The process to create the parchment was lengthy: cleaning the hide, bleaching it, scraping it free of hair and stretching it, scraping again to remove remaining hair, then sanding it down with pumice. This process took several days. On average, one calf yielded about 3.5 pages. When you consider how many pages are in a book, that's a lot of animals to generate one manuscript.

As far as the content within those manuscripts, the writing was copied by hand from one book into another. Space on a page was used as much as possible to prevent needing more pages than necessary so it was not uncommon to see the page filled. It also was not uncommon to find notes in the margin, either to add in a misplaced word or even a forgotten line by the person copying the manuscript. After all, eye strain is a factor no matter what era one lives in. If the scribe or monk caught the error quickly enough, they could actually use a knife to scrape the ink off the page since it was animal skin. If not, in the margin it went.

These manuscripts took a considerable amount of time to create. That said, they were exceptionally pricy, around the cost of a car today. Here is where I confess at having taken some creative liberty with Ella's story. In all reality, Ella would most likely have had about two or three manuscripts - maybe five at most. While the Earl of Werrick was a wealthy man, owning the few dozen manuscripts they had in the solar would have been an extravagant cost and pretty unlikely. Impressive libraries in the 14th century — generally monasteries — would likely only contain a hundred books, of if they were really impressive: hundreds. So, while it would have been historically accurate to only have Ella possess only a couple of manuscripts, I could not (with my reader's soul) give her only those few to read.

I would like to note here as well that there was no mention of blank journal-like manuscripts in my research, ergo this was part of my creative liberty as well. I would assume based on my research that any newly formed stories like the ones Ella created would have been done on individual sheets of vellum or parchment rather than in a blank, fully bound book.

After learning the process of creating a manuscript back in the 14th century, it's definitely given me a newfound appreciation for the books we have today and how plentiful our libraries can be. But no matter how grateful we all are, I would imagine calves, goats and sheep are even more so.

Want to learn a little more about each of the characters and the history of the Borderland Ladies? I have a history of the Borderland Ladies, character bios and free short stories on the supporting characters on my website:

http://www.madelinemartin.com/borderland-ladies/

ACKNOWLEDGMENTS

THANK YOU TO my amazing beta readers who helped make this story so much more with their wonderful suggestions: Kacy Stanfield, Monika Page, Janet Barrett, Tracy Emro and Lorrie Cline. You ladies are so amazing and make my books just shine!

Thank you to Janet Kazmirski for the final read-through you always do for me and for catching all the little last minute tweaks.

Thank you to John Somar and my wonderful minions for all the support they give me.

Thank you to Erica Monroe who saves my life time after time for doing an amazing job with edits and is always there for whatever I need. I swear, you add more years back onto my life with all the help and laughter you bring me.

And a huge thank you so much to my readers for always being so fantastically supportive and eager for my next book.

ABOUT THE AUTHOR

Madeline Martin is a USA TODAY Bestselling author of Scottish set historical romance novels filled with twists and turns, adventure, steamy romance, empowered heroines and the men who are strong enough to love them.

She lives a glitter-filled life in Jacksonville, Florida with her two daughters (known collectively as the minions) and a man so wonderful he's been dubbed Mr. Awesome. She loves Disney, Nutella, wine and could easily lose hours watching cat videos.

Find out more about Madeline at her website:

http://www.madelinemartin.com

- facebook.com/MadelineMartinAuthor
- twitter.com/MadelineMMartin
- instagram.com/madelinemmartin
- bookbub.com/profile/madeline-martin

ALSO BY MADELINE MARTIN

BORDERLAND LADIES

Marin's Promise

Anice's Bargain

Ella's Desire

Catriona's Secret

Leila's Legacy

HIGHLAND PASSIONS

A Ghostly Tale of Forbidden Love

The Madam's Highlander

The Highlander's Untamed Lady

Her Highland Destiny

Highland Passions Box Set Volume 1

HEART OF THE HIGHLANDS

Deception of a Highlander

Possession of a Highlander

Enchantment of a Highlander

THE MERCENARY MAIDENS

Highland Spy

Highland Ruse

Highland Wrath

REGENCY NOVELLAS

Earl of Benton

Mesmerizing the Marquis

Made in the USA
Columbia, SC
02 August 2019